P9-DGZ-758

"With her trademark **hope, humor, and heart-breaking realism,** Laurie Halse Anderson has given us a roadmap to heal. She is a treasure."

—STEPHEN CHBOSKY, *New York Times* bestselling author of *The Perks of Being a Wallflower*

"Laurie Halse Anderson is **one of the best-known writers** of literature for young adults and children in the world."

—SCOTT SIMON, *NPR Weekend Edition*

★"One of Anderson's **strongest and most relevant** works to date."

—*SLJ*, starred review

★"**Anderson at her absolute best**, providing significant and touching realistic fiction."

—*VOYA*, starred review

"Laurie Halse Anderson has been lauded and awarded for her ability to **channel the teenage mind (and heart)** dealing with tough issues."

—*FAMILY CIRCLE*

STRUGGLING TO CONNECT

To make matters worse (was that possible?), I wasn't exactly sure what I wanted with Finn. Did I like him? My opinion about that changed several times a day. Did I want him to like me? Ditto. How could I like him, how could he like me, if we didn't know each other? The little I was able to learn about his family (perfect, middle-class people, apparently) make me pretty sure that he'd run screaming if he ever met my father. That would be a logical reaction, of course, but did I really want to fall in love (fall in "like"?) with someone who didn't give my dad a chance? We had to get to know each other. Gradually. Baby steps. In order to do that, we'd have to break down and talk about things that were more significant than font size in online newspapers and his fevered delusions about his time studying telekinesis with a group of monks in a Himalayan ice cave.

I had no idea how to do that.

— * — * — * —

PENGUIN BOOKS
by LAURIE HALSE ANDERSON

THE IMPOSSIBLE
KNIFE *of* MEMORY

—*—*—*—*—*—*—*—

Laurie Halse Anderson

speak

An Imprint of Penguin Group (USA)

SPEAK
Published by the Penguin Group
Penguin Group (USA) LLC
375 Hudson Street
New York, New York 10014

USA * Canada * UK * Ireland * Australia
New Zealand * India * South Africa * China

penguin.com
A Penguin Random House Company

First published in the United States of America by Viking,
an imprint of Penguin Group (USA) LLC, 2014
Published by Speak, an imprint of Penguin Group (USA) LLC, 2015

THE LIBRARY OF CONGRESS HAS CATALOGED THE VIKING BOOKS EDITION AS FOLLOWS:
Anderson, Laurie Halse.
The impossible knife of memory / Laurie Halse Anderson.
pages cm
Summary: "Hayley Kincaid and her father move back to their hometown to try a 'normal' life, but
the horrors he saw in war threaten to destroy their lives"—Provided by publisher.
ISBN: 978-0-670-01209-1 (hardback)
[1. Fathers and daughters—Fiction. 2. Post-traumatic stress disorder—Fiction.
3. Family problems—Fiction. 4. Veterans—Fiction.] I. Title.
PZ7.A54385Im2014 [Fic]—dc23 2013031267

Speak ISBN 978-0-14-751072-3

Printed in the United States of America

1 3 5 7 9 10 8 6 4 2

— * —

for my father

— * —

—These are men whose minds the Dead have ravished.
Memory fingers in their hair of murders . . .

Wilfred Owen, "Mental Cases"

— * —

Apparently misinformed about the rumored
stuff of dreams: everywhere I inquired,
I was told look for blue.

Carl Phillips, "Blue"

It started in detention. No surprise there, right?

Detention was invented by the same idiots who dreamed up the time-out corner. Does being forced to sit in time-out ever make little kids stop putting cats in the dishwasher or drawing on white walls with purple marker? Of course not. It teaches them to be sneaky and guarantees that when they get to high school they'll love detention because it's a great place to sleep.

I was too angry for a detention nap. The zombie rulers were forcing me to write "I will not be disrespectful to Mr. Diaz" five hundred times. With a pen, on paper, which ruled out a copy/paste solution.

Was I going to do it?

Ha.

I turned the page in *Slaughterhouse Five*, a forbidden book at Belmont because we were too young to read about soldiers swearing and bombs dropping and bodies blowing up and war sucking.

Belmont High—Preparing Our Children for the Nifty World of 1915!

I turned another page, held the book close to my face, and squinted. Half of the lights in the windowless room didn't work. Budget cuts, the teachers said. A plot to make us go blind, according to the kids on the bus.

Someone in the back row giggled.

The detention monitor, Mr. Randolph, lifted his orc-like head and scanned the room for the offender.

"Enough of that," he said. He rose from his chair and pointed at me. "You're supposed to be writing, missy."

I turned another page. I didn't belong in detention, I didn't belong in this school, and I did not give a crap about the Stalinist rules of underpaid orcs.

Two rows over, the girl wearing a pink winter jacket, its fake-fur-edged hood pulled up, turned her head to watch me, eyes blank, mouth mechanically gnawing a wad of gum.

"Did you hear me?" the orc called.

I muttered forbidden gerunds. (You know, the words that end in "ing"? The -ings that we're not supposed to say? Don't ask me why, none of it makes sense.)

"What did you say?" he brayed.

"I said my name isn't 'missy.'" I folded the corner of the page. "You can call me Ms. Kincain or Hayley. I respond to both."

He stared. The girl stopped chewing. Around the room, zombies and freaks raised their heads, awakened by the smell of potential combat.

"Mr. Diaz is going to hear about that attitude, missy," the orc said. "He's stopping by at the end of the period to collect your assignment."

I swore under my breath. The girl in the jacket blew a lopsided bubble and popped it with her teeth. I tore a sheet of paper out of a notebook, found a pencil, and decided that this, too, would be a day not to remember.

—*— 2 —*—

A quick lesson.

There are two kinds of people in this world:

1. zombies
2. freaks.

Only two. Anyone who tells you different is lying. That person is a lying zombie. Do not listen to zombies. Run for your freaking life.

Another lesson: everyone is born a freak.

That surprised you, didn't it? That's because they've been sucking on your brain. Their poison is making you think that freaks are bad. Dangerous. Damaged. Again— don't listen. *Run*.

Every newborn baby, wet and hungry and screaming, is a fresh-hatched freak who wants to have a good time and make the world a better place. If that baby is lucky enough to be born into a family—

(Note: "family" does NOT only mean a biological unit composed of people who share genetic markers or legal bonds, headed by a heterosexual-mated pair. Family is much, much more than that. Because we're not living in 1915, y'know.)

—lucky enough to be born into a family that has a grown-up who will love that baby every single day and make sure it gets fed and has clothes and books and adventures, then no matter what else happens, the baby freak will grow into a kid freak and then into a teen freak.

That's when it gets complicated.

Because most teenagers wind up in high school. And high school is where the zombification process becomes deadly. At least, that has been my experience, both from long-distance observation, and now, up close and personal for twenty-four days, at Belmont.

Where was I?

Right. Detention.

By the time the bell rang, I had written "Correcting a teacher's mistake is not a sign of disrespect" one hundred and nine times.

— * — 3 — * —

Between the attitude chat (lecture) by Mr. Diaz after detention and my stupid locker, I missed the late bus.

There was no point in calling my dad.

I had four miles to walk. I'd done it before, but I didn't like it. I swallowed hard and started down the sidewalks of the neighborhood closest to school, my chin up, fake smile waiting in case an old guy at his mailbox waved at me or a mom unloading groceries from her van checked me out. My earbuds were in, but I wasn't playing music. I needed to hear the world but didn't want the world to know I was listening.

Fifteen minutes later, the safe little houses turned into strip malls and then a couple of used-car lots and then what they call "downtown" around here. I did a quick scan left and right every couple of steps: abandoned mattress store; house with boarded-up windows; newspapers covering a drunk or drugged or dead homeless body that reeked, but was not a threat. A tire store. Liquor store. Bodega with bars on the windows. Two empty lots with fields of gravel and grass and broken furniture and limp condoms and cigarette butts. Storefront church with a cross outlined in blue neon.

Two guys leaned against the church.

Threat

Took my hands out of my pockets. Walked like I owned the sidewalk: legs strong and fast, hips made for power, not playing. The guys would size me up as female, young, five foot eleven-ish, one-sixty. Those facts were the language of my body, couldn't change it. But the way I walked, that made the difference. Some girls would slow down in a situation like this. They'd go rabbit-scared, head down, arms over chest, their posture screaming: "I am weak you are strong I am afraid just don't kill me." Others would stick out their boobs, push their butt high and swing it side to side to say, "Check it out. Like it? Want it?"

Some girls are stupid.

I swallowed the fear. It's always there—fear—and if you don't stay on top of it, you'll drown. I swallowed again and stood tall, shoulders broad, arms loose. I was balanced, ready to move. My body said, "Yeah, you're bigger and stronger, but if you touch this, I will hurt you."

Five steps closer. The guy facing me looked up, said something to his friend. The friend turned to look.

Assess

There was nothing in my backpack worth fighting for. In fact, it would have been a relief if they stole it 'cause I'd have a legitimate excuse about why I didn't do my homework. If they grabbed, I'd twist so that their hands landed on the backpack first. Then I'd shove one of them against the cement church wall and run like hell. They both looked stoned, so I'd have a huge reaction-time advantage. Plus adrenaline.

Plan B: The Albany bus was two blocks away. I'd let them pull off the backpack, then sprint toward the bus, yelling and waving my arms like I didn't want to miss it, 'cause if you act like you're running from wolves on a street like that, people pretend not to see you, but if you're trying to catch a bus, they'll help.

My last defensive option was the empty bottle of Old Crow whiskey carefully set next to the base of the streetlight directly across from the two guys looking at me. The long neck of the bottle would be easy to grab. I'd have to remember not to smash it too hard against the wall or the whole thing would shatter. A light *tink*, with the same amount of pressure you'd use to crack open an egg, that would be enough to break off the bottom. One *tink* and a sorry whiskey bottle turns into a weapon with big, glass teeth hungry for a piece of stoned wolf boy.

I was one step away.

Action

The eyes of the guy who turned to look at me were so unfocused, he didn't know if I was a girl or a ghost. I looked through him to the other guy. Less stoned. Or more awake. Eyes on me, narrow eyes, cement gray with muddy hollows under them. He was the one who smelled dangerous.

For one frozen second I stared at him—*glass bottle at*

eleven o'clock knee his nuts reach for the weapon cut everything— then I nodded curtly, chin down, respectful.

He nodded back.

The second melted and I was past them and past the bottle and the bus rumbled along to Albany, loaded with old zombies staring at me with dead eyes.

I listened for footsteps until the empty lots and closed-up businesses turned into strip malls and then turned into almost-safe little houses. At the end of the last street, past a forgotten cornfield and the ruin of a barn, sat the house that I was supposed to call "home."

—*— **4** —*—

My father wanted me to remember the house. He had asked me over and over when we moved, carrying boxes in from the truck, filling the cupboards with groceries, removing rodent skeletons, washing the windows, "Are you sure you don't remember, Hayley Rose?"

I shook my head but kept my mouth shut. It made him sad when I talked about how hard I tried not to remember.

(Don't think I was crazy, because I wasn't. The difference between forgetting something and not remembering it is big enough to drive an eighteen-wheeler through.)

A few days after we moved in, Daddy got unstuck from time again, like the Pilgrim guy in *Slaughterhouse*. The past took over. All he heard were exploding IEDs and incoming mortar rounds; all he saw were body fragments, like an unattached leg still wearing its boot, and shards of shiny bones, sharp as spears. All he tasted was blood.

These attacks (he'd have killed me if I used that word in front of him, but it was the only one that fit) had been getting worse for months. They were the only reason I went along with his ridiculous plan to quit trucking and settle down into a so-called "normal life." I let him think that he was right, that spending my senior year in a high school instead of riding shotgun in his big rig was a practical and exciting idea.

Truth? I was terrified.

I found the library and a bank and made sure the post office knew that we were back and living in Gramma's old house. On the third day, a girl named Gracie who lived down the street brought a basket of muffins and a tuna noodle casserole cooked by her mom, from scratch. She said she was glad to see me.

Gracie was so sweet—freakishly kind and non-zombified—that I forgot to be a bitch and I fell into like with her by the time I'd finished the first muffin, and suddenly I had a friend, a real friend for the first time in . . . I couldn't remember how long. Having a friend made everything else suck less.

When the past spat Dad back out, he ate what was left of the tuna noodle casserole. (The muffins were already gone.) He went up into the attic and brought down a small box that hadn't been damaged by mice or mold. In the box were faded photographs that he swore were me and his mother, my grandmother. I asked why didn't Gramma keep any pictures of my mom and he said they'd been chewed up by the mice. By then, I could tell when he was lying.

So that day after detention, I made it home from school in one piece, pissed and hungry and determined to ignore all my homework. Dad's pickup was parked in the driveway. I put my hand on the hood: stone cold. I checked the odometer: no extra miles since I left that morning. He hadn't gone to work again.

I unlocked the one, two, three, four locks on the front door of our house. (*Our house.* Still felt weird to put those two words together.) Opened the door carefully. He hadn't put the chain on. Probably slept all day. Or he was dead. Or he remembered that I had gone to school and that I was going to come home and that I'd need the chain to be off. That's what I was hoping for.

I stepped inside. Closed the door behind me. Locked back up: one, two, three, four. Slid the chain into its slot and hit the light switch. The living room furniture was upright and dusty. The house smelled of dog, cigarette smoke, bacon grease, and the air freshener that Dad sprayed so I wouldn't know that he smoked weed.

Down the hall, Spock barked three times behind the door to my father's bedroom.

"Dad?"

I waited. Dad's voice rumbled like faraway thunder, talking to the dog. Spock whined, then went quiet. I waited, counting to one hundred, but still . . . nothing.

I walked toward his door and gently knocked. "Dad?"

"Your bus late again?" he asked from the other side.

"Yep."

I waited. This was where he should ask how my day went or if I had homework or what I wanted for dinner. Or he could tell me what he felt like eating, because I could cook. Or he could just open the door and talk, that would be more than enough.

"Dad?" I asked. "Did you stay home again?"

"It's been a bad day, princess."

"What did your boss say?"

Dead. Silence.

"You called him, right?" I asked. "Told him you were sick? Daddy?"

"I left a message on his voice mail."

Another lie. I leaned my forehead against the door. "Did you even try to get out the door? Did you get dressed? Take a shower?"

"I'll try harder tomorrow, princess. I promise."

— * — **5** — * —

Death deals the cards. They whisper across the shaky table.

Hernandez sticks a cigar in his mouth. Dumbo tucks his wife's letter in his helmet. Loki spits and curses. Roy sips his coffee. We pull the cards toward us and laugh.

I don't remember what my wife looked like, but I recognize Death. She calls for our bets, wearing a red dress, her beautiful face carved out of stone. My friends laugh and lie, already deep in the game.

I remember what my little girl looks like. I remember the smell of her head. The scar on her left knee. Her lisp. Peanut butter and banana. I don't think she remembers me.

Death rattles bone dice in her mouth, clicking them against her teeth. She spits them on the table and they roll.

We bet it all, throw everything on the line because the air is filled with bullets and grenades. We won't hear the one that gets us, but it's coming.

She tells us to show our hands.

We have never been so alive.

—*— 6 —*—

Lunch. First period.

Lunch served at o-dark-thirty. I couldn't figure out why more high school students hadn't risen up in armed rebellion. The only explanation was that the administration put sedatives in the chocolate chip cookies.

The eraser end of a pencil was shoved into my left ear.

"Leave me alone." I pushed away the pencil and the hand holding it, turning my head so that my left ear lay flat against the cafeteria table.

The pencil attacked my right ear.

I gave the classic one-finger salute to my tormentor. "I hate you."

"Twenty vocab words."

"I'm sleeping, watch. Zzzzzz."

"Just my Spanish, Hays. And a little English help for Topher. *Pesadilla*. A quesadilla with fish, right?"

I sat up with a groan. Across the table sat Gracie Rappaport, the casserole-and-muffin-girl. Draped over her was her boyfriend, Topher, Christopher Barnes. (You might have heard of him. When he dumped some girl named Zoe on Labor Day weekend she blasted a disrespectful description of his man-parts all over the Internet. Topher responded with photographic evidence that Zoe was lying. When I asked Gracie about it, all she did was giggle, which was way more information than I wanted.)

"What is 'denotation'?" Topher asked.

"Denotation is when a plot blows up," I said. "And yes, a *pesadilla* is a quesadilla stuffed with fish. You are a genius, Gracie."

"Don't write that down." A shaggy-haired guy with expensive teeth and dark-framed glasses sat down next to me. "She's messing with you."

Topher looked at the newcomer. "Where you been?"

The guy pulled a ring of keys out of his pocket and dangled them.

"You got it running?" Topher asked. "What was it this time?"

"I don't know, but Mom said it cost a ton of money. I'll be doing chores forever to pay her back."

"Dude," Topher said.

"Right?" answered the guy. "So, I'm broke. Feed me."

Topher handed him a ten-dollar bill. "Bring me back a bagel, too."

"Why don't I get paid for doing your homework?" I asked.

Topher handed me a quarter. "Denotation. For real."

"Denotation: a noun that describes the action of a student refusing to take notes during class," I said.

"Denotation," said the new guy. "The precise meaning of a word, without any pesky implications attached to it."

Topher took the quarter back and tossed it to his friend. "Butter, not cream cheese."

"That's it," I said, laying my head back down. "I'm done."

Gracie lobbed a crumpled napkin at my nose. "Just my Spanish, Hayley, puleeeeeze."

"Why, exactly, should I do that?"

She pushed her books across the table to me. "Because you're awesome."

Along with tuna noodle casserole and the muffin basket, Gracie had been carrying a photo album that day she came to our door. In it were pictures of her kindergarten class—*our* kindergarten class, because I had been in it, too. Looking at mini-me in a hand-knit sweater and braids gave me goose bumps, but I couldn't pin down exactly why. The only memory I had of kindergarten was peeing my pants during nap time, but Gracie said that never happened. Then she asked if I still liked peanut butter and banana sandwiches.

(Which, I will admit, freaked me out because they were my favorite and there was no way she could have guessed that.)

I did her vocab and handed it back to her as Topher's friend returned to the table carrying a tray loaded down with bagels and cups of coffee.

"Seven and eighteen are wrong on purpose," I told her. "To make it more realistic."

"Good call," she said. "Thanks."

The flat-screen televisions mounted in the four corners of the room finally roused themselves and blinked on, tuned in to one of the all-news stations. The students who were awake enough to notice gave a halfhearted cheer. I watched for a minute, reading the words that crawled across the bottom of the screen to see if there had been any disasters overnight. Nothing, except for the latest celebrity-worship crap and suicide bombers who blew up a market and a kindergarten on the other side of the world.

"Can I go back to sleep now?" I asked.

"You need to eat your breakfast," the new guy said, handing me a bagel. "Nice hair, by the way. Is electric blue your natural color?"

"I don't do breakfast," I said. "And yes, I come from a long line of blue-haired people."

"What's a 'motif,'" Topher asked, mouth filled with bagel.

"At least have some coffee," the guy said. "You look like you could use it."

"I didn't ask for coffee," I said.

"Motif: a recurring object or idea in a story." The guy pulled a handful of assorted fake and real sugar packets out of the pocket of his green-and-brown-plaid flannel shirt and set them in front of me. "Wasn't sure what you liked."

"None of them. If I want coffee, I'll get it myself. And you forgot structure."

"What?"

"A literary motif is a recurring object, idea, or structure. You forgot structure."

He looked at Gracie, then me, then back at Gracie, a smile slowly spreading across his face. "You were right, Rappaport."

"What about me?" asked Topher. "I seconded the idea."

Gracie said "Shhh" as the boys bumped fists.

"Right about what?" I asked. "What idea?"

"I sort of promised Finn that you would write an article," Gracie said. "For the school newspaper. I told him you were good at English and stuff."

"Is this a joke?" I asked.

Finn (what kind of parent names their kid after the body part of a fish?) pointed his bagel at me. "How long will it take you to pull together two hundred words on 'World of Resources at the Library'?"

"Forever," I said. "Because I'm not doing it."

"What's an unreliable narrator?" asked Topher.

"Come on, Hays," said Gracie. "You haven't signed up for anything, even though you promised you would. You need more friends, or at least a couple of people who will say hello to you in the hall. Writing for the newspaper is the perfect solution."

"I don't need a solution," I said. "I don't have a problem."

Gracie ignored me. "Plus, you two have a lot in common." She counted on her fingers. "You're both tall, you're both quiet, you're both strangely smart, and you are both a little weird. No offense," she quickly added. "Weird in, um, an adorkable way."

"Is 'adorkable' a word?" asked Topher.

"Weird, quiet, and strangely smart?" I asked. "That describes people who make fertilizer bombs. Maybe he does, but not me."

"Fertilizer bombs?" Finn asked.

"Unreliable narrator?" Topher repeated. "Anyone?"

"I'm not writing the article," I said.

The flat screen blinked and pixelated, and the school's mascot, Marty, a white guy with bulging biceps holding a hammer in each hand (we were the Belmont Machinists, God knows why) appeared.

"All hail the demon overlords!" Finn called loudly.

I shot him a glance because I had been thinking the exact same thing, but when he looked back at me, I pretended I was doodling on the back of my hand.

The screen scrolled the morning announcements:

. . . THE FOLLOWING COLLEGES WILL HAVE REPS IN THE CAFETERIA THIS WEEK . . .

. . . MEMORY STICK TURNED INTO THE LOST AND FOUND . . .

. . . NO LOITERING AROUND THE FLAGPOLE . . .

And finally a list of the sorry souls who had to report to the Attendance Office, the Counselor's Office, or go straight to hell and see the principal.

Finn punched me in the shoulder.

"Ow! What was that for?"

He pointed at the monitor. "You made the Doom List, Miss Blue! In trouble with the authorities this early in the year? You'll make a great reporter."

The halls surged with a parade of beautiful strangers. They laughed too loud. Flirted. Shrieked. Raced. They kissed. Shoved. Tripped. Shouted. Posed. Chased. Flaunted. Taunted. Galloped. Sang.

Fully assimilated zombies.

I could laugh at them when I was with Gracie. When I walked through their herd in the east wing hall—alone—I was transformed from my confident freakself into a gawping pile of self-conscious self-loathing. Their shiny-teeth smiles made happiness look easy. They never tripped over their own feet. They could laugh without snorting and tease each other without sounding dumb. They could remember being six years old together and eight and eleven and giggle about all of it.

The flaunts, the taunts, the poses, they were all part of the lie. My brain understood this because I'd heard the whispers. The Honor Society officers who started their day off with a little weed that melted stress like chocolate. The cheerleaders who cut themselves where the scars wouldn't show. Debate team members busted for shoplifting. Mommy's pills being shared like cookies, and the way Daddy's vodka made first-period Latin fly by.

As I walked down the east wing hall, I could feel their sticky fingers reaching for my brain. Puffs of yellow smoke curled toward my ears, my eyes, my nose and mouth. The hivemind wanted to penetrate and infect. Colonize. The danger was so real, so close, I didn't dare open my mouth to ask directions. Or to howl.

—*— 8 —*—

The school counselors shared a waiting room that held uncomfortable chairs, overloaded bulletin boards, a secretary named Gerta with blood-red talons, and a coffeepot that looked like it hadn't been cleaned since the turn of the century.

When I walked in, the doors to all of the counselors' offices were closed. I stood in front of Gerta's desk. Her fingernails had worn off most of the letters on her keyboard.

Only the Q and the X had any pigment left. A girl behind one of the closed doors was sobbing, but I couldn't make out what she was saying.

Ms. Benedetti stepped into the office carrying a cup of coffee from the gas station closest to school. Good call.

"My name was on the list," I said.

"We have a few things to discuss," she said. "Let's talk in here."

I followed her into her private office, a box barely big enough to fit her desk, a file cabinet, and two chairs. It did have a window, however, that looked on to the student parking lot. Some people said that Benedetti filmed the activities out there with a secret camera. Given that her computer looked older than me, I doubted that.

Ms. Benedetti hung up her jacket on a hook, sat at her desk, and took the lid off her coffee.

I sat in the chair by the window, mouth shut.

The trick to surviving an interrogation is patience. Don't offer up anything. Don't explain. Answer the question and only the question that is asked so you don't accidentally put your head in a noose.

"How are things going?" she asked.

I stared at her through the dust that hovered in the air. "Fine."

"I didn't see your name on the community service list for September," she said.

"So?"

"You can't postpone your service requirement, Hayley. All students are required to perform two hours a month, every month. You signed up for," she glanced at her screen, "for St. Anthony's Nursing Home." She handed me a sheet of paper. "There are some sweet old people living there, you'll like it. A staff member needs to sign this attendance log. Be sure to turn it in to Gerta so you get credit for your hours."

"Mandatory community service" seemed like hypocrisy, but Benedetti cared more about attendance lists than philosophy. I took the paper without committing to anything.

"Can I go now?"

"Not yet." She picked up two packets of sugar, the real stuff, and shook them. "You've had detention eleven times since school started."

That was a statement, not a question, so it did not require a response.

"It seems like you're struggling a bit with the adjustment to traditional schooling."

Another statement. She was making this easy.

She ripped open the packets and poured them into the coffee. "Particularly in calculus. How is that going?"

"Precalc," I corrected. "It's fine."

I was fluent in practical math: checkbook balancing; gas mileage calculation; how many gallons of paint it would take to make the living room look nice. Precalculus was taught in dog whistle, a pitch too high to hear. I generally spent the class drawing predatory zeppelins and armies of bears in my math notebook.

"Mr. Cleveland thinks you may need a tutor."

Some statements beg for a response. I shrugged.

"He'll talk to you about it." Benedetti pried the foil top off three plastic containers of chemical milk, poured them in her cup, and changed her angle of approach. "How is your father doing?"

This time, she let the silence draw out, waiting for me to become uncomfortable enough to open my mouth. The sobbing of the girl next door soaked through the drywall and filled the room.

"I can't remember if he played football or basketball," she said. "I'm pretty sure he knew my little brother. Was he with that group of guys who got in trouble for the party at the quarry after the championship game?"

I shrugged again. Dad rarely talked about growing up in Belmont, but I wasn't about to let her know that. The first time we met, Benedetti told me that I could trust her and tell her anything. People who have to announce that they are trustworthy deserve to be lied to.

She waited, eyebrows up, wanting me to say more. I counted the seconds, one after another, watching them drop like heavy rocks down a deep well. Benedetti caved after one minute, twelve.

"The thing is, I'm having a hard time getting ahold of your father," she said.

I did not respond.

"I called his work number, but they said he quit a couple weeks ago. Does he have a cell phone?"

Quit? He quit?

She leaned forward, like she sensed that something was wrong.

"What do you need him for?" I asked.

She stirred her coffee with the black plastic stick. "We need contact information for all of our parents. Where is he working now?"

We had reached that point in the interrogation where I had to cough up some information or risk unnecessary aggravation.

"He's taking time off to write a book," I said.

"A book?"

It wasn't a great lie, but in my defense, I was tired and I really should have eaten that bagel back in the cafeteria. I folded my arms over my chest and watched a red Sentra and a black Mustang scream into the student lot. The Sentra drove up and down the aisles, looking for a spot close to the building and finding nothing.

"About the war," I added.

"Perfect." She stopped stirring. "I want to invite him to be a part of our Veterans Day assembly, too."

"Save your breath," I said. "He hates that stuff."

The Mustang headed straight for the back row, the only row with empty spaces, and parked under a maple tree with leaves so orange it looked like a glowing pumpkin.

"That's what your stepmother said."

The word exploded in front of my eyes and set the ceiling on fire. I forced myself to turn my head and focus on that tree and to count, *two, three, four, five*, before I answered.

"I don't have a stepmother."

Benedetti nodded. "The first time she called, I checked your records. I was pretty sure you hadn't mentioned her. But she was persistent. After several calls, she emailed me the paperwork that proved she had been your legal guardian during your father's deployments."

"He never married her."

"You lived with her," Benedetti checked her screen again, "from the time you were six until you were twelve."

"And then she left."

She stirred her coffee again. "I gather there are still some hard feelings?"

"None, it's just that she's a scum-sucking idiot."

Someone knocked gently before I could slap my own mouth for blabbing.

Benedetti got up and listened briefly to the person at the door. "I'll just be a minute."

A few leaves spiraled down from the maple tree at the back of the parking lot. Six years I lived with Trish, it said that on her computer. Truth? I barely remembered it. I'd get flashes here and there, like fireflies, gone before I could get a good look at them. The years before Trish? Clouds strung on a necklace, the smell of lemons, the sound of bees in a garden. The years of Trish? *Nada. Méi shén me.*

The years after?

After she left, we drifted back and forth across the country in a dented eighteen-wheeler—Dad steering, me navigating—stopping every once in a while in tiny towns that seemed like islands in the middle of an ocean of corn or snow or sand. We'd stay a month or two, until the past caught up to him and blew us out the door again. The miles under the tires helped fade everything we didn't want to re-member into a vague pattern of loosely knit-together shad-ows that stayed just out of reach, where they belonged.

My heart suddenly revved, then raced, and *no, no, no. Not going there. No need. Don't want to. Not going to. Just breathe. It's all good. I'm good. Dad is fine. Focus, focus.*

Orange tree.

Lines of cars. Sun bouncing off windshields.

Asphalt. Lines of tar filling in the cracks.

Just breathe.

The girl next door had stopped crying.

Benedetti came back in and sat down. "Right, where were we?" She took a long swig of coffee and set the cup next to her keyboard, the rim stained with beige lip gloss. "Your stepmother is concerned about you and your father. She told me a few things that contradict what your father said when he enrolled you. That's another reason I need to talk to him."

"She's not my stepmother." I stood up. "She's a cheating, alcoholic asshole who can't open her mouth without lying. She . . . You can't talk to her about me. Can I go?"

She nodded slowly. "I hear what you're saying and I understand. But I still need to talk to your father. If he doesn't want to call me, I can stop by your house."

"He'll call," I said. "I'll make sure of it."

"One more thing." Benedetti opened the top drawer of her desk and pulled out a sealed envelope. My name was written on the front in black, spidery ink, familiar handwriting.

"She sent this." Benedetti set it on top of my books. "The woman who apparently was not your stepmother. She asked me to give it to you."

I opened my precalc textbook and shoved the envelope inside. "I'm not going to read it."

"Your choice. Oh, and don't forget to sign up for your SATs. You're running out of time."

Instead of heading for precalc, I detoured around the technology pod, looped through the music wing, behind the cafeteria, and through the back entrance to the library. I flashed my late pass at Ms. Burkey, the last librarian left standing after the school board fired the rest of the staff, and hurried to the far end of the nonfiction stacks like I was on a mission, the way Gracie taught me. When Ms. Burkey turned her attention to a loud group of guys in the computer room, I emerged to hunt for something real to read so that I could distract my brain from imploding.

A small table covered with a red paper tablecloth had been set up next to the new books display. A cardboard sign with GENOCIDE AWARENESS written on it was taped to the front edge of the table and a banner reading ONE WORLD, hung on the wall behind it. A bulk-sized box of Snickers and a Tupperware container of homemade brownies had been placed on the table next to laminated photos of mutilated bodies. Dark blood pooled on the dirt and ran in slow rivers from the dead toward the photographer. In one picture, a child's hand clutching a rag doll poked out from underneath a heap of broken adults.

An index card showed the price of the snacks: *Brownies $1, Candy $2*.

A tiny girl with rings on all of her fingers sat behind the table reading a tattered paperback.

"Is this a club?" I asked. "A genocide awareness club?"

"One World is more than just genocide." She stuck a scrap of paper in the book to mark her page. "We build schools in Afghanistan and dig wells in Botswana."

"Do members of the club get to travel to those places, you know, to do the work?"

"I wish," she said. "We try to raise awareness. And money. The candy bars are the best sellers. Do you want one?"

"I'd rather have a brownie." I reached in my pocket and sorted through the change while she put a brownie in a plastic bag for me. "Thanks." I handed her the quarters and she handed me my lunch.

"We meet every Wednesday," she said. "Ms. Duda's room, 304, next to the stairs."

I took the brownie. "Do the pictures ever gross anyone out?"

She shook her head. "People don't really look at them."

My math teacher noted the precise time that Benedetti had marked down on my late pass and calculated that I had blown off one-third of his class. He scolded me for so long that I had to hustle to make it to English. I was in luck; Ms. Rogak was still standing in the hall, deep in conversation with the technology teacher who always wore a huge, blue UNION button on his shirt. I scooted past them and through the door.

My usual seat, back row, center aisle, was already taken by Brandon Something, a tennis player who constantly misused the word *literally*. I needed that seat. It had the best view of the door and a solid wall to lean against. If trouble walked in, I'd have plenty of room to maneuver. Yes, I was being paranoid. I knew that Trish was not going to storm my English class with a commando team, but hearing her name, knowing that she was snooping around and could show up to make life even worse had driven me perilously close to a three-alarm anxiety meltdown. Sitting back row, center aisle was not an option. It was a requirement.

"You're in my seat," I told Brandon Something.

"Sit on my face," he said.

"Move," I said.

"What'll you give me?"

A couple of heads swiveled to watch us.

My adrenaline turned up a notch. "How about a swift kick in the balls?"

Before he could respond, Ms. Rogak *click-click*ed in on her stiletto heels, shutting the door hard enough to stop all snickering and conversation.

"Up front, Brandon," she said. "I don't need you scheming back there today. Books open, everyone. Attention on me."

Brandon bumped into me as he carried his books to the empty seat in front. "Bitch," he whispered.

Ms. Rogak had Melody Byrd read a passage: Circe trying to bewitch Odysseus:

> "'Now you are burnt-out husks, your spirits haggard, sere,
> always brooding over your wanderings long and hard,
> your hearts never lifting with any joy—
> you've suffered far too much.'"

I stared at the page until the letters melted into the paper. Trish's envelope waited in my math book. Ticking. Sweat trickled down my neck and soaked into my shirt. I kept breathing, *slow, slow, steady*, but my hands would not stop shaking. Why did she call Benedetti? How did she even know where we lived?

The page started to dissolve into the desk and I closed my eyes.

A knife ripped through the veil between Now and Then and I fell in . . .

> *ripping . . . Daddy holds my hand. A strange woman steps in front of us. She is Trish and I have to love her now . . .*
> *ripping . . . Trish screams louder than sirens, louder than a helicopter . . .*
> *ripping . . . Monsters crawl out of the video game. Daddy's blood fills the couch and drips on the floor . . .*

Ms. Rogak's voice pitched up an octave. "Don't any of you understand what Homer is saying? Please, I'm begging. Anybody."

Had she been emailing Dad? Had she twisted his head around again, was that why he was getting worse? What if she was at the house, manipulating him, lying to him, breaking his rusted heart into pieces?

I have to get home. Now.

Finn was at his locker, just like Topher said he would be.

"Hey." I tapped his shoulder.

His head snapped around, surprised.

"Um," I said. "This is awkward, but I don't have a choice."

He grinned. "Sounds awesome already."

I swallowed hard. The panic was getting worse. "No jokes, please. I need a ride. Home. I desperately need a ride home."

"Okay. Meet me here at two thirty."

"I need a ride home right now. It's an emergency."

"But I have physics." He frowned. "Are you okay? Do you want to go to the nurse?"

"Yes, no, yes, I mean . . ." I pushed the palm of my hand against my forehead, trying not to lose it in front of this guy and the three hundred strangers in the hall. "Nothing is wrong with me. My dad is sick and I need to get home and you have a car and I thought, maybe . . ."

The bell rang so loud I jumped, and then it rang and rang and rang, the halls emptying. Finn said something, his mouth moved, but I couldn't hear him.

"Never mind," I said, hurrying away.

*　*　*

I walked as fast as I dared; *don't run, don't want them to notice.* Down the halls, past open doors that all sounded the same; teachers launching into a lesson, kids restless. Past the auditorium, out the heavy metal doors. Cut straight across the grass around the flagpole, right through visitor's parking and into the student lot.

"Miss Blue!" someone shouted.

I started jogging.

Every step closer to home made me more anxious. *Is she at the house? What does she want? How do I stop this?*

"Hey." Finn grabbed my elbow to stop me, two rows from the pumpkin orange tree. "I'll drive you."

I turned. "Thought you had physics."

"I already know it. Ever heard of Maxwell's demon? Second law of thermodynamics. Cool as shit. Give me those."

"What?"

"You're shaking. Give me your books and put on your hoodie."

He did not mention the fact that there was no wind and the sun was warm. I handed over my books and set my backpack on the ground, then struggled into my sweatshirt and tried to stop shaking, stop sweating, stuff down the explosion that was clawing its way up my spine.

I poked my head through the neck hole and fumbled my hands into the sleeves. "You don't mind if you get in trouble?"

"Trouble is my middle name." He stood soldier straight and bowed. "Finnegan Trouble Ramos, at your service, Miss Blue."

"Stop calling me that."

—*— 12 —*—

I didn't notice too much about his car. It had a windshield, doors, steering wheel, seat belts; that was all I needed. He put the key in the ignition, the engine turned over. He shifted into gear and the wheels rolled.

The gray closed in on me as he was pulling out of the parking lot, right after I gave him the directions. I fought the gray with Dad's tricks: *Say the alphabet. Count in Spanish. Picture a mountain, the top of a mountain, the top of a mountain in the summer. Keep breathing.* It took a few minutes but I won. The gray pulled away from my eyes in ribbons and whispered that it would be back soon.

"You zoned out a bit," Finn said.

"Can you drive faster?" I asked.

"I'm doing the speed limit."

"Nobody does the speed limit."

"I do because I am a good driver," he said. "I'm so good that when I drove my mom to her podiatrist appointment last Saturday, she fell asleep."

"Why couldn't she drive herself? Did her foot hurt?"

"That's not the right question."

"What?"

"You were supposed to ask 'Why did she fall asleep?' The answer was 'Because I was a good driver.' Get it? I was so good she was bored."

"Oh," I said. "Was that a joke?"

"I thought it was."

"Not really."

"Damn." He put on his turn signal, checked all of his mirrors twice, and eased into the next lane. My right knee bounced up and down as I fought to keep myself from grabbing the wheel and slamming the accelerator to the floor.

The light ahead turned yellow. Finn braked so that the car came to a stop a full second before the yellow turned red. The streets in all directions were empty.

Home. I had to get *home*.

"No one is coming," I pointed out.

"What?"

"There's no traffic."

"So?"

"So you can go."

"The light's red."

"It's stuck. Malfunctioning. You can go because the coast is clear."

"We've only been here two seconds."

"More like two minutes. Go."

"I get it." He turned to look at me. "There's a warrant out for your arrest. You've got the FBI, CIA, and Interpol tracking you. What was it—jewel heist? Smuggling pandas?"

"I'm not in the mood to joke around. Even if I were, you are not a funny person."

The light changed to green.

He accelerated slowly. "Are you sure you feel okay?"

"I'm fine."

We drove in silence. I dug my fingernails into my palms as we were passed by three cars and a wrinkled old lady riding a pink moped. A block after he turned right (turn signal activated way too early, every mirror checked and checked twice more—for a right-hand turn, for crying out loud, a right-hand turn made from the far right lane) he eased to another slow stop at a yellow light and nodded to himself as it turned red, as if he were some kind of genius for having predicted that occurrence.

"See?" he asked.

"See what?"

"See what a good idea it was to slow down instead of blowing through that light, the way you wanted me to?"

"I didn't say anything."

"You were thinking it loudly. The words *Just go!* appeared above your head in neon-blue smoke."

"Whatever."

"No, really. Aha! Look! Cop car just rolled out of the gas station back there and pulled up behind us."

I looked in the side mirror. The cop's sunglasses stared at us. His mouth was moving.

Threat

"He's getting ready to pull you over," I said. "Are your taillights out? Have you ever been arrested? You don't have any weed in here, do you? I don't want to get busted. I can't get busted. I have to go home."

"Don't freak out. You're not going to get busted."

My mouth went dry. "Could we be arrested for leaving school?"

He laughed. "Are you kidding?"

I didn't answer. The light changed. Finn drove with both hands on the wheel, his speedometer slowly crawling up to twenty-nine miles per hour.

"Speed limit is thirty-five here."

Assess

I turned around and looked over my shoulder. The police car was six feet behind us. "He can pull you over for driving too slow, you know."

"Not going to happen. We didn't run any lights, nor are we speeding. There just happens to be a police officer driving behind us. He's probably on his way to a diner."

I watched in the side mirror, waiting for the cop to hit his lights and siren. "Don't say 'nor.' Makes you sound like a dweeb."

"Makes me sound like a smart dweeb."

"Really smart people don't flaunt it. Besides, 'nor' is arcane."

"'Arcane' is arcane."

Finn stopped at another light. The cop pulled up so close I could see the grill that separated the front seat of his car from the back, where they stick the suspects. My heart started hammering against my ribs.

"I'll get out here." I tried to swallow the bitter taste flooding my mouth. "It's close enough."

"No, it's not."

"I came up to you in the parking lot." I unfastened my seat belt.

"What are you talking about?"

"If that cop pulls you over, you don't know me. I don't go to your school. I bummed a ride from you in the Byrne Dairy parking lot. You were taking me to the bus station, but then I changed my mind. Understand?"

"I don't understand. What's wrong?"

"Thanks for the ride. I'll write that article for you. I just . . ." I opened the door. "I have to go."

Action

My father's legs stuck out from under the front end of his
pickup. The toe of his right boot pointed to the sky. The other boot pointed so far to the left it was lying on the ground,
like he was asleep, or . . .

My heart skipped a beat, two beats.

He started to whistle. Badly. "Hotel California" by the
Eagles.

I was so relieved I almost barfed.

Spock woofed and Dad rolled out to see why. He sat up
and shaded his eyes, his greasy hands marking his forehead
and the gray buzz cut above it.

"That you, princess?"

I bent down to scratch Spock's ears. "Hey, Daddy."

The dark blue smudges under his eyes were from lack
of sleep, not a fight. He'd woken up screaming three times
the night before. He stood up and pulled a rag out of his
back pocket to wipe his hands. "Aren't you supposed to be
in school?"

"Aren't you supposed to be at work?"

"I asked first."

"Teacher in-service," I said. "Your turn."

"Water pump is going."

The pickup, a 1982 Ford F-150 XL with a five-liter, small-block, V-8 engine, was going to outlive us both. Some days he'd clean and fiddle and fuss over it like the future of the world depended on it being able to shift smoothly and not overheat.

"You should be working on the rig instead." I nodded in the direction of the half-collapsed barn. The cab of his eighteen-wheeler had been parked there since the day we moved in. "You'll never get the price you're asking if you don't."

"Selling it as is." He grabbed a wrench from the tool bench and slid back under the pickup.

I found the other creeper next to the trash can and rolled under the front end next to him. The smell of gas, oil, rust, and coolant relaxed me a little. The half-ton of metal above us kept us safe from everything out there. I took a deep breath and the knot in my stomach loosened.

"Another great day at school, huh?" he asked.

"Hardly," I said. "Did you play football with Ms. Benedetti's brother?"

"I played basketball." He wiped the grime off a nut with his rag. "Lou Benedetti. Haven't thought about him for years. Big kid, so uncoordinated he could barely walk. Spent most of his time on the bench."

"You love football. Why didn't you go out for the team?"

"Because your grandfather wanted me to," Dad answered. "Get me a quarter-inch ratchet, will you? Ten-mil socket."

I rolled out, found the right wrench in the tool chest, rolled back under and handed it to him.

"Why were you talking to Ms. Benedetti?" he asked. "Math?"

"She said I should ask you about partying at the quarry."

"Boring story. Great bonfire, couple of arrests, and one knocked-out tooth. I didn't do it, by the way."

"Doesn't sound boring to me."

"There's a lot of stories about that place. Most of them are bullshit, but a couple kids died there. Not at our party. That's why it was considered boring."

"Ms. Benedetti called your work number. Whoever she talked to said you quit."

The wind blew a few dead leaves under the truck. Dad's mouth tightened. The shrapnel scars along his jaw glowed like a fragments of bone in a bed of cold ash. "What did you tell her?"

"Did you quit or did they fire you?" I asked.

"Doesn't matter."

His tone of voice meant that the discussion on that topic was officially closed, but he was wrong. The difference between walking out or being kicked out meant everything. Moving back here and getting a job was supposed to keep the crazy away.

"Why was she calling me?" he asked.

"Something about a Veterans Day assembly," I said. "I forgot the other thing."

Trish.

Saying her name out loud would be like giving him a cool, sweet glass of antifreeze to drink. It would go down with no trouble, but after a few hours, he'd get a headache and start breathing hard. His legs would cramp up, his eyes would stop working, and he'd slur his words. His organs would shut down, one after another, and he'd die all over again.

"That's not much help," Dad said.

"Something about paperwork," I said. "She said she'd come here to talk to you about it if you don't want to talk on the phone."

"She always was a pain in the ass." He let the loosened nut drop into his palm and removed the bolt. "I'll call her tomorrow."

Crap. "Then I need a favor."

He sighed and turned his head to look at me. "What?"

"We didn't have a teacher in-service today."

I waited for a response. He looked back up at the engine and applied the wrench to the next nut.

"You have to call the attendance office," I continued. "Tell them I had a doctor's appointment."

He whacked the nut with the handle of the wrench.

"Please, Daddy?"

A few flakes of rust landed on his face. "You promised, Hayley. We came back here so you could go to school."

"We came back so you could get a normal job. And keep it."

"Don't change the subject."

"It is the same subject. You quit. Why can't I? Let me take the GED and I'll start online classes in January."

"What, you're going to be my babysitter now?"

I didn't answer. He hit the frozen metal with the wrench over and over, rust raining on his face. The clanking sounded like a cracked bell getting ready to break into pieces.

"Well?" he demanded.

I had to change the angle of attack so he didn't feel like I was disrespecting him.

"It's not about babysitting you," I said, "it's about saving me. That place is awful. They have lockdown drills in case of a terrorist attack. Do you really want me to spend every day in a place like that? Making me go there is cruel and unusual punishment."

The stubborn nut finally moved. He cranked it a few times with the wrench. "Spare me the Eighth Amendment."

"I'll make you macaroni and cheese every night for a year if you let me quit."

He spun the nut off the bolt with his fingers. "Non-negotiable."

"I'll start tonight," I said. "Mac and cheese and mashed potatoes with bacon."

"You're going to school like all the other seniors." He brushed the rust off his face. "But I'll lie about the doctor's appointment if you get me the vise grips and a beer."

−*− 14 −*−

Gracie texted me at 11:30 that night:

> *fin wants your number*
>
> *who?*
>
> *adrkabl fin*
>
> *no*
>
> *ynot*
>
> *cuz*
>
> *ynotynotynot*
>
> *cuzcuzcuzcucuzcuz*

I'd been cyber-stalking Trish for hours. She didn't have any social media pages, at least not public ones. I found a couple of people from her high school class trying to track her down for a reunion, but no one knew where she was. They had all tried the phone numbers and addresses that I found in Texas, Nebraska, and Tennessee, but she wasn't to be found.

Gracie buzzed me again:

> *y dos he wnt yr nmbr?*
>
> *dunno ask him*

Trish was mentioned in her mother's obituary from three years ago. A couple of months after that, she was arrested for drunk driving. The paper didn't cover her trial, if there was one. She probably slithered out of that, too.

I texted Gracie:

so?
    sowht
why does he want my number?
    1 sec

I pulled a lighter out of the top drawer of my desk and lit a vanilla candle. The smell of mold from the wet insulation in my ceiling was getting stronger. (The roof leaked for a few weeks when we first moved in. It was going to be a while before we could afford to replace it.)

    fin sez u stol hz pen
he's a liar
    he wnts it
I don't have his pen
    hes a swmr
?
    finz a swimer buterfly u shuld c him nakd
    the abs omg
when did you see him naked?
    swm teem sutes betr thn nakd

*team
remove head from gutter, G
is he a good swimmer?
made states
he wnts yr lawrs number
lawrs?
*lawyers

I peeked out of the curtains. Dad was still in the driveway.

he wnts yr crimnl hstry
tell him I killed my last lawyer cuz he annoyed me

I slipped my finger under the flap of Trish's envelope and ripped it open. The sharp edge of the paper sliced into my fingertip. I swore and stuck my finger in my mouth.

he wnts 2 no if yr gay
yes
wtf??
????!!!!????
rilly????
want to go out with me? ☺
???
chill, im not gay
???? r u shur
you're not my type G

wats yr typ?
people who can spell
      fin sez he kn spl

It was cold outside, forty degrees. My father was still out there working on his truck, in the cold, wearing jeans and a T-shirt. He said he didn't feel anything.

I pulled my finger out and looked at it under the light. The cut was invisible until I pressed my thumb just below it. Blood welled up, a wet balloon that burst and dribbled over my thumbnail and dripped onto the envelope. I pulled the letter out of the envelope, keeping it folded, and smeared my cut on it.

My phone buzzed again.

      do u no how mny grls wnt fin 2 cll?
cll?
      *call
g'night G zzzzzzz

I turned off the phone, opened the top drawer of my bureau, and pulled out my hunting knife from under my pile of socks. (Dad bought it for me in Wyoming when he decided that I was old enough to walk alone at night to the truck stop bathroom.) I sliced the letter into paper ribbons and stuffed them in the envelope, then carried it, along with the candle, into the bathroom. After I shut and locked the bathroom door and turned off the light and opened the window, I held the envelope into the flame of the candle and watched in the mirror as the fire ate through the paper until I had to drop it in the sink so I wouldn't get burned.

My math teacher had a vendetta against me and as proof I offer the fact that I had not been told about Wednesday's test. Or if I had been told, it was not made entirely clear exactly when the test was going to be, and the fact that we were talking Serious Test, not just a wussy quiz.

1. Find a polynomial with integer coefficients that has the following zeros: $-\frac{1}{3}$, 2, $3 + i$.

2. Matthew throws a Pop-Tart at Joaquim while seated at the table for lunch. The height (in inches) of the Pop-Tart above the ground t seconds later is given by $h(t) = -16t^2 + 32t + 36$. What is the maximum height attained by the Pop-Tart?

3. It just got worse from here to the end of the test.

All of my answers were drawings of armored unicorns. Five minutes before the period ended, the principal's voice lectured the entire school about how badly we'd screwed up last week's lockdown drill. I drew a bomb attached to a ticking clock under one of the unicorns.

Some guy I'd never seen before crashed into me in the crowded frenzy that was the math wing after class, sending my books to the ground and me into the lockers. His buddies, average IQ that of newly hatched turkey vultures, burst into laughter. The geometry teacher standing in her doorway looked me in the eye and then turned away.

"Need some help?" Finn knelt beside me and handed me my copy of *The Odyssey*.

"No." I put the book on top of the stack and stood up.

"I can take him out if you want."

"I doubt that."

"Few people know this, but I am a trained assassin, skilled in jujitsu and krav maga. I can also, with a few folds, turn an ordinary piece of notebook paper into a lethal weapon. Or I can turn it into a butterfly, which is a great trick when I'm babysitting."

I fought a smile. "A trained assassin who babysits."

"Only the Greene twins and only because their family gets every premium channel on the planet." He paused to let a gaggle of freshman girls walk between us. "The skepticism on your face proves that my cover story is tight. That's good, reduces the chance that civilians might be harmed."

"Cover story? You mean the fact that you're a skinny nerd in charge of a nonexistent newspaper?"

"In development, not nonexistent. I am almost single-handedly reviving it. Where are we walking, by the way?"

"English." We swerved around a guy who was roughly the size and shape of a Porta-Potty.

"Ramos," the guy growled.

"Nash," Finn responded.

"Friend of yours?" I asked, once the guy was out of range.

"We train together. Cage fighting. You should hear him squeal when I get him in a Maynard's Kimura hold."

"You just made that up."

"What?"

"Maynard's Kimura. That's not real."

"It totally is."

The bell rang just as we got to Ms. Rogak's room.

"Wait!" He slipped between me and the door. "You promised."

"What are you talking about?"

"You promised me an article."

"Did not."

"Did too, just before you ran away from my car and roughly ten minutes after you coerced me into cutting physics. 'World of Resources at the Library,' that's what you promised."

A small bell went off in my head. *Duh.* This was why he was bugging Gracie for my phone number last night. *I'm an idiot.* He wanted to harass me about the stupid article.

"I didn't coerce you into cutting class. You offered the ride."

"You pleaded."

"I asked."

"You made puppy-dog eyes. That counts as pleading."

"I've never made puppy-dog eyes at anyone in my life. You're a lunatic."

"Gracie said you liked to tease. Hey there, Ms. Rogak. How's Homer doing?"

"Finnegan," said Ms. Rogak with a brief nod. "Do I have your permission to begin my class?"

"Exquisitely executed sarcasm, ma'am," Finn said as he started to walk backward. "Well played."

"And you, Hayley Kincain," she said. "Were you just going to menace us from the doorway or join us?"

—*— 16 —*—

The seat I wanted in the back row was taken, but not by Brandon Something, so I grabbed the empty desk by the drafty window. Ms. Rogak pushed a button on her laptop to show a picture of a buff, tanned guy with long, gray-streaked black hair, shoving a bloody sword toward the sky, his face tilted back, his mouth open in a victory scream.

ODYSSEUS, read the caption.

Before the giggling and obnoxious comments got too loud, she pushed the button again. A tiny, old woman, dressed in a white robe, her hair covered by a long, white cloth, was kneeling on the ground, her arms wrapped around a skinny, half-naked kid who looked on the brink of death. She was holding a cup to the child's lips.

MOTHER TERESA.

The third slide showed the two images side by side.

"Which one is the hero?" Rogak asked. "And why?"

I dozed with my eyes open the rest of the period.

—*— 17 —*—

Finn was waiting for me in the hall after class. "Did you finish the article?"

"I never said I would." I yawned. "Besides, did you think I'd write it in class?"

"Of course." He stayed by my side all the way down the hall. "What do you have now?"

"Gym."

"Perfect! You'll have it done in fifteen minutes."

I shifted my books to my right arm so I could accidentally poke him with their sharp corners. "I'm not writing it."

"But yesterday . . ." He paused as we merged into the traffic that flowed down the stairs. "How's your dad, by the way?"

"Fine." I dodged a group of onlookers who had encircled a brewing fight, then doubled my pace in the hopes of losing Finn. I would have, except for a roadblock by the cafeteria caused by the food line, which had snaked into the hall.

I sniffed. *Taco Day.*

Finn caught up with me in a flash. "I'm glad he's feeling better. I only need two hundred words."

"I. Said. No!" I said.

Well, actually, I sort of screamed it.

The lunch crowd quieted and a few wide-eyed freshman boys with feather-soft baby mustaches scooted toward the walls, opening a path for me. I put my head down and jogged through.

Finn stayed at my heels. "It's just that I really need the help," he said. "Cleveland says the newspaper is back on the chopping block. Getting an article from an actual student-reporter might help him convince the board to leave the paper alone."

I stopped at the girl's locker room door. "Why don't you write it?"

He drew back, wounded. "I'm the editor. I don't write, I edit, with the exception of the sports section, which I write out of love, not duty. Besides—"

"Wait," I interrupted. "Did you say Cleveland?"

"Yep."

"Mr. Cleveland? Calc teacher?"

"Precalc, actually. Also algebra and trig."

"Even if I wanted to, which I don't, Mr. Cleveland won't let me write for the paper. He hates me. Loathes me. If I were you, I wouldn't mention my name to him, ever. Raises his blood pressure."

Two girls walked between us and into the locker room.

"I have to go," I said, hand on the door. "Thanks again for the ride."

"You're wrong about Cleveland." He uncapped a Sharpie, grabbed my arm, and started writing on it before I could react. "That's my email. Two hundred words. Library re-sources."

"What is wrong with him?" I asked, bouncing the ball on the Ping-Pong table. "And what is wrong with you?"

"Me?" Gracie asked. "I'm totally innocent."

"Innocent?" I served the ball so hard she squealed and dove for the ground. "He won't leave me alone! Look what he did to my arm! That's assault."

"Assault with a Sharpie?"

"You dragged me into this. Make him stop bugging me."

"Only if you don't throw the paddle at my head," Gracie said from under the table.

The gym aide blew her whistle. We all groaned and shuffled to the next station. Calling it "gym class" was an exaggeration because Belmont didn't have gym teachers anymore. A couple of years earlier the state had fiddled with the law so school districts could save money by firing all the gym teachers. Students still had to take phys ed, but we only had to be supervised by volunteer "gym aides" (aka parents who couldn't find a job) who took attendance and tried to keep us from breaking the equipment.

The aide blew her whistle again, louder this time, and hollered, "Let's get a move on, ladies."

Two soccer players commandeered the stationary bikes. A group of zombies put together a game of special-rules kickball. The goal was to kick all the balls behind the bleachers and then spend the rest of the period pretending to look for them. I wanted to work on push-ups and pull-ups, but Gracie dragged me to the corner where some fellow freaks were trying to copy poses from a yoga app on a girl's phone.

"I'm not very flexible," I said.

"You need to stretch more," Gracie scolded.

Three girls pretending to have cramps approached the gym aide, whining that they needed to go to the nurse's office. The gym aide wrote out a pass for them and returned to her magazine.

"I hate this place," I muttered.

"Blah, blah, blah." Gracie twisted her body and her legs in opposite directions. "Try this." She lifted her chin up. "I don't know why you're so negative about the newspaper."

I sat with my legs straight in front of me and reached for my toes. "Are you kidding me?"

She untwisted herself and lay down. "You're always complaining about this place. Here's your chance to do something about it."

I leaned as far forward as I could, but stopped an inch short of my sneakers. "By writing about resources in the library?"

Gracie put her arms out on the floor. "That's a test to see if you're any good, which we both know you are. After that you can write what you want. Write about all the stuff here that you hate."

"That is not a yoga pose," I said.

"Is so. It's called 'resting crane.'" She raised her fingertips and bent her wrists back until she looked like a crossing guard stopping traffic in both directions, only lying on a gym floor instead of standing in a crosswalk. "Write for the paper."

I bent my knees a little and grabbed my sneakers. "I have more important things to do."

—*— 19 —*—

The dining room table was covered with newspapers, cleaning rods, a double-ended breech-brush, used patches, and rags stained with barrel oil, solvents, and gunpowder.

Daddy's guns—the rifles, the shotguns, and the pistols—were nowhere in sight.

Why would he clean all of them at once? I capped the barrel oil. *Does he think he's going to need them?*

I headed down the hall, flipped on the overhead light, and knocked on his bedroom door. "I'm home."

"Okay," came the groggy answer.

"Where's Spock?"

"Out back on the chain."

There was a circle of grime around the doorknob from Dad opening it when his hands were greasy. A shredded spiderweb was strung from the top-right edge of the door frame to the shade of the overhead light in the middle of the hall. The house was looking more and more like a place that squatters lived in, instead of what it was: a home that had been in Dad's family for three generations.

"Did you eat anything today?" I asked. *What is going on? I thought.*

"Not hungry."

"What do you want for dinner?" I asked. *Why were you cleaning the guns?*

"Did you hear what I just said?" he asked.

"I think we have some chicken." *Were you up all night again?*

"Let me sleep."

"It's two thirty in the afternoon." *Who are you afraid of?* "Can I throw out the newspaper? On the dining room table?"

There was a pause so long that I began to think he'd

fallen back asleep, but finally he said, "Yeah. Sorry about the mess."

I fed Spock and put away the tools. The tang of gunpowder lingered in the house, so strong that I wondered if he'd opened a couple of shells for the hell of it. Freakish visions crowded in—*Dad smearing gunpowder on his face for camouflage, Dad pouring a thick circle of gunpowder on the floor, sitting in the middle of it and lighting a match, Dad . . .* The only way to get rid of them was to open all the windows and clean the table.

How many of the girls in my gym class had to clean up gunpowder and barrel oil after school?

Ha.

Maybe that was why I want to slap so many of the zombies; they had no idea how freaking lucky they were. Lucky and ignorant, happy little rich kids who believed in Santa Claus and the tooth fairy and thought that life was supposed to be fair.

I scrubbed until my hands ached and I was out of breath, then I found an ancient bottle of lemon oil and rubbed it into the tabletop. The scent of the lemon warred with the gunpowder smell and made my eyes water.

Spock and I went for a walk until the fumes cleared.

—*— 20 —*—

I hitch a ride back to the outpost in a truck filled with ammunition, pork chops, and two guys from Bravo Company. Private first class Mariah Stolzfuss drives, telling me about Jaden, her dancing toddler in Arkansas. We follow a Humvee that is filled with boys barely enough old to shave.

A star goes supernova in the middle of the road.

We fly. Wingless birds.

Shock waves ripple through metal, glass, and flesh. Bone crumbles. Skin explodes. Nerves snap. Brains slosh and spill in dented tin skulls. Arteries spray like high-pressure hoses, painting the world a bright, sad red.

I swim through the smoke. Private Stolzfuss still sits behind the wheel. I wipe the blood off her face to find her mouth, make her breathe. She doesn't have a mouth. She doesn't have a face anymore.

Boys pull me away, strong boys with faces and mouths. They help me sit in the dust and try to get Private Stolzfuss out of the truck. Her arm comes off in their hands. Her blood trickles, drips. Her heart exploded in the middle of her story.

In Arkansas, her son dances, waiting.

Either I never turned my alarm on or I turned it off without realizing it, because what woke me up was not a buzzing phone, but the sound of the bus rumbling down the street.

I swore and threw off the covers.

I could:

A. walk to school

B. wake up my father and tell him he has to drive me and use that warm, fuzzy time together in the truck to ask why he cleaned all the guns

C. stay home because he'd probably sleep all day again and he'd never know the difference if I snuck out a little before two and made a lot of noise "coming home" half an hour later.

Option C had some long-term consequences, but the good part was that they were long-term, so I wouldn't have to deal with them for a while, or at least for a couple of days. C was the winning option, right up until the doorbell rang.

I shouldn't have answered it. I should have gone back to bed. In my defense, I was half asleep and not thinking clearly. I knew it was too early for the mail. Gracie drove in with Topher these days, so it wouldn't have been her. I didn't even think about Trish until I was already pulling the door open.

"Good morning, sleepyhead!" shouted Finn.

Thankfully, I'd left the chain on. As I went to close it in his face, he wedged his foot between the door and the frame.

"Ouch," he said.

"Move your foot."

"No."

"Go away."

"Glad to see you, too."

"What are you doing here?" I asked.

"You missed the bus," he said.

"I'm sick."

"Need chicken soup?"

"Actually, it's my period," I lied. "Killer cramps."

"Chocolate and a heating pad?"

"How do you know that?"

"I have an older sister and my mom is a kick-ass feminist," he said. "I'm probably the only guy in school who can buy tampons without having a seizure. Look at that, I can even say the word. 'Tampon, tampon, tampon.' If you say it enough, it stops sounding like a word, know what I mean?"

"Keep it down," I warned. "My dad is still sleeping."

"Then who just left in the pickup truck?"

"What?"

Finn removed his foot so I could close the door, free the chain, and open the door wide enough to see the empty driveway.

"Big white guy, huge arms, right? Yankees cap, scary sunglasses? I was parked up the block. Watched him pull out of the driveway and head for the city. That's why I figured you needed a ride."

Dad always told me when he picked up a job because it meant the new beginning, the fresh start that was going to change everything right up until the moment a day or two later when it came crashing down around him. Could he have gone to the VA to make up one of the missed appointments? Was he looking for a liquor store that opened early? When would he be back? More important, what kind of mood would he be in?

Option C was no longer an option.

"So," Finn continued, "were you going to put on some pants or go to school pretending that your T-shirt there is a dress?"

—*— 22 —*—

I hadn't paid much attention to Finn's car when I bummed the ride from him on Tuesday. At one point in the distant past, it had been a Plymouth Acclaim, but there wasn't much left to shout about. It had four bald tires, four doors, a trunk that had to be wired shut with a twisted coat hanger, a dented roof, and more rust than paint.

"Somebody must really hate you," I said.

"Awesome, right?" He patted the roof. "Bought it on my own."

The engine started without catching fire. Finn backed down the driveway and shifted into DRIVE. We drove down the road slowly. Part of my head was trying to figure out where Dad went and why. Another part was trying to figure out if it was better to stare out the windshield or to look at Finn and pretend I knew what I was supposed to say in a situation like this. Another part of my brain was trying to figure out what that stench was.

"How much body spray did you put on today?" I blurted out.

"Too much?" He braked for a stop sign.

"You qualify as a hazmat site."

He snorted and laughed and, for some reason, the sound drowned out everything that I was worried about. He turned to look at me, still chuckling, still ridiculously stopped at the stop sign and I realized that for a tall, skinny dude with shaggy hair, he was a little hot. Maybe it was the way he blushed, or the silver hoop in his right ear, or the fact that he had green eyes, the same color green you can see in the summer if you lie under an oak tree and look up at the sun coming through the leaves. And they slanted up a little. And he had killer eyelashes. Just the right amount of beard scruff on his chin.

You know how some babies are blessed by good fairies when they're born, fairies with names like Beauty and Brains and Kindness and Laughter? I was blessed by their evil underworld troll cousins, Gawky and Awkward. I stared at him and my troll fairies whacked me upside the head with their pointy wands, making me spectacularly. . . . gawkward.

I was dressed like a bag lady. Probably smelled like one, too. I hadn't showered, of course. My plan had been to stay in my pajamas all day. I hadn't brushed my teeth, either. I just threw on clothes picked out of the laundry heap, ran a comb through my hair, swiped deodorant on my pits and ran.

OMG, did he put on extra body spray because I smelled this bad on Tuesday? Then why would he let me in his car again?

My good sense bitch-slapped my estrogen and told her to get a grip.

I sniffed the air again: a lethal amount of body spray, a little of my stank, and . . . something that was definitely coming from the engine.

"Do you smell that?" I asked.

"I get it, Hayley. Too much body spray. Point taken."

"No, I'm serious." I sniffed again. "When was the last time you checked under the hood?"

"Um, never."

"What? When was the last time you checked your fluids?"

He accelerated. "That sounds perverted."

"It's not. You're burning oil."

"I thought that was coming from another car."

"Pull over for a second." I leaned toward the dash as the car rolled to a stop. "See that?" I pointed to a wisp of white smoke rising from the edge of the car's hood. "You probably have oil leaking from a valve cover."

He reached for his key. "Is it going to blow up?"

I shook my head. "That's not much smoke, don't panic. Just check the oil the next time you get gas."

"You're sure it's safe to drive?"

"A couple drops of oil hit the exhaust manifold. We're fine. But remember to check it."

He drove in silence.

"You do know how to check the oil, don't you?" I asked.

"Of course."

"Liar." I pushed the button on the armrest to put down the window. Nothing happened. "Are the windows broken, too?"

"No." He jabbed at a button on his armrest. My window screeched down two inches and stopped.

"I thought you said it wasn't broken."

"Well." He braked to a stop as the green light in front of us turned yellow. "It might be a little broken."

"A little broken is still broken," I pointed out.

"But fixable."

As he pulled away from the light, I leaned my head against the shoulder strap and took a deep breath of October morning air. Maybe my blood sugar was low, but it felt like I was in a bubble, a perfect, shimmering bubble moving forward with my eyes closed, air soft as cold silk brushing over my forehead, smoothing back my hair.

And then Finn ruined everything.

"So," he said as we pulled into the parking lot. "That article. You wrote it, right?"

The bubble popped.

"Oh my God, are you still on that?" I asked.

"Why wouldn't I be?"

"'Cause it's stupid! Nobody gives a crap about the resources in the library. Why is that even a word, '*resources*'? It doesn't mean anything."

"That's not the point."

"So?"

"You promised that you would do it."

"Did not."

He pulled into a parking space between a Lexus and a minivan. "I've given you two rides this week."

"I only asked for one. Why are you such a pain in my butt? You don't even know me. Do you always bully strangers into doing stuff they don't want to do?"

As the words came out, I knew I didn't mean them but I couldn't figure out how to unsay them.

Finn shifted to PARK and turned to look at me. "Were you going to blow off school today?"

"Why do you care?" I crossed my arms over my chest. "This place sucks."

"No kidding. You have any homework for Cleveland?"

"Didn't do it. Spare me the lecture."

"What's your average?"

"Can a negative number be an average?"

"How about this—I'll do your math if you write the article. Right now, in the cafeteria." He cut the engine. "Then we'll be even and I won't bug you anymore."

I wrote the stupid article.

I made up names of databases, I put in quotes from students who didn't exist (Paige Turner and Art T. Ficial), and devoted a paragraph—deep in the story—to the "special shelves" where all the banned and challenged books were held. ("'That's where you find all the sex stuff,' said Art T. Ficial.") By the time I was finished writing (and cracking myself up), I was actually in a less-than-cranky mood. The fact that Dad had woken up before noon and taken off in the truck was a good sign, I decided. A great one. He was coming out of the dark place where he'd been hiding for the last few weeks. It was all part of the big adjustment of living normal instead of moving around the country like we were being chased by phantoms. He was having a good day and I was going to have a good day and before I knew it, I'd written a sidebar piece to the library article filled with the URLs of made-up websites for students who wanted help with their homework.

Finn did my math, though I wasn't quite sure how. Every few minutes a new horde of girls would buzz over and bug him about tickets or T-shirts or swim practice. I put in my earbuds and cranked the music.

"Are you a man-whore?" I asked as the loudest group of them teetered away on their high heels. (High heels? Really? At seven thirty in the morning? Shouldn't you actually have breasts before you start wearing heels?) "Or does that stink spray make you irresistible to baby-zombie-bitches?"

"Yes." Finn grinned, eyes glued to the b-z-b butts. "And yes."

But he did my homework. And the look on Mr. Cleveland's face was worth putting up with Finn. Cleveland hadn't gotten around to grading our tests yet, so I left second period feeling almost, kind of, a little . . . happy.

Who says miracles don't happen?

The day only got better after that. Brandon wasn't in English, and Ms. Rogak showed a movie that lasted the entire period. I was awake enough in study hall to finish my Chinese homework, and then health turned into an accidental study hall because the teacher was sick, so I was able to get a nap after all. The sub in forensics was a retired cop who told us real stories about blood-spatter patterns and estimating when a murder had been committed by the age of the maggots and flies on the corpse. Nobody fell asleep.

In Chinese, Ms. Neff gave me and a girl named Sasha extra points for our pinyin homework because we were the only people who had done it. As Sasha high-fived me, I decided that I might do more homework if they made it into a competitive sport.

Even social studies sort of rocked. Mr. Diaz was teaching about the Indian Removal Act of 1830 and he neglected to mention the Chickasaw people. I raised my hand (politely) and pointed out (respectfully) his error. His face turned angry red, but he spent a minute typing on his computer, then reading the screen, and then he said, "Thank you, Hayley. You are correct. The Chickasaw were forced to walk the Trail of Tears, too."

I raised my hand. He grimaced, but called on me again.

"Because thousands of native people died on the Trail of Tears, shouldn't we call it a 'genocide' instead of a 'forced march'?" I asked. "If an African government today did the same thing to their indigenous people, we'd be screaming about it in the United Nations and raising money for the victims, wouldn't we?"

The debate that followed was so awesome I didn't doodle in my notebook once.

—*— 24 —*—

I should have known better.

The laws of the universe dictate that for every positive action, there is an unequal and sucky reaction. So the fact that Thursday had been a somewhat decent day meant that Friday was required to go up in flames.

It started just after midnight. I'd been half sleeping on the couch, waiting, because Dad had gone out for milk and bread right after I got home from school and hadn't returned. Spock barked, that's what startled me awake. The lights of the pickup truck flashed through the front window as it pulled into the driveway.

Spock went to the door, tail wagging. A few moments later, the door opened. Dad smiled when he saw me, grin lopsided, eyes not quite focused. Drunk. When I asked him where he'd been, he called me his sweet girl. He sat down next to me on the couch, leaned his head back, and passed out.

I checked his face and hands; there were no scrapes or cuts to show he'd been in a fight. I threw on a jacket and my sneakers and went out to the truck. No marks on the bumpers, no new scratches in the paint. I opened the door and found empty Budweiser cans in the foot well and an extra hundred and fifteen miles on the odometer.

* * *

Finn hadn't said that he'd pick me up on Friday. In fact, I hadn't seen him since I gave him the library article. But I sort of watched for him while I was standing at the bus stop. He didn't show.

The bus smelled like fresh puke.

The cafeteria was being fumigated, so first period was wasted in the auditorium being supervised by a teacher I had never seen before who had clearly forgotten to take her medication.

Not only did I flunk my math test with a 0 percent (that's right, he didn't give me any points for putting my name on the paper and remembering the correct date), but I also flunked my homework by getting every problem right.

SEE ME! was scrawled at the top of my paper. In red.

Rogak forced a surprise quiz on the lotus-eaters down our throats, we had not one, but two lockdown drills during study hall (we were too loud during the first one), and then we had to go outside for gym because the janitors were doing something sticky to the gym floor.

I had dressed for fall, you know, long sleeves, jeans, boots. Summer had reappeared, choking us with eighty degrees instead of fifty. I had a heatstroke and that's why I zoned in forensics and Chinese and didn't rise to the bait when Diaz asked me what I thought about the legacy of Andrew Jackson.

The final bell rang and my classmates sprinted for the exits. I trudged back down to the math wing.

"There's cheating and then there's felony cheating." Cleveland shook my homework in my face. "It's not even your handwriting, Hayley. How stupid do you think I am?"

I had so much fun thinking about possible answers to that question that I didn't hear much of what he said for the next five minutes. Then an alarm sounded in my brain.

"Excuse me, sir, could you please repeat that?"

"I said I've arranged a tutor for you."

"I don't need a tutor."

He picked up his red pen and circled my test grade again.

"Okay," I said. "I don't want a tutor."

"It's the only way you're going to pass this class, and that's assuming you work your tail off."

"I'm actually kind of, you know, smart," I said. "I don't need a tutor."

He laughed so hard he could barely catch his breath. "Wow." He pulled a couple of tissues out of the box on his desk and dabbed at his eyes. "Whew! I haven't laughed like that in a while." He blew his nose and chucked the tissues in the trash. "Finnegan Ramos has agreed to tutor you."

"No. I want somebody else."

"You want a pony, too? Most of life is doing things we don't want to do, Hayley."

"Thanks for the wisdom, sir, but it doesn't apply here."

"Then I'll set up a meeting with your," he glanced at his screen, "father and Ms. Benedetti so we can discuss which lower-level math class you belong in." He typed on his keyboard and looked at the screen again. "It says here that your father's phone number and email don't work. How can I get in touch with him?"

I chewed the inside of my cheek. How would Dad react? How would he handle himself in a meeting like that? What if Benedetti mentioned Trish?"

"What do I have to do so that you don't call my father?"

He looked at me over the monitor, eyes serious. "Tutoring sessions until you catch up on the work you've blown off. Do your own homework and get your grade out of the toilet by the end of the semester and pass all tests." He stood up. "Also, it wouldn't hurt if you wrote a few more satire pieces for what we hope is going to be a newspaper one of these days."

"Excuse me?"

"Finn showed me your article. He said you wanted a regular opinion column. It might be a good idea, as long as your grade comes up and you don't get controversial. No abortion, no religion, and nothing about today's botched lockdown drill, okay? The board is on the fence about releasing the money for the paper; the last thing we need is to upset them with an actual opinion about something that matters."

I opened my mouth, but words didn't come out.

He handed me back my fake homework. "Your first tutoring session starts now. He's in the library."

—*— 25 —*—

I tried. I really did, but it was ten million degrees in the library, and Finn was being an obstinate jerk. The fans set up in the stacks sounded like jackhammers, and my brain was melting.

I might have said a few things to him that were less than nice.

Finn finally stood up and slammed his book closed.

"This isn't going to work." he said. "I'll email Cleveland."

"No," I said. "I'm sorry. Sorry, sorry, sorry. I didn't mean that."

"You're not even trying."

I almost argued with him about that, but then I remembered that screwing this up meant Dad would get involved and that would end badly.

"I stayed up too late gaming," I said. "Sleep deprivation makes me cranky. It won't happen again, I swear."

He sat back down. "Why do you have such a crappy attitude about math?"

"I don't. I have a crappy attitude about everything."

After that, I did a better job of listening and, eventually, the concept of rational functions started to make a little sense. At least it seemed like Finn was finally explaining it to me in English. The library slowly emptied and we both relaxed a little and before I knew it, an hour had gone by.

"Library closes in thirty minutes," called the aide at the front desk.

Finn started shoving books into his backpack. "Did Cleveland talk to you about your next article?"

"More satire for a column I don't want?"

"I didn't get a chance to mention that, did I?"

I stared at the sea of equations on the page. "Do you really think he'll cut me some slack?"

"He won't pass you just for helping out with the paper." Finn scratched his chin. "But let's say you brought your F up to an almost C—"

"Impossible," I said.

"Stranger things have happened," he continued. "I bet a couple articles might take you from almost C into definite C territory. Or at least really-super-close to a C. Couldn't hurt. What are you doing tonight?"

"Why?" I asked, hackles instantly up.

"Home football game, under the lights. I need you to cover it."

"I don't like high school football."

"Neither does half the team."

"I thought you were the sports writer."

"And editor," he reminded me.

"So why can't you do it?"

He grinned and wiggled his eyebrows. "Got a date."

"Nobody says 'date' anymore."

"Corner table," scolded the library aide, waving her stapler at us. "Keep it down, please."

We leaned our heads together. His body spray was at a less-than-toxic level.

"I'll make you a deal," he whispered, his lips close to my ear.

I tried to ignore the shiver that ran down my spine. "What?"

"I'll pay you ten bucks if you cover the game."

"Fifteen."

"Done." He stood up.

"We have another half hour," I said in surprise. "Where are you going?"

"I have to get ready, remember? Big night." He scribbled a number at the top of my problem sheet. "Call me tomorrow if you forget how to do polynomial functions." He put his books in his backpack. "Aren't you going to wish me luck?"

"How about 'Keep your pants zipped'?"

"Do I have to?"

"First date?"

He nodded.

"If you want a second one with her, then, yeah, you should keep your pants zipped. And your belt buckled."

"Do I get to kiss her, Grandma?"

"Depends."

"On what?"

"On if she feels like kissing you. God, Finn, haven't you ever gone out on a date before?"

"Millions of them. I'm a world-class Casanova, women on five continents swoon at the mere sight of me, *People* magazine—"

I held up my hands. "Spare me the details. I'll see you Monday."

26

All of the bus windows were open on the ride home, but the air that poured through them came straight out of a volcanic eruption. I closed my eyes and thought about a long, ice-cold shower. After that, I'd eat a box of Popsicles, and then I'd call a limo to take me to the megaplex and I would watch movie after movie in air-conditioning so cold I'd need to buy a sweatshirt to prevent hypothermia.

Except that I was broke, so most of that plan was a mirage brought on by the ungodly temperature of the bus.

The shower would feel good, though. Maybe I'd eat a Popsicle in the shower, cool my inside and outside at the same time.

The bus stopped, wheezed open the doors, and let off another group of bedraggled students.

I didn't want to go to the football game. It would be safer to ride my bike than ask Dad to drive me, and that meant I'd be sweat-soaked and gross again by the time I got there. And I'd be even grosser by the time I got home. I should have held out for twenty bucks. Maybe fifty.

The bus stopped in traffic, and the sun beat on the roof, broiling me like a cheap steak set too close to the coils at the top of the oven.

A cold shower, Popsicles, and then I would fill the bathtub with ice cubes and lie in it. The books I'd checked out of the library earlier in the week were still stacked on my bureau, whispering my name and begging to be read.

If Finn wanted me to write about the game, then he'd have to find a way to get me there and home again without me risking heatstroke. I checked the number he'd written in my notebook, dialed it, and listened to it ring twenty times before hanging up.

Who doesn't have voice mail?

The Big Date must have already started. I started to text Gracie to ask if she knew who Finn was going out with, but I deleted the message. The information wasn't worth alerting her Early Warning System. It was probably a girl from another school, anyway. He was a big flirt with an inflated opinion of himself. In fairness, he was sort of funny. And not entirely unattractive. My thoughts drifted to what he must look like in a Speedo, but I yanked them firmly back. The heat was causing my brain to short-circuit.

I stepped off the bus, wiped the sweat off my face, and started walking. Maybe I'd skip the game. I'd find a way to borrow the team statistics and eavesdrop by the jock table Monday morning to pick up a few quotes. That would work. Totally work.

The closer I got to home, the better I felt. I'd treat myself to a reading marathon all weekend. All the ice cream

I could eat, all the pages I could read. *Heaven*.

The mood lasted until I saw the trucks crowded in our driveway: two shiny pickups, a battered SUV, and a Jeep Wrangler with no roof or doors, along with three motorcycles. They were stuffed full of camping equipment, fishing poles, coolers, and covered with military bumper stickers.

The windows of the house were open, shattered, maybe, by the deafening volume of the music being played in the living room. The song stopped and a loud chorus of voices, men's voices, burst into laughter, name-calling, and cursing.

I opened the door. The living room and dining room beyond it were crowded with a dozen guys all older than me and younger than Dad, with military-short hair, black ink on jacked-up arms. They wore T-shirts stretched tight, silver dog-tag chains slipping under the collar. Despite the heat, they all wore long pants, jeans, or camo. A couple had knives hanging off their belts and sat with knees bouncing, eyes restless, darting on involuntary perimeter checks. Soldiers, for sure. Active duty infantry, on leave.

Dad sat in the middle of the couch, pale and tired compared to them, but looking more like himself than he had in months. He raised a can of soda high.

"Hayley Rose! Just in time!"

27

The guys all shook my hand, polite and respectful as Dad introduced me around. The sight of them, the smell of so many soldiers in a room on a hot day, brought back a vague memory of living on base when I was little. I shook my head to clear it away.

"Is there going to be a quiz to see if I can remember your names?" I asked.

"No, ma'am," said several of the guys at once.

"Wait till you see the backyard," Dad said.

As we walked through the house, he explained that they all served with an old friend of his, Roy Pinkney, and were on leave and headed north to Roy's camp near Saranac Lake.

We stepped out of the back door and my mouth dropped open.

"Roy took one look at the backyard, hollered 'Potential!' and sent some of his boys into town to rent a mower," Dad explained with a grin. "It only took an hour or so before they had the whole place squared away."

For the first time in weeks, the backyard had been mowed. Mowed and neatly raked. A fire pit had been dug in the middle, circled with stones and piled with wood, ready to be lit. A soldier stripped to the waist was chopping wood with a splitting maul. Chairs and upended logs waited around the fire pit. Four small tents had been set up, too, poles straight and strings taut.

A tall, bald man walked up to us. "Do not tell me this is your little girl, Andy. No way."

"Hayley Rose," Dad said. "You won't remember him, but this is Roy."

I put out my hand to shake, but the man gathered me into a big hug and kissed the top of my head.

"Not possible," he said, releasing me and smiling. "It is just not possible for you to have grown up this much." He stepped back and looked at me. "I hope you thank God every night that you take after your mom instead of this ugly cuss."

"Yes, sir," I said.

"Do you remember the first time you handed this angel to me, Andy?" Roy asked.

"When we were living next to the PX?" Dad asked.

Roy nodded. "You must have been about, what, five months old?"

"I don't remember, sir," I said.

"Three months, I think," Dad said. "Rebecca was still alive."

My mouth dropped open for the second time because Dad never, and I mean *never*, said my mother's name out loud.

"You're right," Roy said. "I can remember her laughing at me. You see, Hayley, your father handed you to me just as you were starting to do your duty in your diaper. And it was July, as I recall, so all you were wearing was that diaper. I'd just come from, I don't know where, but it was something that required me to be in my finest dress uniform and I looked good."

Dad snorted but Roy ignored him.

"So I sit down in your folk's apartment and your sweet mother leaves to pour me some iced tea and your face goes all red and you start grunting—"

(I said a quick prayer of thanks that the shirtless guy chopping wood could not hear this.)

"—and Andy hands you to me, and I knew nothing about babies so I laid you on my lap. And then your diaper exploded."

Dad and Roy both cracked up and I waited for the earth to swallow me. Roy gave me another hug, and then Dad did, too, and finally I laughed and I realized that there was no way in hell I was going to the stupid football game.

I stayed on the edges of the conversations for the next few hours. I made three dozen deviled eggs, ran the dishwasher, and kept an eye on my father, waiting for him to get drunk. But he didn't. He drank soda and lemonade, even as all the other guys pounded beer and Roy sipped Scotch. This was a new version of my father, comfortable in his skin. Happy to joke about life over there and his scars and the bullshit they all had to deal with from desk-jockey officers and lying politicians.

I couldn't believe what I was watching.

Dad hated talking about the war and never did it sober. Half the time he didn't even want people to know he was a vet. Strangers often said things like, "Thank you for your service," because they meant it and they thought that was the right thing to do, but the problem was it set off a series of detonations inside my father that sometimes ended with him punching a wall or the face of a jerk in a bar. The worst was when he accidentally found himself in conversation with the family member of a soldier who had been killed. The sadness in their eyes would blow another hole in his brain and then he'd go dead quiet for days.

And yet here he was, as sober as Spock and me, and being a soldier was all he could talk about. And he was *laughing*.

Roy had brought a couple of grills and soon the hot dogs and hamburgers were piled high and the guys in the back-yard chowed down. I got a look at the cooler, which was filled with six kinds of ice cream plus whipped cream and a bunch of half-frozen candy bars that Roy told me were going to be chopped up and mixed with the ice cream, and I was a confused, but happy and grateful girl.

Until Michael showed up.

After Gramma died, Michael rented her house from

my father; apparently, they'd been buddies in high school. He moved out when we moved in, but he came back more often than I liked. The way he looked at me creeped me out and I was beginning to think that he was the source of Dad's weed. He'd never done anything that I could complain about to Dad, but whenever he walked in the door, I felt the need to be somewhere else. Roy and his guys would have Dad's back if Michael wanted to do anything profoundly stupid.

Covering the football game for the newspaper seemed like a good idea after all.

—*— 28 —*—

The crowd in the stadium roared so loudly I couldn't hear what the mom manning the ticket booth said.

"Why?" I asked again.

She glared and waited a beat for the noise to die down. "Everybody pays to get into the game. No exceptions."

"But I'm the press," I whined. "On assignment."

"Students get a dollar discount." She put her hand out. "Four dollars or don't go in."

I paid her. Finn now owed me nineteen bucks.

The bleachers were a wall of people dressed in Belmont yellow. For one second, it felt like they were all staring at me, that they all knew I came to the football game alone and didn't know where to sit, but then a whistle blew and the football teams on the field behind me crashed into each other and the crowd cheered and jumped up and down. I was invisible to them.

I turned my back to the stands. On the other side of the field sat the enemy, the Richardson Ravens, dressed in black and silver. Beyond the goalposts at the far end of the field rose a gentle hill that was dotted with people sitting on blankets, little kids zooming around them, cheerfully ignoring the sad excuse for a football game.

The referee blew his whistle and the two lines of players crashed into each other again, grunting and shouting. I couldn't see what happened to the ball, but the Richardson side of the field erupted in cheers.

I texted Gracie:

hey

After a long pause, she wrote back:

at movie ttyl?

I sent a simple smiley face, because my phone did not have a smiley face that was wrapping her hands around her own throat and beating her head against a wall.

The two teams ran to their huddles to plot out their next bit of brilliant strategy. They ended the huddle and ran back to line up, each face inches away from the scowling face of the enemy, feet pawing at the ground like impatient horses. The quarterback grunted, the lines crashed together, and they all fell down again. Everyone in Belmont yellow screamed and whistled.

Should I be writing this down? I looked up at the stands. *Wouldn't anyone who cared about this game be here? Why would they want to read about it?* Answer: they wouldn't. My earlier plan to get the stats and eavesdrop for quotes first period Monday was still viable and even more attractive than it had been on the bus. I just needed someplace to go that was not my house. It was only a quarter to eight. I could probably make it to the mall before nine.

what movie

I texted Gracie.

She didn't answer, which meant she was with Topher, which meant any hope I had of crashing her Friday night plans had just evaporated. How lame would it be for me to go to Gracie's house and ask her mom if she wanted to hang out? Mrs. Rappaport was a big fan of home makeover shows. Last time I was at her house, she'd been talking about redesigning her kitchen. Maybe we could watch a few episodes about countertops.

I shuddered. I'd be better off spending the evening chasing rats out of Dumpsters.

The clock clicked down the last few seconds to half-time, the refs blew their whistles, and people raced for the bathrooms and the food stand.

"This is ridiculous," I muttered as I pressed against the fence that separated the spectators from the field. As soon as the herd moved past, I followed, intending to head for the parking lot, unchain my bike, and ride. Not home, not for a few hours. Just ride in the dark and hope that Topher and Gracie would have a huge fight and she'd call in tears and ask me to spend the night and mention that they had a lot of ice cream in the freezer.

"Great game, huh?"

I turned around, ready to spew venom about parents who were happy to pay taxes for football coaches but would be good-God-damned if they were going to waste their money on librarians or gym teachers.

"I was certain we'd be down thirty points by now," Finn said.

In his left hand, he was holding a flimsy cardboard box loaded with cheeseburgers, greasy fries, and two soda cups. In his right, he held a third cup that was filled with marigolds that looked like they'd been yanked out of somebody's backyard.

"What'd you think of that first-down denial?" he asked. "Great way to end the half, right?"

"What happened to your date?" I asked.

"She's here," he said.

"You brought your big date to this football game? You could have written the article yourself."

"No, I couldn't," he said. "What girl wants to be ignored on a date? Hold this for me."

He shoved the box that held the food and drink at me, pulled his buzzing phone out of his pocket, glanced at it, and typed a reply. Behind us, the marching band took their position on the field, drummers beating a solemn cadence.

"Okay." Finn put his phone away. "Want to meet her?"

"Wouldn't miss it for the world." I followed him through the crowd. "Is she a zombie?" I asked. "I bet she's wearing Belmont yellow. Oh, God, Finn—is she a cheerleader?"

"Definitely not a zombie or a cheerleader or a zombie cheerleader. I'm just getting to know her. Actually, it's sort of a blind date."

"That's gross," I said. "Old people go on blind dates when they get divorced and don't know what else to do. You're only, what? Sixteen?"

"Almost eighteen," he corrected.

"And you already need other people to fix you up?" I laughed.

"This way." He took the box from me and headed for the exit.

"Did you lock her in your trunk?"

"I'm meeting her up on the hill. I thought it would be more romantic than cement bleachers."

The marching band launched into "Louie, Louie," saving him from hearing my answer.

—*— 29 —*—

I followed him past the giggling children rolling down the hills like sausages. Past their tired parents sitting on stained comforters with their arms around each other. Past people critiquing the performance of the band and the flag twirlers. We walked all the way to the top of the hill and into the shadows beyond the reach of the stadium lights.

"She dumped you," I said.

"Not yet." He put the box of food and soda at the edge of a plaid blanket.

"Maybe she had to pee," I said. "What's her name again?"

"Her name is Hayley." He straightened up and handed me the cup of marigolds. "Hello, Miss Blue."

"Me," I said.

"You," he confirmed.

The marching band started playing the theme from the latest Batman movie.

"Why didn't you just ask me?"

"I was afraid you'd say no."

"What if I say no right now?"

"Do you want to?"

I watched the band move in and out of their formations. "I haven't decided yet."

"You could sit and eat while you're thinking about it," he suggested.

We sat on the blanket, the cheeseburgers, fries, and flowers a border between us, watching the little kids and the band until halftime was over. It was marginally less awkward when the game started again, if only because there was so much to mock. Finally, the ref blew his whistle and it was official. The Belmont Machinists had lost their sixth game of the season and I had no idea what would happen next. I didn't know what I wanted to happen next. The stadium slowly emptied; the families on the hill gathered their kids and shepherded them toward the parking lot, and soon we were the only ones left.

"Okay, here's the tricky part," Finn said. "The security guard is going to walk by to see if anyone is up here partying. I'm pretty sure we're far enough away that he won't be able to see us, but we should lie down for ten minutes or so, to be safe."

"That is the lamest attempt ever to get a girl on her back," I said.

"I'm serious. Look." Finn pointed to two security guards at the far end of the football field. "I'm not going to try anything. I swear. I'll move over here so you're comfortable."

He scuttled about four yards away and lay on the grass. "How's this?" he whispered loudly.

I lay down on the blanket carefully, keeping my head turned and my eyes open so I could watch him. "If you touch me, I'll cram your nose into your brain with the heel of my hand."

"Shh," he said.

The lights in the stadium started to click off, one at a time, until darkness took over the field.

"A couple minutes more," Finn whispered, his voice reassuringly far away.

The last of the cars pulled out of the parking lot, tires squealing. The chatter of the security guard's radio moved along the hill below us like a stray breeze. As it faded, I sat up and watched his flashlight bob into the distance. A few minutes later, the guard reached his car and slowly drove away, tires crunching over the gravel.

"Close your eyes." Finn's voice startled me. "Count to twenty."

"After I shove your nose into your brain, I will break your fingers and disable your kneecaps," I warned.

"I'll stay here," he promised. "I'll keep talking so you know I haven't moved. Five. Six. Seven. Talking, talking, talking, okay? Eyes closed? You're lying down? I'm still talking and I am looking for something to talk about but it's tough because this is a bizarre situation. Fifteen. Sixteen. Somehow I failed to anticipate that your response to my well-thought-out date would be to threaten me with violence. I should have been prepared for that. The next time I'm in a meeting with MI5—"

"Can I open my eyes yet?" I asked.

"Twenty," he replied. "Look straight up."

The night sky stretched on forever above me, the stars flung like glass beads and pearls on a black velvet cloak.

"Wow," I whispered.

"Yeah," he said. "I had to pull a lot of strings to get the weather to cooperate, but it all worked out in the end. Can I sit on the blanket now?"

"Not yet." I found the Big Dipper and Orion's Belt with no problem, but didn't know the names of anything else.

Had there always been this many stars in the sky?

"I won't try anything," Finn continued. "Unless you want me to. Of course, if you wanted to try anything, I'd be a very willing participant. Do you want to try anything?"

"I haven't decided."

"Did I mention that the grass I'm lying on is soaked with dew?" he asked.

"I haven't even decided if this is officially a date."

"What would you call it?"

"An anti-date."

"I brought you flowers."

"I like them. It's still an anti-date." I paused. "But I don't want you to blame me if you get sick. You can come back if you want."

"You promise not to maim me?"

"I promise to give fair warning before I maim you."

I watched out of the corner of my eye as Finn's shape stood, walked over, and lay down two inches away from me. I could feel the heat radiating off his skin. He smelled of wet grass and sweat and soap. No body spray.

"Nights like this," he said quietly, "I could look at the sky forever."

I expected him to keep talking, to ramble on about the stars or his adventures as an astronaut or the time he was abducted by aliens (which I might have believed), but he just lay there, staring at the corner of the Milky Way that was smeared right above us. The layers of noise—cars on the road, distant airplanes, the farewells of crickets, the flutter of bat wings—all faded until I could hear only the sound of my heart beating in my ears, and the slow, steady rhythm of Finn's breath.

Somehow my hand found its way to his. Our fingers entwined. He squeezed once and sighed.

I grinned, grateful for the dark.

We left about an hour later so that Finn could drive me home and get back to his house before curfew. Neither one of us had much to say. We didn't talk in the car, either, but that was easier because he turned on the radio. It felt like the time under the stars had delivered us to a new country that we didn't have the language for yet, but I didn't know what it felt like for him because I didn't have the guts to ask.

I finally spoke up just before he turned into my driveway.

"No," I said. "Pull up by those bushes."

"You're having a party without me?" he asked.

"An army buddy of my dad's is here with a bunch of guys on leave. They're headed up to the Adirondacks tomorrow."

I unbuckled my seat belt and opened my door the instant he shut the engine off because I didn't know what I wanted to happen in the front seat. Well, I kind of knew, but

I wasn't 100 percent sure, and it seemed like the safest course of action was to get my bike out of the backseat as soon as possible. The handlebars got caught on the coat hook above the back door, but Finn reached in and unhooked them.

"Thanks." I leaned on the handlebars. "That was a . . . I had a good time."

He leaned against his car. "Can we call it a date yet?"

"No."

"Can we call it a pretty good anti-date?"

I chuckled. "Yeah."

He tossed his keys up and down. "I would like to point out, for the record, that my pants remained zipped and my belt buckled for the entire evening."

"Smart move on your part." I hesitated, because I wanted to kiss him and I was pretty sure he wanted to kiss me, too, but the bike was in front of me, and Finn was several steps away and then two soldiers came around the side of the house and started rummaging in the back of one of the trucks.

"I better go," I said.

"Are you going to be okay?" he asked. "I mean, with all those guys around and everything?"

"You're the one who should be worried. You just took out the captain's daughter without his permission."

— * — **31** — * —

Dad was sitting by the bonfire in the backyard with Roy and a bunch of the others. The conversation died when I stepped into the circle of light.

"Didn't mean to interrupt," I said. "Just wanted to tell you I'm home."

"How was the game?" Roy asked.

"We lost," I said. "But the stars were nice."

"Sleep tight, princess." Dad's face was half in shadow, angular and old-looking. I wanted to sit on the ground next to him and lean against his knee and have him smooth my hair back and tell me that everything was going to be all right, but the awful thing was, I wasn't sure it could be. He was sober, still drinking soda, surrounded by guys who understood everything he'd been through, but his good mood of the afternoon had vanished. He looked lost again, haunted.

One of the younger soldiers got up and offered me a chair, but I muttered a quick g'night, and hurried inside.

Michael was parked in front of the television gaming with a couple of the privates, dribbling chew-stained spit into a paper cup. I went straight to my room without saying a word. Didn't bother with a shower or brushing my teeth. I locked my bedroom door, changed into my pj's, and crawled into bed with a book and my phone.

Finn texted just as I got comfortable:

> am home
> you ok?

yep

I texted back.

I waited, staring at the screen. Should I say anything else? Were we supposed to text all night long?

> ttyt?

he asked.

sure

I hesitated, then held my breath and typed quickly:

flowers were sweet
stars spectacular
thx

He didn't reply and he didn't reply and he didn't reply. I smacked myself in the forehead. *"Anti-date," what was that supposed to mean? He thinks I'm a nutcase now, a total crazy cakes, I said I was going to shove his nose into his brain, who says crap like that?* and then my phone lit up again.

> nxt to you
> i didnt notice any stars
> night

—*— 32 —*—

I woke to the sound of chain saws rumbling in the living room: soldiers snoring loud enough to rattle the windows. I stretched, rubbed the sleep out of my eyes, and found my phone buried in the blankets. No new messages. I reread what Finn had sent the night before to make sure he said what I thought he said.

He did.

My stomach went squirmy. I wanted to text Gracie and ask what I was supposed to do next, but what if he didn't mean it? What if the whole thing was a setup, you know, humiliate the new girl and scar her for life? Plus, if I told Gracie, she'd tell Topher and he liked to exaggerate, so by Monday morning the whole school would think that me and Finn had slept together and Finn would think that I had started the rumor and he'd never talk to me again.

And I'd definitely flunk math.

I read his text a third time. My stomach clenched. I had to find out the truth: Was he messing with me, was I blowing this out of proportion, or . . . or something else?

Deep voices in the hall and the slamming of the bathroom door meant that some of the soldiers were up. If I could get them to stay for the whole weekend, that would distract Dad and give me time to track down Finn and . . .

And what?

Okay, I'd figure that out later. Step One—enlist military babysitters for Captain Andrew Kincain.

The gamers I'd seen the night before had fallen asleep on the couch with the controllers still in their hands. The PAUSE scene looped on the screen, a monster slicing off the head of a green-skinned warrior whose body crumpled to the ground spurting fountains of blood from his neck stump, over and over and over again. I hurried into the kitchen.

"Morning, princess," Dad said.

He stood in front of the stove, watching four fry pans of sizzling bacon, his face tense. The bags under his eyes were swollen, but it didn't look like he'd been crying. He probably hadn't slept at all.

"Morning," I said.

"Perfect timing!" Roy came in from the garage and headed for the coffeepot. "Help me out, Hayley," he said, pouring himself a cup. "I'm trying to convince your old man to come with us to the mountains."

Dad frowned and turned up the heat under the pan. "Knock it off, Roy."

"Cabin, lake, trees," Roy said. "Two days, one night. Time of your life."

Two days and one night? Me with a chance to be on my own, Dad with a chance to get his head straight?

"Are you kidding?" I asked. "It sounds awesome. You have to go."

"I'm not leaving you alone." Dad flipped the bacon. "End of story."

"I'll stay at Gracie's."

"I said no," Dad growled.

"Just for tonight," Roy said. "Hell, you could go home after dinner, the drive only takes a couple hours. Bring Hayley if you want."

Dad shook his head.

I plucked a piece of cooked bacon from the plate next to the stove. I'd seen a glimpse of the old Dad the night before, the guy who was funny and sweet, but he'd gone back into hiding and New Dad, Damaged Dad was cooking the bacon. As much as I wanted some space to think about Finn (and possibly hang out with him), getting Dad to spend more time with Roy was more important.

"I've never seen the Adirondacks," I said. "Might be fun."

"See?" Roy grinned. "Come on, Andy. You know you want to. Man up and get your sorry ass out of this place for a day."

"I'm not going!" Dad snapped. "End of discussion!"

The smoke from the bacon curled toward the ceiling. He stared at the pan. The darkness had settled on his face again. He didn't move when hot grease splattered on his arms.

"It's cool, Andy," Roy said quietly. He reached in front of Dad to shut off the burners, then he turned to me and nodded toward the door.

I was sitting on the tailgate of Dad's pickup watching two soldiers load their duffel bags into a Jeep when Roy came outside. Cold wind gusted from the north.

"Make sure everyone's awake," Roy called to them. "Get all the gear packed and stowed, and make sure the house and yard are cleaned up."

"Yes, sir," they said, trotting toward the backyard.

"When do you have to leave?" I asked.

"After breakfast. We don't have much time to talk." He pulled a pack of cigarettes out of his shirt pocket and shook one out. "Is Andy seeing a counselor or a shrink?"

I shook my head. "He won't go. If I bring it up, he yells at me. And he drinks a lot. Too much."

Roy swore and lit the cigarette, his hand cupping the thin flame to protect it from the wind.

I brushed the hair out of my face. "Are you afraid of overpasses?"

He blew the smoke to one side, away from me. "Come again?"

"Bridge overpasses. Do you turn around if you see one so you don't have to drive underneath it?"

"No." He studied the burning end of the cigarette. "But I'm guessing Andy does. Why?"

"Snipers," I said. "First it was overpasses, then toll booths. He'll take huge detours around Dumpsters or trash cans 'cause they could be hiding an IED. He knows that's stupid, but knowing doesn't stop the panic attacks. Sometimes, he won't leave the house for days."

"What about a job?" Roy asked.

"When we first got here he worked for an insurance company, then the post office hired him. That didn't last long. A couple weeks ago, the cable company fired him, too."

"What's the problem?"

"His temper. He blows up about stupid things and then he has a hard time calming down."

"Does he get any disability money?"

"A little."

"This was your grandmother's house, right? Is it paid for?"

In a flash, I saw myself . . .

. . . standing on a chair at the kitchen table, helping Gramma put packs of gum in a brown box. We fill it up with gum and cigarettes and books and a picture of the sky filled with birds that I drew with my crayons. Gramma tapes it up and we take it to the post office and mail it to Daddy. . . .

I dug my nails into the palms of my hands until the memory disappeared. "I think so."

Dad's voice boomed across the backyard, but with the wind, I couldn't make out what he was saying.

Roy took another drag of the cigarette. "What's the story with this Michael dude?"

"They went to school together. He's the only friend Dad has around here. I think he's a dealer."

"Shit," Roy said.

"Why is he getting worse?" I asked. "It doesn't make sense. He's been back for years."

"The blood is still flowing."

"No, it's not," I said. "Everything's healed up, even his leg. Has been for a long time."

"How old are you now?"

"Eighteen," I said. "Well, I will be. In April."

"His soul is still bleeding. That's a lot harder to fix than a busted-up leg or traumatic brain injury."

"But it can be fixed, right? People can get better."

"Not always," he said. "I probably should sugarcoat it a little, but you're old enough for the truth. Andy needs to take charge of this. He needs to get help."

I hopped off the tailgate. "Make him go with you. Talk to him. He'll listen to you."

"That's the hardest part." Roy frowned. "If he doesn't want to go, there's nothing I can do."

"So stay here with him," I said. "I'll go to my friend's house."

"I wish I could, Hayley, but I made a commitment to the guys."

"Just for one night?" I hated whining, but couldn't help it. "Please?"

"I'm sorry." Roy stubbed out his cigarette on the bumper and carefully put what was left of it back in the pack. "I'll talk to some people when I get back to base, make sure that someone from the VA checks in with him. This shouldn't be on your shoulders."

He looked like he was going to say more, but we were interrupted by a skinny, acne-scarred soldier. "Everyone's awake, sir, and cleaning up."

"Make sure they put out the fire completely," Roy said.

"Captain Kincain just built it up again, sir. He told me to leave it alone. And, ah . . ." he hesitated.

"What is it?"

"Sir, Captain Kincain wants us leave ASAP. He was pretty loud about it."

—*— 33 —*—

Dad emerged from his room after they left and joined me at the bonfire, carrying a six-pack of beer. He threw on a couple sticks of wood and sat on a folding chair without a word.

"It was nice of them to stop by," I said carefully.

He picked a thin stick off the ground and threw it into the fire. "Yep."

I pulled the buzzing phone out of my pocket. It was Finn:

> good morning
> want 2 go 2 paris?

"Who's that?" Dad asked.

"Friend from school." I quickly typed:

> yes plz
> later

and put the phone away.

"Not what's-her-name up the street?" Dad asked, cracking open a can of ten-o'clock-in-the-morning beer.

"Not Gracie." I said. "A new kid. New to me, I mean."

He grunted, beer can on his right knee, left leg jiggling

like he was listening to fast music I couldn't hear. He leaned forward and poked the fire with an old broom handle. "Thought you had homework."

That was my signal to leave him alone. I couldn't, even though I knew I should. Beer for breakfast was freaking me out. The wind rattled the dried cornstalks in the field next door. I tossed a stick onto the fire, sending up sparks, and tried for a safe path through the minefields of Dad's mood.

"He said I looked like Mom." I cleared my throat. "Roy did. It was weird to hear him say that."

Dad grunted.

"So was he like a best friend or something back then? I mean, if he remembers what Rebecca looked like."

He poked at the fire again. "He and his girlfriend lived in the apartment below us when you were born. I don't remember her name. She and your mom were friends."

"You never said I looked like her."

"You don't." He drained the can and popped open another one. "You look like yourself. Nobody else. Trust me, that's a good thing."

I picked up a rock the size of my thumb and tossed it in the fire. "You don't think I look like you? Not even around the eyes?"

He stretched his neck to the right until the bones popped. "Don't do that."

I threw in another rock. "What?"

"Sedimentary rocks can explode in a fire. The moisture in them turns to steam, then *boom*."

"You're not my teacher anymore."

He poked at the fire again, lifting the logs to get some air underneath them. "Why are you in such a crappy mood?"

There was no way to answer that without getting into trouble. He was the one with the mood, with the crazy demands, chasing his friends out before they could eat the breakfast he'd cooked. He was the one acting like a kid, making me figure everything out on my own. Roy handed him the perfect opportunity to get his head straight and Dad basically spat on it. Made me wonder if he liked being a miserable hermit, if he enjoyed screwing up my life as much as he was screwing up his own.

"Are you gonna answer me or what?" he asked, daring me to mouth off.

All of his stupid anger about Roy was being aimed at me. I didn't deserve it, not this time. I pitched another rock into the flames, trying to stay calm because this was dangerous, my heart beating this fast, my mouth bitter and dry. I'd been angry at my father before, but this was different. I'd leveled up without realizing it. This new landscape was cave-dark.

"Did you hear what I said about the rocks?" he demanded.

I scooped up a handful of pebbles. "Yep."

"Ah," he said as if enlightened. "You're pissed, is that it? Have a crush on one of the soldier boys? You're crazy if you think I'd let any of them near you."

The north wind gusted again, stoking the fire and sending my hair writhing in all directions. A loud *pop* came from inside the flames. Dad flinched. A rock had reached its boiling point.

"How come you didn't go with them?" I asked.

"Didn't want to."

My phone buzzed. I didn't answer it.

"Talking to Roy might have helped," I said.

Smoke billowed.

"There's nothing to talk about," he said.

"Roy thinks you should talk to someone from the VA."

"They're the ones who did this to me."

"Dad—"

"Enough, Hayley. I don't want their help."

"Okay, so don't go to the VA, but at least go up to the camp." My phone buzzed again. "You were actually laughing last night, Roy—"

Dad roared, "I don't like the woods, damn it!"

Oxygen swooped into the gap he'd opened under the logs. The bonfire flared. For a second, I wished the grass was still long and dry so that the fire would catch and burn everything—the house, the truck, everything—and force him to see what a jerk he was being.

I started to walk away.

"Get back here," Dad ordered.

"Why?"

He cold-stared at me without answering until I walked back and sat on an upturned log. The phone vibrated again. Either Finn was texting me an entire novel, or Topher and Gracie had just broken up.

"You looked like you were having fun last night," I said quietly.

"I was," he admitted. "But when I went to sleep, the nightmares were still there, bigger and badder than ever."

He sipped from the can and stared into the fire as if he'd forgotten me entirely. I took a chance and checked my phone. The messages were from Finn, asking if I wanted to go skydiving, if I wanted to hunt for gold, if I wanted to ski down Mount Everest. Part of me wanted to go in the house, call him, gossip, flirt, do anything except talk to my father. I wrote back quickly, told him I'd call when I could.

Dad put out his hand. "Give that to me."

"Why?"

"'Cause I'm tired of listening to it buzz."

The fire crackled. I fought to keep my mouth shut because if I said what I wanted to say, the nuclear fallout would kill everything for hundreds of miles.

I put the phone on the ground. "I won't answer it. I promise."

"I want to see who you're talking to. I'm your father. Give me the phone."

"You?" I stared at him through the shimmering waves of heat. "Act like a father?"

He stood up. "What did you say?"

Something inside me boiled. "You're a mess, Daddy," I blurted out. "No job. No friends. No life. Half the time you can't even take the dog for a walk without freaking out."

"That's enough, Hayley. Shut it."

"No!" I stood up. "And now you're all 'I'm the dad' but it doesn't mean anything because all you do is sit on your ass and drink. You're not a father, you're—"

He grabbed the front of my sweatshirt. I gasped. His jaw was clenched tight. The bonfire danced in his eyes. I had to say something to calm him down, but he looked so far gone I wasn't sure he'd hear me. He tightened his grip, pulling me up on my tiptoes. His free hand was balled into a fist. He had never hit me before, not once.

The wind shifted, swirling the smoke around us.

I braced myself.

The smoke made him blink. He swallowed and cleared his throat. He opened his hand, let go of my shirt, and started to cough.

I let out a shaky breath but didn't move, afraid to set him off again. He turned his back to me, bent over with his hands on his knees and coughed hard, then spit in the dirt and stood up. The smoke shifted direction and I breathed in. Breathed out. On the inhale I was angry. On the exhale . . . there it was again. Fear. The fear made me angry and the anger made me afraid and I wasn't sure who he was anymore. Or who I was.

High above his head, an arrowed flock of geese was flying south. The sound of their honking moved slower than their bodies, floating down to the bonfire a few heartbeats after they moved out of range. A cloud moved in front of the sun, dimming the light and shrinking the shadows.

My phone rang and Dad jumped up as if it had given him an electric shock. Without a word he grabbed it and pitched it into the fire.

—*— **34** —*—

Small, ancient men lead us up the mountain to their village. I can't speak their language. My interpreter claims he can.

Yesterday, the enemy set up grenade launchers on the flat roof of a house here. They fired at our outpost, corrected the angle and fired again. And again. Every shot looked like a small, red flower blooming across the valley. They rained destruction on our heads, distracting us so that we weren't ready for the men who poured into our camp, weapons blazing.

Nine of my soldiers had to be evacuated. Two died before they made it back to base. We killed four insurgents and captured four more.

At the end of the battle, our air support fired missiles through the front door of the house, turning it into a hole in the side of the mountain.

The old men take us there. A tiny hand, stained with blood and dust, pokes out of the rubble. The old men shout at us.

"What are they saying?" I ask.

"We got the wrong house," the interpreter says.

We blew up a house filled with children and mothers and toothless grandmothers. The insurgent house sits empty, a stone's throw away.

The ancient men yell at me and shake their fists.

I understand every word they say.

—*— 35 —*—

"Fifty people saw you at the game," Topher said. "Stop lying."

The first-period cafeteria was quiet, everyone in mourning for the death of another weekend.

"I'm not lying," I repeated. "The whole thing was weird. He's weird. Isn't he, G?"

Gracie nodded, absently chewing on a fingernail. Something was up with her; she hardly had any makeup on, her hair was pulled back into a ponytail, and it smelled like she hadn't brushed her teeth.

Topher reached across the cafeteria table and tore a piece off my muffin. "He said he tried to text you a million times."

"He exaggerated," I said. "He texted me twice. Then my phone died."

(I was not about to explain how.)

I'd spent the rest of Saturday watching cooking shows. Dad stayed by the fire, his back to the house. When I woke up at noon on Sunday, a brand-new phone, expensive, sat on the kitchen table next to a note that read *Sorry*. He came home a few hours later, his arms heavy with grocery bags. I put the food away and made a pot of chili. He watched football, the volume turned up loud enough that I could hear it in my room, even with my music cranked as high as it would go.

I knew that he was waiting for me to say thanks, but I didn't want to. Buying me a new phone we couldn't afford was pathetic. His "sorry" didn't mean anything.

Enough. Thinking never helped.

I pulled myself back to real time. "It doesn't matter what Finn told you," I said to Topher. "We were not on a date. He's making it all up."

"Typical guy," Gracie murmured, starting in on a thumbnail. "Lies and more lies."

"Babe." Topher gently pulled her hand away from her mouth. "You promised you weren't going to do that anymore."

Gracie glared at him. "Shut up."

There was something not-good going on between the two of them. I pretended to study Chinese words for breakfast foods.

Gracie pointed at me. "Don't you say anything, either."

"Babe!" said Topher. "Relax."

Before I could open my mouth, Finn plopped himself down on the seat next to me.

"Hey," he said.

"Um," I responded, articulate and witty as ever. He was wearing a tight black T-shirt with the logo of a band I'd never heard of, jeans pulled a little low, and new sneakers. He had cut his neck shaving. He smelled like spice.

"Um," I repeated.

"I hate it when you call me 'babe,'" Gracie said to Topher. "I'll chew my nails if I want. When did you become such a jerk?"

"Whoa!" Topher raised both hands. "Sorry, it's just—"

"It's just nothing." She blinked back tears, got up, and ran for the door.

"What's up with her?" Topher asked me.

"Probably her period," Finn suggested.

"Do you have any idea how insulting that is?" I asked.

"Do you know how much women loathe it when guys think every show of negative emotion is tied to our menstrual cycle, like we're sheep or something?"

(From a poorly lit corner of my brain came the thought that picking a fight with Finn about the stupid things boys say about periods when girls are acting weird might be a bad decision. This was drowned out by the next thought, which screamed loud and clear that if he was dumb enough to think that periods were the root of all female aggravation, then I wasn't going to waste my time with him.)

(But, damn, did he look good in that shirt.)

I switched my attack to Topher. "Did you guys have a fight this weekend?"

Topher shook his head. "Not me. It's either her period or her parents."

"It's not her period," I insisted.

"Well, she won't talk about it." He stole another piece of my muffin. "I took her to the movies Friday night? She didn't say one freaking word. Didn't want to, you know, do anything after, either."

"Don't you think you should go find her?" Finn asked, motioning toward the door.

"Why?" Topher asked.

"Because you're her boyfriend, douche bag. You're supposed to help. See what she needs."

"Really? I should do that?"

"Yes, Toph, really," I said. "Go. We'll watch your stuff."

As soon as he left, a horrifying silence fell over the table.

I could feel Finn sitting next to me. Smell him, too. It wasn't just the faint hint of spice, he had definitely brushed his teeth. Maybe used mouthwash. Would that be a good conversation starter, asking about his preferred mouthwash brand?

Probably not.

"So." His voice cracked and he hit a soprano note. He cleared his throat and tried again. "Right. So when are you going to turn in the football article?"

I had not thought about it all weekend. "Do you really need it today?"

"Sort of. As soon as you turn it in, the paper will have a grand total of," he frowned and counted silently on his fingers, "a grand total of two articles. We could have an official staff meeting this afternoon and figure what else we want to write about."

"No, thanks."

He was fumbling with his container of chocolate milk, trying to open the waxed cardboard top. "You have something better to do? A bank to rob? Small nation to invade?"

"Something like that."

"Will you come to the meeting if I give you ten bucks?"

"You still owe me nineteen from the football game."

"I'll make it an even thirty. But not a penny more."

"Do you pay everyone on the staff?"

"Why, is that a bad thing to do?"

"How many people are working on this thing?"

"Counting me? And you? Two."

I laughed. "You are the worst high school newspaper editor ever, aren't you?"

"My proudest achievement to date." He finally opened the milk and gulped it down. When it was finished, he wiped his mouth on the back of his hand. "So do you hate me?"

"Because you said a dumb thing about women's periods?"

"I was thinking more about the fact that you didn't call or answer my texts after Saturday morning."

"It was my phone."

Finn groaned. "Come on, Blue Girl, something original, please." He took a deep breath. "I know . . . I was . . ." He sighed. "I ambushed you with the date thing. I'm sorry if it pissed you off."

"Pissed me off?"

He leaned forward and banged his forehead on the table three times.

"Stop that!" I put my hand between his head and the table. "Are you crazy?"

"Certifiable," he said.

"Look. I wasn't making it up." I dug Dad's guilt-present phone out of my backpack and handed it to him. "My old phone was killed on Saturday, just as you were texting me.

I got this one yesterday and I don't have anyone's numbers and I couldn't ask Gracie because, well, things at my house were weird."

"Weird with your dad or weird with the 10th Mountain Division?"

"With my dad," I explained. "And those guys were the 101st, out of Kentucky. They left early Saturday morning."

Finn perked up. "So you weren't ignoring me because you hated me because I lied to you about Friday night and, in fact, if you recall our conversation, offered to pay you for what turned into a date?"

I hesitated while I picked through all the clauses he'd shoved into that question. "Ignoring you, no," I said. "And we agreed that it was an anti-date, remember?"

He relaxed and laughed. "Excellent! I was starting to feel a little less than confident about the whole thing. But!" He pointed at me, then leaned so close that my vision blurred and made two faces of his one. "Now the truth can come out. You were on a secret mission all weekend. Black ops. Which was the real reason those soldiers were there. Don't worry," he sat back up, "you don't have to explain the details. I understand everything."

"Everything?"

He opened his second container of chocolate milk. "I spent the weekend contacting sources and bullying reluctant suspects. I know it all: your years working for the British secret service, the favor you did for the Swedish royal family, and the fact that you speak twenty-seven languages fluently."

I took the chocolate milk from him and sipped. "Twenty-eight."

"What?"

"I speak twenty-eight languages. You probably forgot Udmurt. Most people do."

"Udmurt?" He laced his fingers together behind his head, showing a shocking amount of bicep and pec definition under the thin material of his shirt. "You are flirting with me, Miss Blue."

"Don't flatter yourself," I muttered, blushing so hard I expected the sprinkler system to activate.

"Oh, yeah," Finn said, grinning. "I'd like to go on record as stating that if you come to your senses and decide never to talk to me again, I will cherish this moment forever. Udmurt. That was awesome."

Before I could deconstruct that sentence and figure out if he was mocking, teasing, or paying me a compliment, Topher burst in through the door and ran over to us.

"You better come," he said, panting. "She is seriously freaking out. In the bathroom."

Based on his panic level, I expected the hall to be filled with a SWAT team and hostage negotiators. Instead, I found a group of girls standing in front of the bathroom door, waiting like excited spectators at a medieval hanging.

"You can't go in there," the tallest one said to me, stepping in front of the door.

"Yeah," chimed in the one wearing pajama pants and furry boots. "Our friend needs some privacy."

Inside the bathroom, Gracie sobbed.

"Your friend?" I asked.

"She's having a really hard time," said the third girl, her voice oily with drama.

"What's the problem?" I asked.

"She's depressed," said the tall one.

"Suicidal," said Pajamas.

"Or it could be her period," said the third one.

The slack-faced, highlighted zombies stared at me, trying on different expressions of concern and self-righteousness they'd memorized from reality shows. I looked around, hoping to see someone who actually knew what to do in a situation like this, but found only Topher and Finn, a few steps behind him.

"Do you know her name?" I asked the girls.

"What?" asked Pajamas.

"What's your friend's name?" I asked. "The one who is in there crying?"

"Her name is Gwen," said the third one. "I think she's in my gym class."

"Get out of my way." I pushed between them and opened the bathroom door.

Gracie raised her head as I entered. She was sitting on the floor by the radiator under the window that was guaranteed never to open.

"Go away." She wiped her eyes on the sleeve of her brown sweater.

I thought about it and said, "I don't think I should. What's up?"

She shook her head, closed her eyes, and leaned back against the radiator.

"Do you want me to get the nurse?"

She snorted. "Because a Children's Tylenol and a glass of orange juice will fix everything? Right."

The bathroom smelled like cigarette smoke, vomit, and perfume. Two of the three stall doors had been removed. I dampened a paper towel in the sink and handed it to Gracie.

"What's this for?" she asked.

"Put it on your eyes," I said. "It will feel good."

She did as I asked, sighing a little when the cool paper touched her skin. Out in the hall, Topher was arguing with the drama zombies.

I sat next to Gracie because I didn't know what else to do. From the floor, I could see the bases of the three toilets and the undersides of the sinks. Couldn't tell which was more disgusting, but I was pretty sure that the biology and chemistry teachers never needed to pay for mold or bacteria kits again.

"He cheated," she murmured.

"Topher?"

"No." She squeezed the paper towel and watched the drops puddle on the dirty tile. "My dad. He cheated on Mom."

"Are you sure? I've been to your house. Your parents are perfect."

"They're good at pretending. This has been going on for a long time. It's a cycle—he cheats, gets caught, they fight, go to counseling, fall in love, he takes her on a romantic vacation. Six months later, he finds a new girlfriend and starts the whole thing over again."

"I don't know what to say."

"You could say it's really shitty," she suggested.

"That's really shitty," I echoed.

"You bet it is," she said quietly. "And it's gross, especially the sex part. Who wants to think about their parents having sex? You don't want to hear them fight about it, either. Trust me."

"I trust you," I said.

"He says he loves Mom. Last Christmas they renewed their vows. Garrett and I had to stand up there with them in front of everybody, all of us pretending. Sometimes I wonder if he cheats on us, too, if he's looking for new kids who won't disappoint him."

"I never thought about anything like that," I said.

"I wish I could stop thinking. They keep saying, 'High school is so important. You have to get serious, Grace Ann, this affects your entire life,' and then they get drunk and shout at each other for hours." She sighed and let the paper towel fall to the floor. "The whole weekend sucked. Last night was the worst it's ever been. I thought for sure the neighbors would call the cops."

"Did he hit her?"

"My dad? Never. She threw a coffee cup and hit him on the nose. And then she felt awful, because she really, really loves him, you know? She felt bad because she hurt him," she sniffed, "and then she felt worse because it doesn't matter how much she loves him, he's not going to change."

Gracie's father was an engineer, her mother, an accountant. I couldn't picture either one of them yelling or throwing things or having affairs. I could see my dad doing stuff like that. Trish sure did. But Dad carried a war in his skull, and Trish was a drunk. Gracie's parents didn't have anything like that to deal with, but their daughter was falling apart on the bathroom floor.

"Why can't they just be parents?" She sniffed again. "They used to be awesome. They'd tease each other and kiss in front of us, and Dad would write silly poems and Mom would bake him muffins, and now . . ." Her voice pitched up on the last word and her bottom lip quivered and, as her face crumpled into sadness, she looked over at me and for the first time, I remembered her; I saw her the way she looked in kindergarten the day she'd fallen off the monkey bars and scraped up both knees.

"Oh, Gracie." I opened my arms and she leaned toward me and sobbed against my shoulder. I smoothed down her hair, and whispered, "Shh . . . shh," rocking us back and forth until she quieted down. By the time the bell rang, her tears had stopped and she was breathing regularly. As we stood up, she laughed a little and reached over to wipe away my tears.

"Why are you crying?" she asked.

"Allergies." I sniffed. "So what happens next?"

She looked in the mirror and used the corner of a paper towel to mop up the eyeliner rolling down her cheek. "Mom said this was the last time. She's going to a lawyer."

"Yikes."

"She tried to explain to Garrett what divorce meant this morning. He's in second grade; why does he have to understand a word like that? He got so upset that he puked up his breakfast and hid in Dad's closet." Her lower lip quivered and she blinked quickly. "If it was just me, I could deal with it. I don't want to live in two houses, but if it means the screaming ends, then let's do it. But the look on my brother's face . . ."

The stampede was underway in the hall. The door opened a few times, but Finn or Topher stopped whoever it was with a line of BS and pulled it closed.

"Do you want to go home?" I asked.

"Ha!" Gracie laughed, shaking her head. "Only if you have a time machine." She bent over the sink and splashed water into her face. When she stood up, I handed her more paper towels. "It doesn't matter where I go, I don't want to be there. And then I get to the next place, and I don't want to be there, either." She reached in her purse and pulled out a small tin of mints. "Want one?"

She opened the tin and held it out to me. I started to reach in, but then saw what was inside: large oval pills the color of a robin's egg. "Those aren't mints."

"Duh. Mints wouldn't do much good right now, would they?" She set the box on the edge of the sink, swallowed a pill, then took a swig of water from the faucet. "It's okay, they're legal. One of my mom's prescriptions. You should take one. It might make math fun for a change."

I stared at the pills and then at her. She still looked like kindergarten Gracie around the eyes, but around the mouth, under the zits and the makeup that didn't quite hide them, she looked like someone I didn't know at all.

I closed the box. "No, thanks."

She looked at me in the mirror. "Can I go to your house after school?"

"Can't. I have to go to the nursing home for my service hours." I closed the box and handed it to her. "Come with me."

—*— 37 —*—

The receptionist at St. Anthony's Nursing Home and Care Center clamped a phone between her ear and shoulder and wrote down the arrival time on my form with a well-chewed pen. She pointed to the elevators and held up four fingers, then she told the person on the other end of the phone that she had to work a double shift and some days it felt like she'd never get out of this damn place.

Gracie followed me into the elevator. She hadn't said a word on the bus. I suspected that she was a little bit stoned, but she was with me and that counted for something.

The elevator doors closed. "How long do we have to stay?" she asked.

"Benedetti said I need four hours."

"Four?" Gracie sighed dramatically. "I don't like old people that much."

"I bet they don't like you, either," I said. "At least an hour, okay? It's better than going home."

She frowned as the elevator doors opened. "Barely."

A nurse sent us to an Activity Room. Whoever named it that had a sick sense of humor. Of the dozen residents there, only one seemed to have a pulse, a lady in a faded flowered dress pushing a walker so slowly it was hard to tell what direction she was moving in. Most of the others sat slumped and sleeping in wheelchairs lined up in front of a huge television screen, all tethered to oxygen tanks like withered balloons. The television was turned off. My nose wrinkled; the room smelled like cherry cough drops, used diapers, and bleach.

A skinny guy in a uniform with a long, black ponytail pushed a cart past us. "First time here?"

"The last," Gracie muttered.

He pointed to a table in front of the window. "Doris likes to play cards. Mr. Vanderpoole, sitting across from her, is a jigsaw puzzle fan."

Doris was the size of a garden gnome (minus the hat) with thick glasses that magnified her gray, watery eyes. She stared at Mr. Vanderpoole's puzzle, a picture of an old-fashioned fair. Half of the Ferris wheel and a few pieces from a cattle pen were missing, but there were no extra pieces on the table. Mr. Vanderpoole, wearing a suit and tie, his face perfectly shaved, slept in his wheelchair silently, like a statue.

Gracie walked over to a low bookcase and examined the puzzle and game boxes stacked there. "Think they have a Ouija board?"

"Why?" I asked.

"More interesting than puzzles, for one thing," she said. "Maybe the dead will tell me how to deal with my parents."

"Come on, G," I said. "The whole point of dragging you here was to get your mind off that."

She flipped me the "whatever" hand.

I pulled out the chair next to Doris and sat down. "I'm Hayley Kincain, ma'am. Do you want to play cards?"

She blinked like an ancient owl and asked, "When is my sister coming?"

"Um . . ." I looked around desperately for a gnome-sized old lady who looked like Doris or, even better, a nurse.

"When is my sister coming?" Doris repeated. Her eyes puddled up.

"I'm not sure," I said. "Does she live here?"

"Your sister will be here soon," Gracie said over her shoulder. "Right now you're supposed to play cards, Doris."

"She's right," I said with more enthusiasm than I felt. "Bridge or Go Fish?"

Doris smiled and nodded. "I like Fish."

Crisis over, I shuffled the cards. "How did you do that?" I asked Gracie.

"Do what?" Gracie carried a stack of dented boxes to the table. "Can you believe they have Candy Land?"

Someone down the hall moaned regularly, like a bored ghost. I silently cursed Ms. Benedetti, cut the cards, and cursed again. I dealt seven cards to Doris and looked at my own hand: five aces and two seven of hearts. I opened my mouth to say we needed a different deck but closed it again when I saw how carefully Doris was organizing her cards, and how calm she looked, as if she hadn't just been on the verge of bursting into tears about her sister.

One minute passed. Two. After a short eternity, Doris finally put one card facedown on the table and pulled another from the draw pile.

"Your turn," she said.

I looked at my cards. "Do you have any sevens?"

She looked at me blankly. "Why?"

We were clearly playing by Doris Rules. I mimicked her; one card down, another taken from the pile. It was like playing with a three-year-old. (Was that disrespectful, thinking of her like that?)

Gracie lifted the lid off the Candy Land box and frowned. Then she took the lids off the Monopoly box and two jigsaw puzzles. "These are a mess. The pieces are all mixed together. How can they play anything?"

Mr. Vanderpoole snorted and shifted in his sleep.

Doris reached across the table and tapped my hand. "When is my sister coming?"

*　　*　　*

Fifty hands of Doris Rules Go Fish later, Gracie had spread out the contents of the boxes on an empty table, sorted the pieces into piles, and gone to the Activity Room at the other end of the floor in search of the missing pieces. Doris was in a happy world of her own, picking one card from the deck at a time, laying them down, and announcing "I win" every once in a while. She talked to herself quietly. Once she said "Annabelle." Another time it sounded like she mumbled "cotton candy."

I wasn't sure why I had to do this in order to graduate, but the longer I sat, shuffling and dealing, shuffling and dealing, the less pissy I became. This room had no connection to the outside world. Did Doris know what year it was? Probably not. Did the old people in this room know who the president was, the price of gas, which war we were fighting now? How many of them could even remember their names?

I shuffled. Dealt another hand. I wound up with six aces (two hearts, two spades, a club, and a diamond) and the jack of hearts. Doris hummed and put her cards in some kind of order that made sense to her.

If Gramma had lived, would she have wound up in here? I'd spent so many years trying not to think of her that I could barely remember what she looked like. I didn't even know how old she was when she died. Did it happen in the grocery store? Was I at school? Did I find her? I'd remember that, right? The questions filled in the glacial pauses while

Doris decided which card to lay down. A wristband poked out from the sleeve of her cardigan. It had her name printed on it, along with the name of the nursing home and a phone number. Did Doris really not know who she was or where she lived? Which was better: being alive (if that was the right word) but not remembering anything, or being dead?

That was a Finn question. He'd probably answer it with an obscure quote from *The Tibetan Book of the Dead* or gibberish about runic interpretations, but there was a chance he'd really think about it, and then we might get somewhere.

Half an eternity later, a nurse wearing a top decorated with dog cartoons walked over, crouched down to next to Doris, and asked if she wanted to go to the accordion concert before dinner.

"Will my sister be there?" Doris asked.

"I hope so," the nurse said kindly. She helped Doris stand and said to me, "Thanks for coming. Janine's on the desk. She'll sign your form."

Nurse Janine wore a plain beige top, no dogs. When I walked up to her, she closed the binder she was writing in and said, "Let me guess. Belmont?"

"How did you know that?" I asked.

"I have a sense about these things. Do you want to be a nurse?" she asked. "Physical therapist? Pharmacist?"

I shrugged. "Never really thought about it."

She rolled her eyes. "I told them to stop sending kids like you. We only want volunteers who care about this kind of work."

"I'll tell my guidance counselor." I handed her my attendance sheet. "Does Doris's sister live here, too?"

She scribbled on the paper. "Annabelle? She died more than seventy years ago."

"That's awful."

"Not really. Doris loves her. She always thinks that Annabelle is going to walk through the door in just a few minutes. Imagine how awful it would be if she realized that she'd never see Annabelle again." She handed the paper back to me. "Bus comes on the half hour. Tell your guidance counselor to send you to the Girl Scouts next month."

—*— 38 —*—

I found Gracie sitting on a wooden bench bolted to the patio in front of the nursing home. I sat next to her and waited, but she just stared, sniffing, at the river flowing at the bottom of the hill.

"Nurse Janine told me not to come back," I said.

"It's not like they can afford to be picky," she said.

"She didn't like my career goals."

Gracie wiped her nose on her sleeve. "Do you have ca-reer goals?"

"Of course. I plan on lifting the zombie curse from our fellow students." I pulled a wadded-up tissue out of my pocket and handed it to her. "Don't tell Ms. Benedetti."

She blew her nose. "Okay."

"You gonna tell me what's wrong?" I asked.

"They have three Candy Land games and no red pieces." She kept her eyes on the river. "Everybody wants to be red, the whole world knows that."

"You're not crying about the red pieces."

"No." She tucked her hair behind her ear and sighed. "Mom blew up my phone 'cause I wasn't on the bus. Left a million messages begging me not to go to the quarry."

"Why would you go there?"

"Every couple of years someone jumps and kills them-self. If you ask me, there has got to be a better way to go. Anyway, I called Mom back to tell her I hadn't killed myself and then we got into a fight. Why? Because I didn't make my bed this morning. That's when I started crying again." She tossed the tissue at a trash can and missed. "And now I'm a lump of snot."

"A useless lump of snot who can't even throw out her Kleenex."

"Jerk," she said with a faint smile. "Who won the card game?"

"I never figured out the rules." I picked up Gracie's used tissue and a couple of cigarette butts and threw them in the trash. "The nurse thinks that Doris is lucky because she can't remember her life. She doesn't understand how much she's lost."

"My nonna died of Alzheimer's," Gracie said. "The last ten years of her life she didn't recognize anybody, not even Grandpa, and he visited her every day."

"Was she in here?" I pointed at the building.

Gracie shook her head. "Connecticut. A week after we buried her, Grandpa died, too. Mom barely talked for a month after that."

"What made her start again?"

"Talking?"

"Yeah."

"Garrett." She pulled a pack of gum out of her purse, handed a piece to me, and folded a piece in her mouth. "One day he told Mom he wanted to visit Grandpa in his grave. We packed a lunch and ate it at the cemetery. At first I thought it was gross, but it was actually kind of sweet. Hanging out with our dead grandparents became a thing. We go a couple times a year now."

"You go to a cemetery on purpose?"

"Yeah," she said. "Isn't that the point?"

A gust of wind rose from the river, shaking the last gold leaves of the fragile birches planted around the patio.

"Sounds creepy."

"It's not like we dig them up. We have a picnic. Tell them what's going on in the world. Garrett brings his report card and soccer photos. Haven't you been to your grandmother's grave yet? Didn't your dad take you?"

Gracie had spent months patiently weaseling the hows and whys of our return to Belmont out of me. She didn't know everything, of course, but she knew enough to be able to ask questions that could mess with my head.

"Time to go." I stood up and pointed. "The bus is coming."

—*— 39 —*—

Dad and I had spoken only a few words to each other since the bonfire incident. This was becoming more of a habit, the not-talking, but it still made me uncomfortable. Not-talking with him was like trying to walk after my foot had gone to sleep. Everything felt weird and heavy.

I took a deep breath and knocked on his door. "You awake?"

The door opened. He was dressed in jeans and a long-sleeved Syracuse Orangemen shirt and he was freshly shaved, to my surprise. Over his shoulder, I could see an open email on his computer screen, but it was too far away to see who he was writing to or what he was saying.

"You're home late," he said. "Everything okay?"

He smelled of soap. Not weed or booze, not even cigarettes. This was another part of his apology, maybe, for what had happened on Saturday.

"Where's Gramma buried?" I asked.

His eyes opened wide. "Don't remember the name of the place. It's near the river. Why?"

"I want to go there," I said. "Now."

"Can't. It'll be dark soon."

"I don't care." Pins and needles shot through me, that dreadful, awkward feeling of something waking up inside. "I really want to see it."

"We'll go tomorrow," he said. "After school."

"You don't have to come with me. If you draw me a map, I can ride my bike there."

"What's the rush?"

"I was at the nursing home after school," I said, "for my volunteer hours. It made me think of Gramma and I don't know why, but I really want to see where she is. It's important."

I hadn't planned on telling him the truth. It had become easier to lie about most things because it didn't hurt as much when he ignored me. In my defense, I hadn't planned on finding him clear-eyed and sober, either. It was hard to know how to play the game when the rules kept changing.

He looked over his shoulder at the window. "We're gonna need jackets."

*   *   *

The old headstones at the front of the cemetery were so worn that the blue jays and chickadees mocked me for trying to read them. We walked quickly for a few minutes, then Dad stopped at a crossroads where the stones were easier to read. He was squinting against the falling sun, trying to figure out the right path. I studied the family plot.

ABRAHAM STOCKWELL 1762–1851

RACHEL STOCKWELL 26 FEB 1765–22 FEB 1853

THADDEUS STOCKWELL 1789–12 NOV 1844 REST IN PEACE

SARAH D. 1827

Four small headstones topped with stone lambs lay on the other side of Sarah.

BABY 1822

BABY 1823

BABY 1825

BABY 1827

"Know what they call this?" Dad asked, his voice back in teacher mode.

"A graveyard?"

"No, silly. This time of day."

"Sunset?"

"When the sun is below the horizon, but it's still light

enough to see, it's called 'civil twilight.' There's another word, too, an older one, but I can't remember it." He reached up with his right hand and rubbed the back of his neck. "They're farther back, I think. Next to some pine trees. Let's hustle, it's almost dark."

"They?" I asked. "Who's they?"

He was already six strides ahead, despite the limp. I caught up with him at the top the hill.

"Found them," he said quietly before heading down the other side.

I shivered. A wide valley of the dead spread out below me, hundreds of them gently tucked into the ground in neat rows, their whispers frozen into the stones above them: *I am here. I was here. Remember me. Remember.*

I zipped up my jacket and jogged down the hill, past graves decorated with flowers—some plastic, some real and faded—and small flags on wooden sticks. Dad was waiting by a headstone speckled with pearl-green lichen near a row of tall, dark pine trees. He knelt and tried to brush off the lichen. It was stuck fast, like it had been growing for a long time. He took out his pocketknife and scraped at the words and dates with the blade:

REBECCA ROSE RIVERS KINCAIN 1978–1998
BARBARA MASON KINCAIN 1942–2003

"I didn't know that she was here." I pointed at the top name. "My mother."

(The word sounded like a foreign language. Like I had pebbles in my mouth.)

"Becky got along so well with Mom that it seemed like the right thing to do," Dad said. "Your grandmother taught her how to cheat at bridge. That's what I imagine they do in heaven."

"Where's your dad buried?"

"Arlington. Mom didn't want him there, but he insisted. Always had to do things his way."

I studied the names again, waiting for tears to bubble up. It was hard to figure out what I was feeling. Confused, maybe. Lonely. I wondered if Gramma could see us standing there, looking lost as the shadows grew deeper around us. I tried to picture her. I didn't remember what she looked like and that made me more upset than anything.

"Do you miss her?" I asked. "I mean, them?"

"I miss everybody." Dad stood up, folded his knife and put it back in his pocket. "Doesn't do any good to dwell on it." He brushed his hands together to clean off the lichen. "Should have come sooner to clean this up."

I pointed to the headstones in the next row. "How come those have vases built into them and ours don't?"

"Mom ordered the stone when Becky died," he said. "She didn't like cut flowers, my mom. Preferred flowers that were planted. Maybe that's why she didn't order the kind of grave marker that came with a vase."

"We should do something to make it look nicer."

"I guess." He stood next to me and pointed to the empty grass to the left of the grave. "That's where you need to put me when my time comes."

I swallowed hard. "You're not going to die." I leaned my head against his shoulder. "Not for a hundred years."

He put his arm around me. I closed my eyes and took a deep breath of pine and damp earth. Only a few birds were singing and, far away, an owl called. Leaning against my father, the sadness finally broke open inside me, hollowing out my heart and leaving me bleeding. My feet felt rooted in the dirt. There were more than two bodies buried here. Pieces of me that I didn't even know were under the ground. Pieces of Dad, too.

"Gloaming," Dad said.

"What?"

"That word I couldn't remember. Gloaming. That short, murky time between half-light and dark." He hugged me quickly and let me go. "Night's here, princess. Let's head home."

—*— 40 —*—

Finn texted me Tuesday morning to ask if I wanted a ride to school. I was kind of surprised, but I said yes and then I put on a cleaner shirt. By Thursday, we had fallen into a sort of pattern. Right around six thirty in the morning, he'd text:

?

and I'd text:

K

and by the time I got to the corner a block south of my house (no way was I going to let him pick me up where Dad might see), Finn would be sitting there, his engine smoking because he hadn't fixed the leaking oil valve yet. He also slid into the habit of eating breakfast burritos and drinking chocolate milk at first-period lunch with me and Gracie and Topher, in addition to meeting me in the library after school to try and convince me that precalc wasn't some enormous joke that got out of hand.

I was beginning to understand why people were horrified when they learned that instead of attending school from grades seven through eleven, I'd been riding shotgun in my dad's semi. It wasn't that my life was ruined because I never sang in a holiday choir or that I missed the thrill of reenacting the Battle of Gettysburg with water balloons and squirt guns. It was that I didn't know The Rules.

I hadn't even known The Rules existed before that week.

I was not a totally ignorant feral recluse. Watching Animal Planet had alerted me to the existence of mating behavior. Plus, having eaten a lot of bologna sandwiches in truck stops, I'd heard the kinds of things that grown men say to other grown men about these issues. But I was pretty sure that the blue-footed booby's courting dance wasn't going to get me anywhere with Finn, and if I approached him in the way that truck drivers recommended, it wouldn't end well.

Things were complicated even more by the fact that there was something weird about Finn. Not zombie weird. He was more of a cyborg with a vivid imagination. But he'd spent enough time around the zombies to adopt some of their ways. He knew The Rules. I didn't.

Finn would show up at my locker one day and then he wouldn't the next. Was I supposed to return the gesture and go to his locker before he could take the next step, make the next move, whatever that might be? One minute we'd be riffing about conspiracy theories, the next we'd be arguing so loudly about mandatory military service (I was for it; he, being a privileged wuss, was not) that we got kicked out of the library. And then we didn't say a word to each other the whole drive home.

Which was another thing—I couldn't talk about this to him. And/or he couldn't/wouldn't talk about it to me, assuming he wanted to, assuming the entire drama wasn't a product of my estrogen poisoning or a symptom of a brain tumor caused by eating so many gallons of artificially colored, high-fructose corn syrup–enhanced plastic food products when I was younger. (Truck stops are not known for their selection of organic fruits and vegetables.)

I watched all the couples and almost-couples around me, frantically trying to understand how this stuff worked, and was more confused than ever.

Gracie was no help. The situation at her house went to DEFCON 4 when her dad moved out. The next day, her little brother refused to go to school. Mrs. Rappaport carried him out to the car and tried to shove him in, even though he was kicking and screaming. Gracie grabbed her mom's arm to make her stop and Mrs. Rappaport turned around and slapped Gracie's face. The neighbor who saw the whole thing called the police.

The only relationship I'd ever seen my father in was with Trish, and for most of those years he was on the other side of the world from us. When he was finally discharged, the two of them turned our apartment into a battlefield.

Even if their relationship had been less than awful, there was no way to talk to him. The gloaming that closed over us in the cemetery had crawled inside his skin. He didn't want to talk or eat. He just sat in front of the TV.

So I couldn't talk to Finn about what I wanted to talk to him about, I couldn't talk to Gracie about anything other than how awful her parents were, and my dad was a bigger mystery than ever.

To make matters worse (was that possible?), I wasn't exactly sure what I wanted with Finn. Did I like him? My opinion about that changed several times a day. Did I want him to like me? Ditto. How could I like him, how could he like me, if we didn't know each other? The little I was able to learn about his family (perfect, middle-class people, apparently) made me pretty sure that he'd run screaming if he ever met my father. That would be a logical reaction, of course, but did I really want to fall in love (fall in "like"?) with someone who didn't give my dad a chance? We had to get to know each other. Gradually. Baby steps. In order to do that, we'd have to break down and talk about things that were more significant than font size in online newspapers and his fevered delusions about his time studying telekinesis with a group of monks in a Himalayan ice cave.

I had no idea how to do that.

I started to cyber-stalk him late on Wednesday night, but it made me so disgusted with myself that I played hours of *Skulkrushr III* instead and thus flunked the next day's

Chinese vocab quiz. I wrote an apology note to my teacher in Chinese. She told me that I had actually written something about pigs and umbrellas.

At one level? None of this mattered. It was hard enough surviving day to day, both navigating the hordes at Zombie High and listening to the bomb that had started ticking inside my father's head. A little flirting with Finn? That wouldn't hurt. But I concluded that it couldn't go any further. When we met after school for precalc tutoring, I made sure that there was always a table between us. And when I was in his car, I kept my backpack on my lap, my face turned to the window and my attitude set to the frost level of "Don't Touch."

Despite this strategy, the hordes gossiped about us. Girls in my gym class asked me flat out what Finn was like. That's how I found out that his family had moved to the district only a year earlier and that he had led the swim team to the state title but decided not to swim this year, and no one could figure out why. I also learned that those same girls were pissed off; they'd assumed he was gay, because why else wouldn't he have tried to hook up with them before?

I dialed up my serial killer glare and eventually they walked away.

Even the teachers noticed. Mr. Diaz walked past my locker when Finn was there and said, "For the love of all that is holy, you two, please don't breed."

Seriously?

The sex thing, that was the undercurrent, the electrically charged wire that ran through all of this nonsense. I'd been eavesdropping on zombie sex conversations since school started. Most of them, I thought, were totally made up. But now I found myself doubting that conclusion. What did The Rules say about this? If everyone was really having sex, then why was it paradoxically a hush-hush-whisper thing and a scream-it-online-and-in-the-cafeteria thing? If everybody was really having sex, why weren't more girls sporting baby bumps? I knew the statistics. I also knew the closest abortion clinic was more than a hundred miles away. Most of my classmates couldn't remember to tie their shoes in the morning. I had no faith in their ability to use birth control. Either nobody was getting laid and everybody was lying about it or the school was putting contraceptives in the oatmeal raisin cookies.

No wonder the zombies were crazy. They thought they were supposed to practice breeding before they learned how to do their own laundry. They talked about it, thought about it, maybe did it, all while going through the motions of attending class and learning stuff so that they could go forth and become productive adults. Whatever that was supposed to mean. It was enough to make me want to flee into the mountains and live out my life as a hermit, as long as I could find a hideaway that had a decent public library within walking distance and toilets that flushed, because Porta-Potties were the worst.

Then I'd see Finn in the hall, or I'd catch a glance of his profile out of the corner of my eye while we were driving to school, and he would turn to me and smile. And I didn't want to be a hermit anymore.

—*— 41 —*—

He was waiting for me when I got out of detention on Friday.

"Rogak?" he asked.

"Diaz."

We fell into step next to each other and headed for my locker. "What did you do this time?"

"It wasn't my fault."

"That's what they all say."

"I just pointed out that calling it the 'Mexican–American War' falsely gives the impression that the Mexicans started it, and that in fact, in Mexico they call it the 'United States Invasion of Mexico,' which is the truth, or the 'War of 1847,' which is at least neutral-ish."

"You got detention for that?" Finn asked.

"Not exactly. Mr. Diaz, who really needs to work on his anger management issues, yelled at me for disrupting his class with what he called my 'pedantic quibbles.' Then this idiot named Kyle lost it because he thought 'pedantic' meant the same thing as 'pedophile,' and I sort of melted down a little." I handed him my books and dialed the combination on my locker. "And I wasn't being pedantic or quibbling. Diaz was being an imperialist first worlder."

"How do you know such a bizarre amount of history?" Finn asked.

"Dad was a history major at West Point. I know more about the fall of the Roman Empire than the Romans did." I lifted the latch. The locker didn't open. I dialed it again. "But that's the wrong question. Ask why everyone else is so pathetically stupid and why they're always whining about how hard American history is. Instead of getting detention, I should get a medal for not slapping people in the face every day."

The latch still would not open. I kicked the locker, remembering too late that I was wearing sneakers and not boots.

Finn nudged me to the side and spun the dial. "You whine about precalc."

"That's different," I said, trying to stand casually on the foot that wasn't throbbing in pain. "The zombie overlords numb our brains with math so they can implant their devious consumer-culture agenda in us."

Finn pulled up the latch. My locker magically opened.

"I hate you," I said.

"I'm not being obtuse," he said as he crossed his arms over his chest, "but you're acute girl."

"What's that supposed to mean?"

"It's a math joke."

I shoved my books into the locker. "'Math joke' is an oxymoron, Fishhead, like 'cafeteria food' or 'required volunteer community service.'"

"I think we should take each other to the limit to see if we converge," Finn said.

"Shut up," I said.

"I'm flirting with you, Miss Blue, flirting in the perfect language of calculus. It's a sine I think you're sweet as pi. Get it?"

I paused. He'd said "flirt" twice. My detention rage contracted into a small, spinning ball. Finn raised his eyebrows, waiting, maybe, for me to say something. What was I supposed to say to an irritatingly good-looking guy using stupid math puns to flirt with me in an empty hallway on a Friday afternoon?

"You are the biggest dork in the history of dorkdom," I declared.

"Even though you have a mean value," he said with a grin, "one of these days I know you'll want to integrate my natural log."

"Okay, that's just awkward," I said.

"Maybe," he said. "But you stopped scowling."

"The library is closing in five minutes so you don't have to tutor me today." I slammed the locker closed. "But can I get a ride home with you?"

"Um . . ." He suddenly frowned and spun the dial on

the locker next to mine. "Yeah . . . about that."

"What? Is your car dead?"

"No." He lifted the latch to check if he had broken in. He hadn't. "I was thinking maybe we could do something. Together. Do something together."

"Now?"

"Well, yeah. Now."

"Like what? Write another article?"

"Um, no." He jiggled the locker latch again. "I was thinking more like a movie. Or maybe we could go to the mall."

"A movie or the mall? Are you asking me on a date?"

"Not quite." He brushed his hair out of his eyes. "What was that word you used at the game? 'Anti-date'?"

"Yeah, an antidote to the stupidity of dating. An anti-date by definition can't be a brain-dead movie or a spirit-crushing trip to the mall."

"What could it be?"

The conversation had suddenly veered into dangerous waters. "I don't know. I guess we could go to the mall if we liberated all the animals in the pet store."

"We'd be arrested and put in jail," Finn said.

"That could be fun."

"No, that would screw up my chances of getting into a decent college, which would freak my parents all the way out."

"It would give you the best material ever for a college essay."

"Our mall doesn't have a pet store."

"Okay, so that's a real problem," I said. "Liberating hot dogs at the food court doesn't sound as interesting. What would you normally do on a Friday afternoon—stuff your face and game yourself into a coma?"

He shook his head. "I'd probably head to the library. No one uses the computers there on Friday afternoons."

"That's pretty lame for a guy whose middle name is Trouble," I said. "What about the quarry?"

He blinked. "You want me to take you to the quarry?"

"What's wrong with that?"

"It's not exactly the kind of place to go in the daylight."

"Well, duh, it is if you actually want to see it."

He looked very confused, which made two of us, and I decided that was better than being confused alone.

42

The quarry was closer to my house than I realized, hidden from Route 15 by a grove of old maple trees with flame-red and caramel-orange leaves. We drove past the trees onto a dirt road and started up a steep hill. The quarry was on my side of the car, beyond a tall chain-link fence and about twenty feet of dirt and rock. I felt the emptiness before I saw it.

At the top of the hill was a large plateau; Finn swung the car so that it pointed toward the fence and parked. "The view is better at night."

"You keep mentioning that," I said. "Will we get arrested?"

"Doubt it." He turned off the engine. "The cops only patrol at night when the view is better and conditions are ripe for all sorts of things."

I unbuckled my seat belt, and unlocked and opened the door.

"Where are you going?" he called after me. "Hayley?"

The fence was fairly new: ten feet tall and built with steel mesh nearly as thick as my pinky finger. I stuck my foot in a hole, reached up, and started climbing.

"Wait," Finn said.

"You coming?" I asked.

"You're not supposed to do that."

"So?" I reached, pulled, and climbed.

"In fact, that sign we passed back there?" he continued. "That definitely said no trespassing."

I lifted my left foot, found another opening. "We trespassed by driving up here." My right hand was just below the top of the fence.

"Yeah, but you're taking it to another level."

I clutched the top bar and slowly worked my feet up until I could swing one leg over, then the other, and climb down the forbidden side.

"Ta-da!" I threw my arms in the air, victorious. In front of me, uneven granite sloped up to the quarry's edge. It made me think of an ancient map. Like if we went over the edge, we'd be lost forever in the "Great Unknown." *Here be dragons* . . .

"Now what?" Finn asked.

"I'm going to walk over there and look down."

"Oh, no, you're not." He leapt at the fence and started climbing. "Don't move, don't you dare. The whole thing could crumble."

"I am standing on a block of granite, Finnegan. It's not going to crumble for another billion years."

He swung his legs over and quickly climbed down

the inside of the fence, sweating and breathing hard even though he was in way better shape than I was.

"What if an earthquake hits?" He stood in front of me, right hand clenching the fence tightly, his knuckles bone-white.

"The only natural disasters around here are blizzards. It's fifty degrees out, so I think we're safe for the next ten minutes or so."

"Fracking." He licked his lips and swallowed. "Earthquakes can happen anywhere now because of fracking. You could be walking to your seat at the movies, your face in a box of popcorn, and *boom*, a massive earthquake rips open the ground and thousands die."

"Another reason to avoid the movie theater and the mall," I said, taking a step away from the fence.

"Don't!" he shouted. "I mean, it's dangerous, going to the edge."

"You don't have to come with me."

"I do," he said miserably. "It's a Man Law."

"You did not just say that."

"I don't make the rules. I just have to follow them."

"That's ridiculous and patronizing." I took another step.

"Stop, please," he said with a groan. "Can you do it on your butt?"

"What?"

"Like this." He let go of the fence and sat, hyperventilating. "Scootch on your rear end. It'll be safer. Please?"

I sat and scootched a few feet. "Will this make you happy?"

"No, but it'll reduce my terror to panic."

"You can stay there, you know. Guard the fence."

He shook his head and muttered, "Man Law," then sat and scootched behind me.

When I got to the edge, I crossed my legs and took a deep breath, enjoying the view. From one side to the other, the quarry was almost as wide as a football field is long. Scraggly bushes and grass grew on thin ledges in the sheer walls, with a few birds' nests tucked into them. The surface of the water was at least fifty feet below me. There was no telling how deep it went.

According to Finn, an underground spring had flooded the quarry decades earlier. The ghosts of the workers killed in the flood still haunted the place, he said, operating the skeletons of the dump trucks and earthmovers underwater. (The ghosts of the people who killed themselves were probably here, too, but I didn't mention that.) A gravel road sloped up out of the water on the far side. Trees grew through the roof of a building over there, and heavy chains stretched across the road, maybe to protect the ghosts.

Finn moved a few inches at a time, breathing like he was sprinting.

"You okay?" he asked.

I chuckled and inched forward until my legs could dangle over the edge. The smooth rock warmed my butt; the wind ruffled my hair like a giant hand. The quarry water rippled and reflected the dizzy clouds above. The whole place felt alive, somehow, like the ground knew we were here, like it remembered every person who had ever stopped to enjoy this view. Or maybe every person left something behind: fingerprints, DNA, secrets whispered near the rock face and recorded, hidden and kept safe until time ended. Maybe the flood was the rock protecting those secrets so that men would not dig them out with monstrous machines.

"This place is amazing," I said.

Finn scootched once more and, a body length behind me, caught his first glimpse of the quarry. "Oh, God." He bent his knees and leaned his forehead against them, hiding from the sight.

"We're okay. We're safe," I said. My heels bounced lightly against the quarry wall. "This rock isn't going anywhere. Touch it."

He didn't answer but his hands slowly came out of the pouch of his hoodie and spread out across the sun-warmed granite. "How far down to the water?"

"Not that far."

He craned his neck for a brief look and shuddered. "Ohgodohgodohgod."

"Don't like heights?" I asked.

"What was your first clue?"

"You're a swimmer. Don't you ever jump off the high dive?"

"Hell no," he said. "Please don't tell me you're the girl who can do double flips off it and come up laughing."

"Hell no," I echoed. "I can't even swim."

"What?" He stared at me. "Everyone can swim."

"Not me."

And there it was, that awful knife again . . .

ripping . . . sun glaring off the pool grown-ups crowded I can't find him music so loud nobody hears when I slip into the deep-end water closes over my face I open my mouth to yell for Daddy and water sneaks in my mouth my eyes watching the water get thick and then thicker and grown-ups dancing . . .

"Why not?" Finn asked.

A couple of birds flew by. Their shadows floated across the water.

"Never learned," I said.

ripping . . . in the water above the water flying like a cloud grown-ups screaming grown-ups splashing in the water still can't find him . . .

Finn scooted forward a few more inches and wiped the sweat off his face with his sleeve. "I'll teach you."

"Seriously, I don't do water, except in the shower."

"Chicken."

"You never hear about chickens drowning."

He scootched at an angle to come closer to me. "I'd like to point out that right now I'm confronting my fear of heights, precariously perched on this ledge in an attempt to impress you."

"Puh-leez, Finnegan. You're at least a meter from the edge."

"If I make it to the edge will you let me teach you how to swim?"

I laughed. "Your feet have to dangle."

He shot me a dirty look and slowly inched forward, his legs straight in front of him, until the soles of his sneakers were technically inhabiting space a millimeter past the edge of the cliff.

"I did it," he croaked, his voice breaking on the last word. Sweat had beaded on his forehead again and he was shaking, even though the rock under us was radiating heat like a furnace.

"Isn't it fun?" I asked.

"No," he said. "The opposite of fun. This is like dealing with subway rats, antibiotic-resistant infections, and the cafeteria's mystery nuggets all rolled together and magnified to the tenth power. Why aren't you scared?"

"The higher, the better." I yawned and closed my eyes.

"When I was little I used to pretend I could fly because I had wings hidden under my skin. I could unfold them," I stretched my arms out, shoulder height, "lean into the wind and—" My butt shifted on the rock, sending pebbles rattling down the quarry wall. My eyes flew open as Finn yelled and grabbed a handful of my shirt, yanking me backward and sending both of us sprawling.

"I'm sorry," he said quickly. "You almost went over. I'm not even exaggerating. You jerked forward and I really, really thought you were going to fall. Oh, God. You hate me now, don't you?"

I sat up, rubbing the back of my head where it hit the ground. I didn't almost fall. It felt more like something wanted to pull me into the air, but that was crazy, right? Nothing like that could ever happen.

"So do you?" Finn brushed dirt out of my hair. "Do you hate me? Should I drive you home now? I don't want to, but I will."

I blinked twice, three times, and pretended I had dust in my eyes so I could rub them hard, trying to rub out the sensation of almost launching myself over the edge.

"I don't hate you," I said. "Do you hate me?"

He sighed and smiled. "I could never hate you, even if I wanted to."

43

After we left the quarry, we hung out at the library (Finn scoured the Internet for proof that the fear of heights was a sign of intelligence; I read some new manga) and went to Friendly's for ice cream. I had one scoop of pumpkin. He had a hot-fudge sundae with chocolate-almond ice cream, whipped cream, and sprinkles. After the waitress brought the ice cream to our booth, we got stuck in one of those agonizing silences that are so uncomfortable you start thinking about escaping out the bathroom window.

"So," I said. (*Brilliant, Hayley. Utterly brilliant, witty, and dazzling.*)

"So," he agreed.

I licked my ice cream and said the first thing that popped into my head. "So why aren't you on the swim team this year? Gracie said you're not that bad."

"That's boring." He stuck a straw into the bottom of his sundae and tried to suck ice cream through it. "Tell me about the time you met the Russian prime minister while hunting wild boar on the taiga."

"Swim team first."

"Nearly naked young men, plunging into pools of warm water? Why would you want to hear about that?"

"What part didn't you like," I asked. "The water, the guys, or the nearly naked?"

"The coach." Finn plucked sprinkles off his sundae and laid them in a line down the middle of the table. "He turned every meet into a life-or-death situation."

"But you won states, right? If you swam this year, couldn't you get a scholarship and go to college for free?"

"That's such bullshit," he said bitterly. "Mythology repeated by parents because it lets them force their kids into sports and push them too hard by pretending that in the end it will pay off with the holy scholarship. You know how many kids get a free ride? Hardly any. Like, maybe fourteen."

"Fourteen sports scholarships in the whole country?"

"Okay, maybe fifteen. The point is, parents and coaches believe the myth. The Belmont coach made swimming suck, so I quit."

I pressed my fingertip against a sprinkle ant and put it in my mouth. "What did you like about it, back when it was fun?"

He studied me for a moment before he answered. "Exploding off the block at the start of a race. It'd be all crazy noise and I'd hit the water like a missile and then the crowd disappeared. I can swim underwater for thirty-five yards. I hated coming up for air."

"Okay, so swimming is great, coaches and parents suck."

"Pretty much."

He chopped at his sundae with his spoon and we plunged into another excruciating, razor-blades-under-the-finger-nails lull in the conversation.

"You going to college or straight into the CIA?" I finally asked.

He smiled and—like a dope-slap upside my head—I suddenly realized that I wasn't the only one feeling totally awkward when we ran out of things to say.

"I gave the best years of my life to the CIA," Finn said. "I won't go back even if they beg me." He stuck a spoonful of ice cream in his mouth. "The real question is how can I go to college when my parents have no money for it?"

I held up my right hand and made a circle with my thumb and pointer finger. "Where you want to go." I did the same thing with my left hand. "Where you can afford to go." I slowly brought my two hands together until the edges of the circles overlapped a little, then I brought them up to my face and looked out of the smaller circle that they made like it was a telescope. "What college is here in the middle?"

"You just made a Venn diagram sexy," he said. "This could make our tutoring sessions so much more interesting."

"Shut up. College. Where?"

"Honestly? Swevenbury, which is totally unrealistic. I couldn't afford to go there even if I sold my soul. Which is why," he shoveled in a huge spoonful of ice cream, "I'm going to be a good little boy and visit some SUNY school next week. Mom set it up." He licked the back of the spoon. "Where do you want to go?"

"Haven't thought about it much. Online classes, I guess." I licked up the pumpkin ice cream dribbling down the back of my hand. "Can't leave home."

"Why not?" he asked.

The bright lights in the restaurant reflected off the tables and the chrome-plated walls. The hard surfaces amplified the buzz of the conversations around us and the shouting in the kitchen. The noise might have made me wince.

"You really don't want to answer that, do you?" he asked.

I shook my head.

"Okay, next topic," he said. "Nostril cams: fascinating biological journey or humiliating fad? Discuss."

"Where did you live before you came here?" I asked.

"The moon," he said smoothly. "We left because the place had no atmosphere."

"No seriously. I want to know."

He took a deep breath and tried to balance the saltshaker on the edge of its base. "Outside Detroit. My dad was a marketing guy for Chrysler. One day he got to work and *poof.*" The saltshaker fell on its side. "No job." He picked up the saltshaker. "And then *poof.*" He let it fall. "No house." He shook salt into a small mound in the middle of the table.

"My mom got a job here, that's why we moved. Dad is a consultant in Boston. We only see him once a month or so. My parents are tired and miserable and it's mostly a disaster."

"What about your sister?" I asked.

He looked up, startled. "How do you know about my sister?"

"You told me about her. The first morning you picked me up, remember?"

He frowned, poked his finger in the middle of the salt mound, and slowly circled it into a spiral. "We don't talk about her."

The sadness on his face was unexpected. I held my cone so that a few drops of melting ice cream landed in the middle of the salt painting.

"Nostril cams prove that the apocalypse approacheth," I said in a low voice.

He chuckled and tossed salt at me. After that, we swapped outrageous lies about our childhoods until the waitress said we had to either order more food or free up our table for new customers.

The gloaming had come and gone while we were in Friendly's. Night had arrived, held at arm's length by the bright streetlights and fast-food places. Finn started the engine and pulled out of the parking lot.

The quiet inside the car made things weird again.

I couldn't get comfortable. I kept shifting, looking out the window, checking the side mirror, staring at my phone, willing Gracie to call, and then looking out the window again, wondering what I should say, if I should say anything. The tension built the closer we got to my house until I found myself thinking about bailing out at the next stop sign, the way I had the first time he gave me a ride.

Finn checked his mirrors and put on his signal to turn onto my street.

"Don't go in the driveway," I reminded him.

"I have to," he said as he turned the corner. "It's dark." He signaled again. "After a date, even an anti-date, I have to deliver you to your front door. It's a Man Law. I screwed up last week because I thought your dad's friends all had submachine guns. Can't do that again."

Before I could say anything, he turned into the driveway, the headlights running across the siding and stopping on a pile of logs in front of the garage. They hadn't been there when I left that morning. The garage door was open and the lights were on inside, but the only sign of my father was the splitting maul leaning up against the stump he'd been using for a chopping block.

I relaxed. He was probably passed out on the couch.

Finn put the car in PARK and unbuckled his seat belt.

"What are you doing?" I asked.

"I have to walk you to the door."

"I know how to walk."

The hurt look on his face made me want to pinch myself. We were flirting again. Or were we? Maybe not. Why couldn't there be a light in the middle of a person's forehead to indicate flirting status and other confusing social behaviors?

Finn rubbed his thumb on the worn plastic of the steering wheel. He had strong hands, but no calluses. He bit his lip. I waited. (*I should leave.*) He opened his mouth like he was going to say something.

He didn't say anything.

I didn't say anything. (*I really should leave.*)

He put his hand on the emergency brake, turned toward me a little. Was he going to kiss me? Tell me I had chocolate sprinkles stuck in my teeth? Why was this so complicated?

It wasn't complicated, I scolded myself. It was stupid.

I pushed the button on my seat belt. It retracted and smacked against the door, making us both jump. I put my hand on the door handle.

Finn cut the engine and turned off the headlights. The dim blue light from the garage barely reached us. Shadows fell under his cheekbones. He raised his eyes to look at me. To look through me. I finally figured it out, late as usual: I did not want him to kiss me.

I wanted to kiss him.

My heart pounded so loudly I was sure it was making

the windows vibrate, like we had the radio on, booming heavy bass through the best subwoofers on the planet. I put my hand on top of his, horrified by the questions racing through my head. Eyes open or closed? What should I do with my tongue? How bad was my breath? How bad was his? Was I the only seventeen-year-old in America who had never kissed someone before? He'd know it as soon as our lips touched. Why did I care what he thought? And when in the course of the day had I turned into a babbling idiot?

I couldn't stop the questions any more than I could stop myself from leaning toward his lips.

He brought his face close to mine.

And stopped.

His eyes grew wide. I hesitated. Had I made a mistake? Was being kissed by me so terrifying that it paralyzed him?

"Don't move," he whispered, staring over my shoulder.

"What's wrong?"

"Big guy. With an ax." His voice was so hoarse I could hardly understand him. "By your door. I think he's going to kill us."

"Hayley Rose!" My scowling father knocked on the window and motioned for me to get out.

Shit.

"We studied at the library," I whispered to Finn. "And we ate ice cream. Not a word about the quarry."

Dad knocked again. "Out!"

I turned and put my face to the glass. "Hang on!"

"Ask him to put the ax down," whispered Finn.

"It's not an ax, it's a splitting maul."

"I don't care. Just ask him to put it down."

"Drive away as soon as I get out." I reached for the door handle. "I'll call you tomorrow."

"I can't," he said.

"Why not?" I asked.

"It's your father," he said. "I have to meet him, right?"

"No, you have to leave." I pointed at my father. "Back up, Daddy, and put that thing down!"

It took some arguing, but he finally walked to the garage, leaned the maul against the chopping block, crossed his arms over his chest, and watched as I climbed out of the Acclaim. Unfortunately, Finn got out, too.

"Man Law," he whispered.

"Idiot," I said.

"Who are you?" Dad growled as we walked toward him.

"Daddy, this is my friend, Finn."

"Pleasure to meet you, sir." Finn stretched his hand out to shake. "I'm Finnegan Ramos. I go to school with Hayley."

Dad kept his arms crossed. "I didn't give you permission to take my daughter out."

I tried to smile. "He doesn't need permission."

"The hell he doesn't," Dad said, slurring.

It took a lot of booze to make him slur.

"Go home," I told Finn.

"It wasn't a date, sir," Finn told Dad. "We were at the library."

"Sure you were," Dad said. "Did this boy touch you, Hayley Rose?"

Something was wrong with his eyes, too. They weren't red, but pupils were tiny and he didn't seem to be focusing.

"It wasn't like that, Daddy. You're overreacting."

He glared at me. "So you let him touch you, is that it?"

"I didn't touch her, sir," Finn said. "Can I explain?"

Dad pointed at Finn. "You arguing with me?"

"Stop it!" I shouted.

"No, sir." Finn's voice got louder. "But you're jumping to the wrong conclusions."

I stepped in between them. "Finn's the editor of the school newspaper. I have to write for that paper. Benedetti thinks it will help with my attitude. You're the one making me go to this school. You can't get upset when I follow the rules and try to act like the other kids."

He grunted.

"Please go," I told Finn.

He nodded and shuffled backward. "Yeah. I'll . . . I'll see you."

I lifted my hand and waved good-bye as Finn backed his car down the driveway. He didn't wave back.

Dad put a log on the chopping block.

"I can't believe you just did that," I said.

"What do you want from me, huh?"

Without waiting for an answer, he swung the splitting maul so hard that the two halves of the log flew off at different angles, one disappearing into the dark, the other one almost taking me out at the knees.

"It's your own damn fault," Dad muttered. "Stand that close and you're gonna get hurt."

—*— 44 —*—

Gracie showed up after noon on Saturday with a duffel bag and pounded on the door until I woke up. When I opened the door, she announced, "You have to let me stay here."

I rubbed my eyes. "You don't want to do that."

"If you don't let me, I'll sleep in the park."

I yawned. "What's going on?"

"Garrett is at Dad's and I'm stuck with Mom. Blood will be shed, I swear, but I don't know if its going to be hers or mine. Maybe both."

"My dad's sick," I said. "You can't stay here."

"Then come with me," she urged. "My mom won't lose it if you're there, she'll act like everything is normal. I'm begging, Hayley, please."

I sighed. "Give me five minutes."

I stood outside the door to Dad's bedroom and told him I was going to sleep over at Gracie's.

He muttered something, half hungover and half still-drunk.

"What?" I asked.

"I said leave the door unlocked!" he shouted. "Michael's on his way over."

I packed fast.

Gracie talked nonstop as we walked to her house. Not only was her mom a wreck and her dad feeling guilty and her little brother angry enough to break his favorite toys, but Topher's old girlfriend, Zoe, had been texting him and asking him for help on an English paper and other incredibly slutty things.

"How is asking for help on an English paper slutty?" I asked.

"Are you kidding me? It's Shakespeare! Look at *Romeo and Juliet*; they're what, like, fourteen years old, and they meet at a party and *bam*, jump in bed. They hook up in her bedroom with her parents in the house, and then they get caught and everybody dies."

"It's a little more complicated than that."

"Slutty fourteen-year-olds and gang violence. I can't believe they make high school kids read it." She kicked a rock down the street. "I hate Zoe."

I decided to wait for a less bitchy moment to tell her what happened when Dad met Finn. I had already decided not to tell her—or anyone—about what had happened at the quarry. I still hadn't figured it out myself. If I'd been afraid of heights like Finn, it would have made sense: dizziness, followed by a drop in blood pressure brought on by anxiety. But heights didn't make me dizzy, they made me laugh. Maybe there's something in the rock, a weird magnetic pulse that messed with my brain or my sense of balance. Maybe nobody ever planned to kill themselves there. They'd just gone up to enjoy the view and the rock energy messed with their heads and they'd tried to fly.

At Gracie's house, we baked cinnamon scones and chocolate chip cookies and bread that refused to rise. As the first batch of cookies went into the oven, her mom pulled into the garage, where she stayed for ten minutes, sobbing and yelling into her phone, before she backed out again and drove away.

Gracie told me to leave the mess that we'd made, but I couldn't. I said that I liked washing dishes and then Topher called her and she walked up the stairs yelling into her phone at him, her voice sounding so much like her mother's that it gave me goose bumps.

When we'd moved back to town, Gracie had taken me all over the place to help me remember living there: the church basement where we went to Sunday School (Gramma had played the organ, she said), the graveyard where we once played hide-and-seek and got hollered at by guys with shovels, the grocery store where we'd push our kid-sized carts behind her mom, the park where the slide got so hot in the summer that it would burn the back of your legs if you went down it too slow. It was like listening to a fairy tale or the life story of a total stranger. It upset Gracie when I said I didn't remember any of it so I started lying and pretended that, yeah, of course I remembered the time we made cookies with salt instead of sugar, and the time Gracie's old dog got skunked and we poured all of her mom's perfume on him to cover up the smell.

Gracie and Topher were still arguing when I finished the dishes. I wandered down the hall, past the school pictures of Gracie and Garrett hung in chronological order, and into the family room.

(*Is it still called a "family room" after your parents split up?*)

The photos on the wall and on top of the piano were of younger Gracie and toddler Garrett and Mr. and Mrs. Rappaport, all four of them at Disney World and a zoo and on a beach, always squinting into the sun. There were no photos of Gracie's grandparents or anyone else. It was like the four of them had magically appeared and lived, happy for a while, in a plastic bubble with bright lights. I picked up a photo of five-year-old Gracie in an angel Halloween costume and carried it to the coffee table.

The house smelled like a bakery. Gracie was still arguing upstairs, but at least she wasn't cursing anymore and her voice was quieter. I curled up on a couch and flipped through the shiny pages of Mrs. Rappaport's magazines. The pic of little angel Gracie watched me. I kept looking up, half expecting her to flap her wings.

I didn't like admitting it, but the truth was that my memories were starting to surface. First in Ms. Rogak's class after I got Trish's letter and then in the quarry. Maybe Gracie was right. Maybe visiting childhood places helped. Or maybe it was because I was older or angrier, or maybe because I was forgetting how to not-remember. It was also possible that we'd finally stayed in one place long enough for our yesterdays to catch up with us.

And now. Sitting alone in the not-family room, paging past recipes and haircuts and celebrity baby sightings, there, just out of the corner of my left eye, I was seeing myself playing with a cat, with a kitten, black and white. I kept turning the pages (fifty fabulous turkey recipes, whittle your middle like the stars) because if I looked at it head-on, the memory would evaporate. . . .

 . . . *a black-and-white kitten playing with yarn,*
  . . . *yarn in my hand, the sound of needles clacking,*
   . . . *clicking and the sound of women and the smell*
  of lemons and face powder, clicking,

. . . clacking, the yellow yarn in my hand and the green yarn that went from the basket up to Gramma's needles,

. . . her voice with other women chattering like birds in a tree, laughing, the laughter floated down to the floor like feathers and

. . . I leaned my head against my grandmother's knee.

I went back to the kitchen to rewash the pans in very hot water.

When Gracie stopped fighting with Topher, I piled a plate with chocolate chip cookies, put it on a tray with a quart of milk and two glasses, and carried it up to her room.

"Well?" I asked.

"He promised never to speak to her again." She blew her nose and tossed the tissue on the pile by her desk. "He's mad at me for not trusting him."

There was no safe reply to that. I bit into a cookie.

"Wanna watch a disaster movie?" she asked, picking up the remote. "Something where everybody dies?"

"Sounds perfect," I said, pouring the milk.

As the movie started, she fished her mint tin out of her purse, swallowed one of the pills in it, then handed it to me. It had more pills in it than before, different ones: small yellow ovals and pale pink diamonds and white circles.

"Did you steal all these from your mom?" I asked.

"Bought them," she admitted. "You want one or not?"

"What do they do?"

"Depends." She pointed. "Those ones make you sleep, that one wakes you up, the rest of them make the world suck less. It's not like they get you high or anything. Why are you looking at me like that?"

"I'm not looking at you like anything."

She shrugged. "My parents started it; they put me on ADD meds when I was in fifth grade. You watch, by the time we have kids, they'll have a pill for everything, even cheating boyfriends."

"He's not cheating, Gracie."

"Everybody cheats." She closed the box. "Want some popcorn?"

Her mom walked in without knocking an hour later, and stopped, confused to see me there. "Oh," she said. "Hello, Hayley."

"Hello, Mrs. Rappaport."

"Hey, Mom." Gracie smiled, her glassy eyes wide and innocent. "Hayley has to stay here tonight. We made cookies, want some?"

"I don't remember giving permission for a sleepover," Mrs. Rappaport said.

"I told you," I said to Gracie. "I'll go home."

Gracie pushed me back down. "No, you won't." She turned to her mother. "Her dad went away for the weekend. We can't let her stay alone, can we? What if someone breaks in?"

"Where did he go?" her mom asked.

I thought fast. "Hunting. With some army buddies. I'll be fine, really. He'll be back tomorrow."

Mrs. Rappaport sighed. "All right, you can stay. Just keep it quiet. I have a migraine."

Finn never called. Never texted, either.

Some time during the second movie, the box of mints that were not mints placed itself on the bed next to me and opened its lid and before I knew it a pill was in my mouth and I washed it down with milk.

I thought I had taken the waking-up pill, but soon my eyes started to close themselves and I drifted off as Gracie talked about going to Fort Lauderdale for spring break. I curled up under a quilt on her bed, her ancient cat perched on my hip and purring, and I sank into a heavy, soft sleep as Gracie's voice faded. The rumbling purr of the cat sounded like a well-tuned diesel engine, and I was on the road again, at night, safely buckled into the passenger seat as Dad's truck shot through the dark, the driver's seat empty, the steering wheel too far away for me to reach.

—*— 45 —*—

We drink tea made with dirty water over an open fire near the village, far from the mountains. The radio cuts in and out; we can't account for the interference. We swirl the tea in metal cups, waiting. Not sure what we're waiting for.

Then the screaming starts.

Fire boils in the desert-colored sky, breathing poison down his lover's throat and eating her children. A moving mountain, alive, hungry, thundering toward this village, our tents: simoom.

We throw the tea in the fire. Shout in seven languages, guns, arms, fingers all pointing to the wind coming for us. We race. We hide. Pray.

The crippled camel-girl limps. The hungry wind is coming and all she can do is limp. I turn around. Someone grabs my arm, pulls me inside, screams in my head, but I watch her. The red scarf is torn from her hair. She limps. The village disappears. The wind is a lion, jaws open wide. He swallows the crippled camel-girl and scours the color from her eyes.

Sand fills my mouth, stuffs my head with the stench of the lion. Pours into my ears the screams of every corpse. The winds of the desert have names. They feed on the bodies of broken children and rip out the beating hearts of men.

46

Gracie's mother woke us up on Sunday morning and said that Gracie had to go to church with her and that I could join them if I was in the mood. She didn't want me tagging along, I could tell, so even though Gracie looked like she wanted to strangle me, I said I had too much homework and, after a small bowl of cereal, packed up my stuff.

"We never go to church, this is ridiculous," Gracie said as we stood on her driveway.

"Maybe she wants to ask God to help her get back together with your dad."

"As if He cares."

I went to the park and sat until I saw Mrs. Rappaport's car speed away, Gracie slumped in the front seat, staring at her phone. I walked back to their house and keyed in the entry code that opened the garage door. (This took no skill; I'd seen Gracie do it—112233—at least a dozen times.)

I set the alarm on my phone to make sure I'd be out of there long before they returned.

Back in the not-family room, I paged through the magazines again and then the photo albums that stood in a neat row on the bottom shelf of the bookcase, but saw nothing out of the corner of my eye. The pages stayed flat and shiny. The room didn't share any secrets or replay scenes that happened more than ten years earlier.

The person who went upstairs to Mrs. Rappaport's bathroom looked a little bit like me. I saw what she did, watched it in the mirror. She opened the medicine cabinet, took out each pill bottle, and read the label, then put them back. Except for one. She poured the pills into her hand. They looked like generic vitamins or allergy medicine, something ordinary. Could it be this simple? She spilled the pills from one palm to the other like they were coins or cheap pearls. Her father swallowed pills to make the hurt go away. A long time ago they came in white bottles that had labels printed with the pharmacy's phone number and the doctor's name. Now they came in empty cans of chew or old baggies. It didn't matter where he got them. They didn't fix anything. They blurred the lines and turned the voices into ugly static.

Her face in the mirror melted, morphed one centimeter at a time the way pictures in a flip book do when you slide your thumb down the edge of the pages. She waited to see what or who she'd turn into. Her skin lightened. The freckles vanished. The color drained from her lips and then her hair. Her eyebrows and lashes turned white, then transparent, and then they no longer existed. Her chin faded away next, then her mouth and her nose. The eyes smudged like they were being wiped off with a fat pink eraser, and then they were gone, too. The mirror was empty.

I blinked.

When I opened my eyes she was gone and I was back. My eyes. My freckled nose. My absurd hair. My sweating, shaking hands that poured the pills back into the bottle. I ran out of the house before I turned into someone I didn't want to know.

Our living room smelled a lot like chicken wings and pizza and a little like weed when I walked in the front door.

Dad looked up from the television. "Hey, princess," he said with a grin. "Have a good time?"

I hung up my jacket in the closet.

"Giants are playing," he said. "Philly, first quarter. I saved you some pizza. Double cheese." He frowned. "What's that look for?"

"You're joking, right?"

"You love double cheese."

"I'm not talking about the pizza."

"Is it the wings? You gave up being a vegetarian two years ago."

"Are we going to play 'pretend'?"

"Vegetarians can eat double-cheese pizza."

"It's not the food," I said.

"Are you still upset about the cemetery?"

"What?"

Dad muted the television. "I was thinking about what you said. I'll call the cemetery and find out how much those special vases cost. Mom didn't like cut flowers, but she hated being outdone by her neighbors, and that headstone looks awful. Good idea?" He let Spock lick the pizza grease off his fingers. "Why are you still wearing the pissy face?"

"Did you run Friday night through the Andy-filter so instead of looking like a total ass, you can feel like you were a hero or something?"

He turned the television off. "Andy-filter?"

"You don't think I have a right to be upset?"

"I don't know what you're talking about. Friday night I split wood and fell asleep reading about the Spartans."

"What about when I came home?"

"You never went out," he said.

"You don't remember?"

He frowned. "Remember what?"

When we first hit the road, I'd been clueless. I was twelve, confused and brokenhearted about the way we left home and about Trish. Getting by minute to minute was my strategy. It was at least a year before Dad started to take unapproved "sick days," and a year after that before I connected the dots that led from him spending the night in a bar to him waking up, puking, and moaning. He got fired a couple times for it. That always led to months of clean living and on-time deliveries until he'd stumble again and fall down the rabbit hole. But he'd never gone this far. He'd never forgotten what he did the night before.

"This is stupid." Dad picked up the remote. "I'm not going to be interrogated by my own kid."

I snatched the remote. "You blacked out, Daddy."

He pressed his lips together.

"When I got home you were waving the splitting maul around like the crazy bad guy in a horror movie. You humiliated me in front of my friend."

Spock jumped off the couch, shook himself, and fled for the kitchen.

"What did I say to her?" he asked.

"To who?"

"Your friend."

"It was him, not a her. Jesus, you don't remember any of it. Was it just booze or did you take pills, too?"

He paled, but narrowed his eyes. "There's no law against a grown man getting a little shit-faced in his own house."

"There's a difference between getting drunk and getting so drunk you black out," I said. "That's a bad sign, Dad. A really bad sign."

"Pack the attitude away, young lady. I drink. Sometimes I don't remember. That's how it works."

"This has happened before?"

"We're done talking. You want pizza?"

"Give it to the dog," I said.

47

I'd been at Gracie's for only one day, but dirty dishes filled the sink, and the trash can smelled like sandwich meat gone bad. Directions to Roy's camp still hung on the wall, stuck on a nail. In the living room, the Giants scored and the crowd went nuts.

I was hungry for pizza and wings, but I wasn't going to give him the satisfaction. The peanut butter was in the cupboard next to the stove and the bananas and bread were on the counter. After I made the sandwich, I opened the fridge for something to drink and stopped. On the top shelf, next to a cloudy jar of pickles and a tub of expired cottage cheese, sat a stack of mail.

Another first. Dad never left mail lying around anywhere, much less in the refrigerator.

The catalogs for garden supplies and special tools for arthritic hands still arrived monthly, even though my grandmother had been dead for more than a decade. Dad got a couple of credit card applications and a VFW magazine that I knew he'd throw out without reading. The last two envelopes were addressed to him, too. I poured myself a glass of milk.

It's wrong to open another person's mail, right? Especially if that other person is your parent, because parents are supposed to be in charge and they're supposed to make all the decisions, and there might be things in the mail that are none of your business, because even in high school you're still a kid. Or at least sometimes, you want to feel like you are.

I carefully opened the first envelope, from the bank. Dad had overdrawn the checking account by $323.41, plus fees. I took a bite of my sandwich and a sip of milk and opened the second envelope, a note from the VA that listed all the appointments he'd missed and "strongly urged" him to call their office. I wasn't so hungry after that. I washed the dishes and emptied the garbage. After I put a clean bag in the trash can, I dumped the catalogs in it. That's when the third envelope, addressed to me, fell out of the gardening supply catalog.

Roy sent it.

He said that he'd talked to Dad on the phone a couple times, but he didn't think it would help. He apologized for not being able to do more. He apologized for how short the letter was, but his unit was leaving earlier than planned.

I know it's not fair, but you have to be the strong one,
he wrote.

You have to be patient with him, even when you don't want to be. He's still wounded, don't forget that. I'll call when I can.

Gotta hop.

"Uncle" Roy

I made Spock sit between us on the couch, the demilitarized dog separating Dad and me like the zone that keeps the peace between North and South Korea. I ate a slice of pizza and three chicken wings. That made him happy. I stared at the screen and tried not to wince when Dad yelled at the refs. The teams crashed into each other, helmets hitting helmets, necks snapping backward, bodies falling. Dad twitched and jerked with every hit. Out of the corner of my eye I could see a mirror, and in the mirror we were sitting on that couch, me twenty years old, thirty years old, then forty, then fifty, and Dad, always the exact same age, timeless, unshaven, dirty, eyes bloodshot and empty. The Eagles quarterback was sacked at the beginning of the third quarter and taken to the locker room. From that point on, the Giants scored at will.

After the game, I took Spock for a walk, the envelopes in the pouch of my hoodie, resealed as best I could. We walked until night fell and the safe, little houses on our side of town had all closed their curtains. Our curtains were still open. Dad was asleep on the couch, beer bottle in hand. I put the mail back in the mailbox and hoped the next day would be a better one for him.

— *— 48 —*—

I took the bus Monday morning. Finn was never going to drive me anywhere again.

I didn't see him in the cafeteria first period. Didn't actually go to the cafeteria. Went to the library. The Genocide Awareness table was gone. Nothing had taken its place. Tried to fall asleep in a corner where no one could find me. Couldn't sleep. Counted the holes in the ceiling tiles, decided they were probably made of a chemical that was causing cancer to bloom in my lungs.

Each tile had 103 holes.

I trudged through the day. Classroom. Locker. Hall. Classroom. Caught a glimpse of myself in the reflection of the tall windows along the corridor to the B wing. I was shuffling, books weighing down my arms. Defeated, like a zombie who'd been dragged from the grave and bitten, but who didn't feel the hunger yet. Wasn't quite assimilated into the hivemind of delirium.

Ms. Benedetti stopped me in the hall, complained about playing phone tag with Dad, and shoved SAT paperwork into my hands, babbling away about the need to shift my paradigm and look over the next horizon. I threw the paperwork away as soon as she was out of sight. In English, Brandon Something pegged me with spitballs every time Ms. Rogak turned her back. I picked them out of my hair before she noticed. I really didn't care enough to do anything else. Found out in gym class that Gracie had gone home sick. I told the aide that I was going to puke and spent the next two periods staring at the tiles above the cot in the nurse's office. They were smaller than the ones in the library. Maybe they didn't leak as much cancer.

I had let down my shields, that was the problem. The crazy inside Dad had infected me, weakened me so that when Finn smiled, I'd been vulnerable. I'd dropped my shields and let myself pretend that somebody like Finn would want to be with somebody like me.

I was an idiot.

In history, Mr. Diaz misstated so many facts about the issues that led to the Civil War that I was sure he was baiting me. He stopped me when I was headed out the door at the end of the period to ask if I was okay.

"I'm fine," I told him.

I was first in line when the bus pulled in. Took the seat on the left, two rows from the back. Stared at the zombies on the sidewalk dramatically reciting their lines, stalking to the edges of their stages, playing at life.

Looking out the window, I wondered how many of those kids had parents who were losing it, or parents who were gone, taken off without a forwarding address, or parents who had buried themselves alive, who could argue and chop wood and make asses of themselves without being fully conscious. How many of them believed what they were saying when they blathered on about what college they'd go to and what they'd major in and how much they'd earn and what car they'd buy? They repeated that stuff over and over like an incantation that, if pronounced exactly right, would open the door to the life of their dreams. If they looked at their parents, at their crankiness and their therapy and their prescriptions and their ragged collections of kids, step-kids, half-kids, quarter-kids, and the habits that had started in secret but now owned them, body and soul, then they might curse that spell.

And then what?

Despite my best intentions, I was beginning to understand how my dad saw the world. The shadows haunting every living thing. The secrets inside the lies wrapped in bullshit. Even Gracie's box of mints was beginning to make sense.

"Excuse me?" a voice said. "Can I sit here?"

I turned to say no, but he was already sitting down.

Finnegan Trouble Ramos.

I opened my mouth, but he put his finger on my lips.

"Shh," he said. "Please. Let me say this before I chicken out again, okay? First, I'm sorry I didn't call or text you or show up this morning." He swallowed, his Adam's apple dropping down and bouncing up like a basketball.

"I really like you, Hayley Kincain. I want to be with you as much as I can. I get that it's weird at your house, scary maybe, and your dad can be a jerk. You don't have to tell me about it if you don't want to, but it kills me because you are so beautiful and smart and awesome and I don't want anything to be scary for you, I just want—"

He paused for a breath.

I reached out and put my hand at the back of his neck; I pulled myself close to him and I kissed him until everything that hurt inside me melted into a pool of black water so deep I couldn't touch the bottom. As long as I was touching him, I wouldn't drown.

—*— 49 —*—

So. *That.*

Right?

That feeling in your stomach when you hear him whistling off-key, down the hall. That way your heart trips and then hammers against your ribs when he sees you and he grins like a little kid at the top of a steep, shiny-hot slide. Call it hormones, an early-stage bacterial zombie infection, or a very pleasant dream I was experiencing; I didn't care.

I liked That.

— * — **50** — * —

Two days later, I came home to find that the hood of Dad's pickup was warm and ticking, like he'd just pulled in the driveway. I opened the door to check the odometer. Twenty-three miles had been put on since I left for school.

"Hop in!" Dad called from the garage.

His cheery tone of voice made me suspicious. "Why?"

He stood up, holding a hand pump and a basketball. He bounced the ball once and grinned. "Got a surprise for you."

I hesitated. Since Sunday, he'd been quiet, but not sober. "Are you okay to drive?"

He laughed. "I'm running on coffee and sweat today, nothing else." He bounce-passed the ball to me. "It'll just take a couple minutes. Get in."

I didn't notice the paint until we were on the road: two shades of yellow and a dark blue dotting his forearms and knuckles. He had paint on his shirt and jeans, too. He sang off-key with the radio, his breath smelling of mint gum, his hands steady on the wheel and gearshift. I was beginning to see a pattern. After the bonfire argument, he'd made nice and taken me to the cemetery. After his ax-murderer bit in the garage and the fight we had about it, here he was acting happy again. Well, happy-ish.

My phone buzzed. It was probably Finn, but I didn't take it out of my pocket. I didn't want to trigger Angry Dad again.

The song ended and an obnoxious commercial for a used-car dealer came on. Dad turned the radio off.

"I ran into Tom Russell in the grocery store." He took a deep breath. "He was buying carrots."

I had no idea where this was going. "Were they on sale?"

He turned left and stopped along the curb in front of a small park I'd never seen before. The swing set was empty. A couple of old people sat on a bench watching dogs chase tennis balls that they tossed onto an empty basketball court.

"Didn't notice," Dad said. "The point is that Tom's a contractor. Small jobs mainly: roof repair, gutters, painting, that kind of thing. Anyway, he was buying carrots, like I said, and he recognized me from high school. We got to talking and one thing led to another, and it turned out he'd had a guy not show up for work today." He pointed to a small house with green shutters across the street from the park.

"Voilà."

"Voilà?"

"I painted the kitchen and the laundry room in there.

Only took five hours. Tom paid me cash, everything under the table. Not too shabby, huh?"

His face lit up with real excitement, not the kind that comes in a bottle or a bong. I couldn't remember the last time I'd seen him like this. "That's fantastic, Dad."

"I thought you'd like hearing that."

"Tell me more," I said. "Is this going to be a part-time thing? Full-time? Did you know any of the other guys?"

"I worked alone," he said. "Had tunes playing and the windows open. It was a good day, princess."

"What time does he want you tomorrow?" I asked.

"Who?"

"Your buddy there. The guy who hired you."

"Tom?" He turned the key enough to glance at the time, then took the keys out. "Said he'd call if something else came up." He picked up the ball and opened the door. "We haven't shot hoops in forever. C'mon."

It took him a long time to find his rhythm. I fetched the balls that clanged off the rim and bounced off the backboard. For about ten minutes, he made one shot for every five he took.

"Painting took more out of my arms than I thought," he said.

"It's been a while," I said.

I ran through topics in my head, trying to find something to talk about that wouldn't lead to trouble. I couldn't bring up Finn, for obvious reasons. He didn't want to talk about work. I didn't want to talk about school. Politics was completely out of the question. Spock had started to gnaw on a hot spot on his hind leg, but to talk about that we'd have to talk about a trip to the vet and that would lead to talking about money and how we didn't have any because of everything else we couldn't talk about.

By the time he'd started to sweat, his bad leg was dragging a bit, but his hands were remembering what to do. He dribbled, one, two, three, leaned a bit on the good leg, pulled in his shooting elbow and launched the ball in a beautiful arc that fell, *swish*, through the basket.

"Nice!"

He grinned and made three more shots in a row. "What time is it?" he asked as I grabbed the rebound.

I passed him the ball and checked my phone. (Finn had texted five times.) "Quarter after. Why?"

"Just curious." He dribbled with his left hand. "Finally got ahold of your guidance counselor today."

"Ms. Benedetti? Don't listen to her. She lies about everything."

"Don't worry. She likes you."

"What did she want?" I asked carefully.

He bounced the ball between his legs and passed it to me. "Still struggling in math, huh?"

I put the ball on my hip. "I have a tutor."

He wiped his face on his shirt. "Sounds like you're

spending a lot of time in detention."

I dribbled the ball. "Cruel and unusual punishment, re-member?"

"Maybe you should work on your diplomacy a little bit."

I shot and missed. "They're all lunatics."

"Teaching kids like you?" He chuckled, grabbed the re-bound, spun around me, and made a layup. "Can you blame them?"

I caught the ball and dribbled it behind my back. "What else?"

"Nothing else."

I passed him the ball and watched him make a couple of layups. Maybe Benedetti hadn't talked to him about Trish or she had and he didn't want to discuss it with me. A loud motorcycle headed toward the park. A couple of guys had arrived and were shooting at the other basket. Dad watched them for a minute, dribbled to the foul line, sank a free throw, and raised a triumphant fist.

"Not bad for an old guy, huh?"

Asking about Trish would spoil everything. It wasn't worth it.

"Watch this," Dad said.

He dribbled, cutting left, then right, like he was faking out an invisible opponent. He spotted up and tried to jump, but stumbled, landing hard and wincing. The ball sailed over the backboard.

"Oh, God, I said. "Are you okay?"

"Fine." He limped a few steps. "Just need to walk it off. Get the ball, will you?"

I found the ball under an SUV across the street as the engine of the motorcycle revved loudly, then cut out. I stood, then ducked back down, trying to keep out of Dad's sight. He looked around once, then hurried over to where Michael sat straddled on his Harley. The exchange— something in Dad's hand, something in Michael's— happened so fast nobody else would have noticed it.

My phone buzzed and I took it out of my pocket.

Sup?

Finn wrote.

have you been kidnapped by aliens?
are they torturing you?
helicopter is gassed up and ready I can
rescue you

I wrote back:

i wish

As we were walking to gym the next day, Finn asked me to go to see a school with him.

"We're already in school, dummy," I said.

"No, goof." He gently hip-checked me. "College. My mom set up an interview for me, tomorrow. I don't really want to go, but if you come with me, we can make it into a road trip. An epic road trip."

"*Epic* is a stupid word," I said. "Ninth graders call the cafeteria nachos 'epic.' That actress, what's-her-name, the stoned one, she says her dog is 'epic.' And her lipstick."

"It'll get us out of here for a day," he said. "And my mom will pay for the gas."

"Seriously?"

He nodded.

I kissed him. "That's potentially epic, I'll grant you that much."

Forging my father's signature on the excused absence card was cake, and it felt good, in a bizarre way, to watch Ms. Benedetti's face light up as she officially approved the absence. I wrote a note on my hand to bring her back a souvenir.

* * *

He picked me up at the corner the next morning. I thought he'd be buzzing on energy drinks and the epic-ness of the adventure, but he hardly said a word. Barely looked at me. When we got to the Thruway, he took a hard right into the commuter parking lot instead of driving through the tollbooth.

"What's going on?" I asked. "Did the oil light just come on? Is the engine overheating?"

He shook his head, but I craned my head for a look at the dashboard, just in case. The indicator lights showed no impending disasters. Finn sighed heavily, but still didn't say a word.

"Want me to drive?" I asked.

"You said you didn't have your license yet."

"Not technically."

He didn't even smile at that.

"It's not the car, is it?" I asked.

He sighed again, watching the line of cars rolling through the tollbooth. "I had a fight with my mom this morning," he said. "Before she even had her coffee."

"Why?"

"She was telling me a bunch of stupid, ass-kissing things to say in this interview and then she got on me again for quitting the team. Next thing you know, she was bitching about the rent going up again and what a rotten son I am. For the first time ever, I yelled back." He pounded the steering wheel gently with his fist. "I made her cry. Didn't think that would happen."

"Call and apologize," I suggested. "Text her, at least."

"I already did. That's not the point." He leaned forward and wiped the condensation off the windshield with his sleeve. "This interview is a waste of time. I don't want to go to Oneonta."

"Where do you want to go?"

"Told you the other night. Swevenbury."

"What's so great about it?"

"Swevenbury College, home of The Wanderers? Voted Strangest Small College the last three years in a row? You get to design your own major; there are, like, only two required courses and everybody has to study overseas for a year. Swevenbury is what all other colleges want to be when they grow up. They say the grounds are seriously hallowed. Set foot on the campus and it changes you forever. It's . . ."

He paused like he was searching for the right word, something I'd never seen him do before.

"It's Nerdvana!" he finally declared.

I nodded. "How far away?"

"One hundred eighty-three miles, north by northeast."

I shrugged. "Let's go."

"So I can be tortured by the magnitude of its awesomeness? No, thanks. I'd need a winning lottery ticket to go there."

"That's not why we're going, numbnuts," I said. "Road trips can make things look different. Trust me."

He sighed. "I don't know."

"You have nothing to lose," I said. "The look on your face when you said Swerva-whatever—"

"Swevenbury," he corrected.

"See? Just saying it makes you smile." I said "You promised me 'epic,' Finn-head. Point this car to Nerdvana and floor it. Or at least try to make the speed limit."

I tried to goad him with stories of my years stalking ivory poachers in Southern Cameroons and the time that the Dalai Lama and I got snowed in on a mountaintop and played checkers until dawn, but Finn wasn't interested in talking. He drove hunched over the steering wheel, his face stuck between a frown and pout (a prown? a fout?). I finally gave up and crawled into a book. Three and a half hours and one thick novel about dragons later, we drove under a massive stone arch with the words SWEVENBURY COLLEGE carved into it. A few minutes later, the forest opened up and the main campus came into view: old stone buildings, impossibly green lawns, and expensively dressed students. It looked like a supersized, Americanized version of Hogwarts, without the robes.

We parked and got out of the car.

"That grass looks like it's been combed," I said.

"Whatever," Finn grumbled. "This way."

The admission office was in a red stone castle, complete

with turret and winding staircase. The receptionist there explained that we'd missed the first tour group, but we could join the next group after lunch.

Finn grunted.

She handed us a stack of glossy brochures and badges that had GUEST printed on them in red block letters.

"You'll need these to get into the library and student center," she said. "Those coupons are good for five dollars off your meal."

"Doesn't matter." Finn handed back his badge and the coupons. "We don't have time." He walked out of the office without another word.

"Sorry." I took back the badge and coupons. "He needs some chocolate milk. We'll be back for the tour, thanks."

She winked. "Good luck."

I caught up with Finn at the top of the front steps of the building. "What's your problem?"

"You want a tour? I'll give you a tour." He pointed behind me. "Over there is the School of Teaching Rich Kids How to Become Richer. Behind that—"

"Get over yourself." I followed him down the stairs. "This place is amazing. Look at how that stone is worn down in the middle." I pointed to the marble steps. "Worn down by people carrying books! How cool is that?"

"I shouldn't have let you talk me into this. Did you see the cars in the student lot?"

"Not really," I admitted. "I was looking at the castles."

"Give me the name of one college you've visited that didn't have a castle on it. We should leave."

"No!" I said. "I've never visited a college before, asshole, and I want to see it. Stop whining. You're smarter than most people on the planet, you have nice teeth, and your parents can afford your glasses. Your life does not suck that bad." I started down the steps. "I'll meet you in the parking lot at three."

"Wait." He stepped in front of me. "Can we back up? You've never visited a college before?"

"Yeah, so?"

"Not even when you were in middle school, like on the way to a band competition or something?" Finn tilted his head to the side a little, like he was confused, like he couldn't imagine a life that didn't include college visits on the way to band competitions.

I'd given him bits and pieces of my peculiar life, but colored softer and funnier than they had been. I'd painted my dad as Don Quixote in a semi, on a quest for philosophical truths and the best cup of coffee in the nation. I'd explained Dad's craziness with the ax as a rare night of too much drinking and avoided the subject ever since.

He raked his fingers through his hair. "Your dad never took you?"

I wasn't going to ruin the day by discussing my dad's parenting style.

"Go to the library," I said. "Absorb the dork energy. I'll find you when I'm done walking around."

He bit the inside of his cheek. "Am I really being an asshole?"

"Yes."

He stared at the students walking up and down the steps for a moment, absently nodding his head like he was having a conversation with himself. Finally, he took a deep breath and exhaled hard.

"Please forgive me, Mistress of the Blue." He rolled his right hand in front of his belt buckle, then swept a low bow in front of me. "This day shall henceforth be dedicated to your education of all things related to, but not exclusively concerning, this institution of post-secondary, ivy-choked, divine education."

"Rise, knave," I said regally. "Rise and let the merriment begin."

Finn was right; we didn't need a tour guide. He'd memorized every inch of the campus from the website. He showed me the new behavioral sciences building, the athletic center, where one vast room was filled with treadmills, each with its own television monitor, and a massive swimming pool, and a student center filled with people who looked impossibly comfortable and happy. When he told me the number of books in the library, I didn't believe him, so I asked at the reference desk, and the dude showed me a screen with a summary of their collections. It made me so faint I had to sit with my head between my knees for a while.

Better than all that was the simple act of walking down hallways where classes were being held. We lingered by a few open doorways, catching random bits of lecture and arguments about Kant and Indonesian history and bonding equivalencies and scansion and *King Lear*. We peeked through the windows into lecture halls and argued about whether a board filled with symbols was physics or astrology.

Finn gradually transformed from *Grumpasourous maximus* into my hot, skinny, almost-boyfriend. (I hadn't decided if I was using that word yet.) We used our coupons to buy lunch and sat underneath an ancient oak tree in the middle of the quad feasting on subs, chocolate milk, and a peanut butter cookie the size of my face. Halfway through the cookie Finn lay back in the combed grass with a sigh.

"Nerdvana?" I asked.

"Not yet, but I am slightly less despondent. You were right. It was a good idea, coming here."

The bells in the clock tower boomed. I pointed at a dude riding a skateboard from one end of the quad to the other, typing on his phone. "You really want to be like him?"

"If he's here on a full scholarship and majoring in political science, I'd give my left nut to be that guy. Maybe minus the skateboard."

"Then go," I said. "Be nice to the admissions reception-ist and ask if you can get an interview with somebody. Any-body. Give it your best."

"But if I get an interview and apply and get in, what do I do then? And worse, what if I apply and they turn me down?"

"If they can't see that you're perfect for this place, then they suck. And if you're smart enough to go here, then you should be smart enough to find a way to pay for it, right? Now go."

I watched until he'd disappeared inside the red stone castle (practically skipping), then I stretched out on the cool grass. This was not hallowed ground. It was dirt, brown dirt, crawling with ants.

I found the college's website on my phone and looked up the application. Stupidest thing ever. How could filling in a bunch of blanks and writing a fluffy essay about the "moment of significance" in my life let them know if I was good enough to go here? The other essay prompts were just as bad:

Recount an incident or time when you experienced failure.

Reflect on a time when you challenged a belief or idea.

Discuss an event that marked your transition
from childhood to adulthood within your culture,
community, or family.

Who wrote these things? What the hell did they have
to do with how smart a person was or how ready she might
be for college?

I tried to hop on the school's Wi-Fi because we couldn't
afford the data charges. The passwords I guessed (welcome,
guest, wanderer, spoiled, nerdvana) failed, which pissed me
all the way off. I wanted a map so I could find a shortcut to
get home.

—*— **52** —*—

I gave Ms. Benedetti a Swevenbury Owls pencil at the end
of fourth period the next day.

"What did you think?" she asked. "Want to go there?"

I snorted. "No way."

"There are lots of scholarships," she said, her forehead
wrinkled into the earnest lines of sincerity.

"Not for me," I said on my way out the door. "But
thanks."

*   *   *

After school on Thursday, we parked in a secluded place and made out until the alarm on his phone went off. We adjusted our clothes and buckled up.

"Do you know what you're going to wear tomorrow?" he asked as he started the car.

A simple question, right? Maybe it should have raised a flag or something, but I was still swooning, because *daaaang* that boy could kiss. He could have asked me anything, like what's the specific gravity of honey or what kind of bra did Marie Antoinette wear, and I would not have found it odd.

"Hayley?" He waved his hand in front of my eyes. "I said, do you know what you're wearing tomorrow?"

I blinked, still not getting it. "No, not yet."

"I know, right?" he replied.

Had I been less swoony it might have struck me as weird that he was asking about my wardrobe, but a block from my house we parked again and got tangled up in a good-bye kiss and I forgot all about it.

My Chinese homework, that was partly to blame, too.

I'd started it, but then I had to go online to look something up and one thing led to another and suddenly I found myself gaming with Finn in a distant galaxy. Totally pwnd him. His manly pride took offense at that and so we had to play again. And again. We would have played until dawn—me winning, him losing—except that I got a text from Sasha, who had become my drill partner in Chinese, asking me if the test was just going to cover chapter four or everything since the beginning of the year.

I don't know what came over me. You could blame the kissing, I guess. His saliva had infected me with a strain of Finnegan Ramos Conventional Success Syndrome. I stopped gaming and stayed up past three trying to memorize eight weeks' worth of Chinese characters.

I woke up with my face on the keyboard, my phone screaming inches away from my nose.

"I've been waiting out here for ten minutes," Finn's voice said. "Are you okay?"

I hadn't changed into pj's the night before, so I didn't have to waste any time getting dressed. I grabbed my stuff, staggered out the front door, down the street and into the Acclaim, which smelled more like burning oil than ever.

My first glance at Finn made me wonder if I were still asleep.

"Like it?" he asked, pulling away from the curb.

I was speechless.

He pointed to the cardboard cutout of an old-fashioned pipe sitting on the dashboard. "Can't you guess who I am?"

"What's on your head?"

"A deerstalker," he said. "It's a detective hat. This," he plucked at the ugly gray thing he was wearing over his shoulders, "is a cape. I should have on fancier shoes but they don't fit anymore. Looks good, huh?"

"I just woke up, Finn. You're confusing me. What's going on?"

"Elementary, my dear Kincain," he said in a lousy British accent. "It's Halloween!"

He filled me in on the details as we drove (almost reaching the speed limit for several thrill-filled moments), but I didn't believe him. My mistake.

Our principal was dressed as a spider. The secretaries were all convicts. The janitors had transformed themselves into Luigi clones. All of the teachers were in costumes. The cafeteria ladies, too: beehive hairdos and poodle skirts from the 1950s.

Gracie was wearing a T-shirt that said DISFUN on the front. Topher's T-shirt said CTIONAL. They were as keyed up as six-year-old kids at a birthday party with unlimited candy and cupcakes.

"I don't understand," I said again. "Why is the staff more dressed up than the kids?"

"Because they get to make the rules," Gracie said.

"Because the students all wanted to be inappropriate," Topher said.

"It's a game," explained Sherlock Finn Holmes. "A game

afoot! The challenge: to walk the thin line of costuming that separates what the administration has labeled—"

All three of them made bunny-ear quotation marks with their fingers: "Distractions!"

"And those that are merely, ahem . . ." Sherlock stared at me.

"Lame," finished Gracie. "Your ignorance is mind-boggling. What time should we pick you up?"

"Who is 'we' and why are 'we' picking me up?" I asked.

"Trick or treating, duh!"

The entire day was surreal. Ms. Rogak taught English dressed as the Bride of Frankenstein. My Chinese teacher was a ham-and-cheese sandwich. She canceled the test and let us watch a movie. My forensic science teacher was dressed as a crime scene, dusted with fingerprint powder, sprayed with Luminol, and wrapped in yellow police tape. As the day wore on, I found myself liking it, actually loving it. Halloween—the day when we could pretend to be whatever we wanted—seemed to be letting everyone be who they really were. Wearing face paint and masks gave everyone in school permission to drop the zombie act. Even the kids who were hinting at actual zombification by the way they walked and moaned seemed more human to me than ever before.

When I was called down to the guidance office at the end of last period, I took my sweet time getting there so I could admire the decorations that made the music hall look like the palace of Versailles. (The chorus teacher and band instructor had dressed as Mozart and Scarlatti.) If every day could be like this, I bet test scores would go through the roof.

Gerta, the guidance secretary, was completely covered by orange rubber fish scales. An enormous clam, opened to show a pearl inside it, sat on her head.

"No costume?" Gerta asked as I signed in.

"I'm going to wear something different tonight," I said. "Right now I'm disguised as a rebellious, irritating teenager."

"Very convincing. I hardly recognized you."

Ms. Benedetti, dressed as an old-school, guaranteed-to-piss-off-the-Wiccans witch with a pointy hat, wart on the chin, cobwebs and plastic spiders nestled in her wig, opened her door.

"Ger-a agh-agh allowee," she mumbled, beckoning me in and brushing aside the thick cobwebs that drooped from the ceiling. "Ome ee."

I had to squeeze by an inflatable cauldron and step over life-sized plastic rats to get to the chair.

"I o oou own my—" Benedetti began.

"Ma'am." I interrupted and pointed at her fake teeth. "Would you mind?"

"Oh." She pulled out the teeth and took off her hat. "Feels so natural, after a while you forget you're wearing them."

It took all my strength, but I resisted the temptation to comment.

She pushed a plastic orange bowl across the desk. "Candy corn?"

I didn't want to take anything from her, but my stomach overruled my head and I snagged a handful.

She waited until my mouth was full.

"Hayley, we have a bit of a problem."

I stopped mid-chew, mind racing with the countless disasters that could follow an opening statement like that.

"I had a meeting with Mr. Cleveland," she continued.

I started chewing again.

"He said he'd set you up with tutoring."

I nodded, hoping she didn't notice the blushing because my tutoring sessions no longer had anything to do with math.

"And yet your grade hasn't improved at all."

I shrugged and took another handful of candy.

"He said you had shown some interest in helping revive the school newspaper, but that has fallen by the wayside, too. In addition—"

"Did you tell my father about Trish?" I asked. "He said he talked to you."

"We didn't talk about Trish," she said. "We discussed her concerns."

"What were those, exactly?"

"Most had to do with your father's unconventional approach to your homeschooling. He confirmed that he had not been entirely truthful about your lessons."

"Was he angry?"

"Not at all. He simply asked if I thought you were struggling in any subjects. According to your teachers you haven't had any problems with the material, with the exception of math, of course."

"You said 'most.' What else?"

"In trying to understand the whole student, it's helpful to have a picture of the larger family dynamic."

"That sounds like a load of crap," I said. "Did you ask Dad about this 'dynamic'?"

"I tried." She picked up a piece of candy corn with her fingernails. "I got the impression that you'd have more to say about that than your father."

The final bell cut her off.

I jumped up. "Can we talk about this on Monday?"

"I imagine so." The witch sighed and popped the candy in her mouth. "Be careful tonight."

—*— **53** —*—

Our washer and dryer stood at the bottom of the basement steps. I led Gracie past them and opened the door to the rest of the basement.

"Whoa," Gracie said. "It didn't used to look like this."

When we first moved in, Dad had spent an afternoon trying to deal with Gramma's old stuff in the basement.

I helped him until we got in a stupid argument about some ancient books of his. They stank of mold and I said we needed to throw them out and he'd yelled at me so I'd stormed out. This was the first time I'd ventured past the washer and dryer since then. It looked like Dad had stopped working as soon as I'd left.

"I swear to you this wasn't here then," Gracie said, pointing at the rickety metal shelving unit half filled with plastic tubs and cardboard boxes. "There was a little round table and three chairs, and a rug and a toy chest—"

"Knock it off, will you?" I asked. "You're freaking me out. Your memory is unnatural. I bet you have a brain tumor or something."

She stuck her tongue out at me. Her mood had been better since her parents had declared a temporary truce after their family therapist had threatened to quit.

"This is ridiculous," I said. "We'll never find anything. How about I just carry an open umbrella and say that I'm a rainstorm?"

"Such a pessimist." Gracie pulled a bin from the shelf, set it on the ground, and opened it. "Eww! Old wigs and mouse poop." Two bins later, she shrieked in triumph; she'd found our old dress-up clothes and a box of arts and crafts supplies that were free of rodent turds. I pointed out that we had grown a bit in the past decade and she called me an ungrateful bitch and we dumped everything on the floor and started pawing through it to figure out a costume for me.

"How about Sexy Princess?" Gracie asked, putting a bent tiara on her head.

"Absolutely not," I said.

"Sexy Cowgirl?" Gracie held up a kid's holster and six-shooter.

"I'd rather be warm than sexy," I said, holding up an old shawl. "It's going down to the twenties tonight."

She rummaged in another bin. "Feathers!" she shouted triumphantly. "You could be Sexy Big Bird!"

"That's disgusting," I said.

Before she could reply, heavy footsteps hurried down the wooden stairs. My gut tightened.

"Dad?" I called.

He stopped in the doorway. "What are you two doing down here?"

"I need a Halloween costume," I said quickly. "Gracie asked me to help her take her little brother trick or treating."

"It'll be supersafe," Gracie added. "We'll only go to the houses of people we know and—"

She stopped when my father held up his hand.

"That's great, sounds like fun," he said, "but where's the vacuum cleaner?"

"What?" I asked.

"The vacuum cleaner," he repeated. "I can't find it. Or the thing you use to clean the toilet."

"Toilet brush is in the holder in the garage. Vacuum cleaner is in my closet."

"Thanks." He studied the mess we'd made on the floor. "What time are you heading out?"

"I'll make dinner before I go," I promised.

"Don't worry about that, I got it."

"Remember, I'm spending the night at Gracie's," I said.

"I remember!" he called. "Have fun!"

"You can count on that!" Gracie whispered as she danced a few steps.

"Shh!" I warned. Finn's mother had taken an unplanned trip to Boston because his dad had the flu. She wasn't going to be home until Sunday night. Maybe Monday. So we had an empty house for the whole weekend.

"Hey!" Dad's footsteps thudded back down the stairs, and his face poked around the corner. "No parties and you don't go near the quarry, understood?"

"Of course it is, sir," Gracie answered super sincerely. "My parents have the exact same rules."

"Good," Dad said. "Glad to hear it. You girls leaving soon?"

An alarm bell clanged in my head. *Michael.*

"I don't know, Dad," I said. "Maybe I should come back here. What if a million little kids show up or some idiots egg the house? It'll drive you nuts. If I stay, you won't have to deal with any of it."

"You go," he said firmly. "I'm having a friend come over for dinner. Between the two of us, we'll take care of it."

Definitely Michael. My heart sank. Would it be better to

spend the night here to make sure that creep did not cause a catastrophe or go to Finn's and spend all night worrying?

"Mr. Kincain, do you have a date?" Gracie teased.

Instead of losing his temper or being rude, my father grinned and cleared his throat. "Well, maybe," he said. "Maybe not. I'll let you know tomorrow, how's that?"

Dear gods above. Michael has hooked my father up with a skank piece of trash.

—*— **54** —*—

It took the rest of the afternoon, a raid on Mrs. Rappaport's closet, and a cheeseburger (medium rare, spicy mustard, toasted bun), but by the time Finn and Topher got to Gracie's house, I was costumed.

"Well?" Gracie asked the guys as she spun me around in the driveway. "What do you think?"

"Aaah," Topher said, incapable of looking at anyone other than his girlfriend. Gracie's Sexy Nurse costume had robbed him of the power of speech.

"Erm," said Sherlock Finn, eyes wide. "Do I get three guesses?"

"If you say Sexy Big Bird, I will punch you in the throat," I warned.

"Wouldn't dream of it," Finn said.

"Come on!" Iron Man, aka Garrett, grabbed his sister's hand and pulled her down the driveway. Topher followed, his eyes still on Gracie.

"Come on, you guys," Gracie called to us.

"In a minute," I promised.

The wind was picking up, blowing hard enough to send the last of the leaves to the ground and make little tornadoes, the tiny funnels gathering speed and spinning down a street filling with superheroes, witches, and monsters who giggled as they ran from house to house, their bags already drooping with candy.

Finn waited for our friends to get a little farther away, then he drew me into the shadows. "I like the mask."

I kissed him.

"The wings are cool, too," he eventually said.

I'd woven an entire bag of feathers into an old shawl of my grandmother's. Gracie had pinned the most colorful feathers in my hair. She'd also dug into her treasure chest of makeup and painted bold streaks of violet, gray, and turquoise around my eyes. Under the shawl, I was wearing black tights and a black football jersey of her dad's that went down to my knees. As long as I kept my wings on, no one could see the name and numbers on the back of it.

The wind stirred my feathers. I touched the fat piece of amber-colored glass hanging around my neck. In the bottom of my grandmother's jewelry box, it had looked like a garage sale leftover. In the half-light, with the wind gusting, it glowed, transforming me.

"This is a magic amulet," I whispered into his ear. "I am an owl, bird of the night. I see everything. I know everything."

"Do you know what I'm thinking?"

"Yes. Beware, boy, or I'll turn you into a toad and eat you."

We followed Garrett for hours: running up driveways, cutting through yards and gardens, begging him to share his loot and laughing as he found a million and one reasons why he wouldn't. His Iron Man costume was one of the best out there, but I don't think he cared. For a while, we walked with some of his buddies. Their parents wore costumes, too, video game characters and football players and vampires, lots of middle-aged vampires, some sipping from coffee to-go cups that did not have any coffee in them, given how often they tripped over their own feet.

Topher spent a while on the phone, lagging behind and talking into it so quietly I couldn't hear what he was saying. Gracie gave him a dirty look when he caught up to us and pulled away when he tried to put his arm around her waist.

"What's going on?" Finn asked.

"Party at the quarry is hot." Topher kept his voice low enough that the parents ahead of us wouldn't hear him.

"No," Gracie said.

"The place doesn't have ghosts," Topher said. "I asked. But it does have Jell-O shots, dancing, and the possibility of a bong or two."

"Nothing good happens there," Gracie said. "I'm not going."

"All those stories are exaggerated," he said. "It's just a way to get girls nervous so they'll want their boyfriends to hold them tight."

"Well, maybe you should find a different girl," Gracie said.

All that magic in the air, squealing kids, spooky music, free candy, and those two had to fight. I was beginning to see signs of zombification in both of them, but Halloween was the wrong time to bring up the subject and, besides, I had better things to do.

Finn and I took advantage of every shadow to sneak in kisses. When thin-boned fingers of clouds raced over the moon, it felt like I could soar.

Gracie's mom had given permission for Finn and Topher to hang out until midnight watching movies with us, so when Garrett's bag was full, the four of us headed back toward the Rappaports'.

"I think you need some sweats," Finn said for the fifti-eth time. "You can't claim to be a very wise owl if you get pneumonia."

"I'm not just an owl, I am Athena." I flapped dramatically, twirling so he wouldn't see my teeth chatter. "Goddess of wisdom and weaving and weapons and cheeseburgers. Goddesses do not wear sweatpants."

"They do when they're in human form. I'm pretty sure it's a Goddess Law."

I sneezed. "Goddess Law? I am so using that."

"I'm not kissing you again until you get something warmer."

"How can you be boring and hot at the same time?"

We caught up with Gracie, Topher, and Iron Man and told them we were detouring past my house and would meet them in a few minutes. Finn insisted on draping his coat over my shoulders, and did it gently so I wouldn't lose any feathers. The warmth felt better than I wanted to admit.

The rental car parked in the driveway brought me crashing back to Earth.

"Ugh," I said. "My father has a date. Stay outside, okay? The sight of her might blind you."

They froze, caught in the act of laughing.

A blue cloth covered the dining room table. Two long, white candles stood in the middle of it, flames jumping. A glass beer mug filled with grocery store flowers sat between the candles, next to matching salt- and pepper-shakers I'd never seen before. Music was playing from a phone at the end of the table, the crappy, soft oldies Dad hated.

My father stood quickly. The napkin that had been in his lap fluttered to the ground. "I thought you were sleeping at Gracie's."

"I need my sweatpants."

He'd shaved. Found the iron, too, because his khakis didn't have any wrinkles. Neither did his shirt, a white button-down with the sleeves rolled up. His old watch was strapped on his left wrist. He was wearing a tie, too, an honest-to-goodness tie, knotted with military precision.

I hit the switch to the left of the door and turned on the living room lights.

"Didn't think you'd be home till tomorrow," Dad said, blinking. "Yeah, um . . . well."

Trish reached out and muted the phone.

Threat

"Why is she here?" My voice sounded like it came out of someone else's mouth, someone calm, someone whose heart beat slowly.

Under the table, Spock whimpered.

"I invited her," he said.

"Are you crazy?" I asked, still calm, though my hands were damp.

"Hello, Hayley." Trish stood up, setting her napkin beside her plate. She took a few steps in my direction and stopped. "Wow. You look so grown-up."

"Wow," I said, *calm, calm, calm*. "You look old. No, not 'old,' that's not the right word. 'Diseased,' maybe."

"Whoa, princess." Dad put his hands up as if he were being held at gunpoint. "That's not necessary."

"Not necessary?" I asked. "When did this happen, this invitation? Was it before or after you told me she was coming? Oh, wait. You didn't tell me, did you?"

The polite mask fell off his face. Adrenaline shot into my heart.

"You didn't tell me because you knew I'd say 'Trish? The drunk who abandoned us?'"

There was a knock at the front door.

The snake opened her mouth. "Hayley," she said, "you have to give me a chance."

"I don't have to give you shit!"

"Enough!" Dad's voice shook the walls.

The noise in my head was so loud I barely heard him. I

had crossed the floor. I was in her face. "Get out now or I'm calling the cops."

The knock sounded again. Spock headed for the door as it opened.

"Excuse me," Finn said. "It's just . . . you were yelling. Everything okay?"

"We're fine," Dad said.

"Miss Blue?" Finn asked.

Assess

Trish hadn't flinched. She met my gaze, having to look up a bit because I was taller than she was. She wore contacts instead of glasses. Concealer that couldn't hide the dark circles under her eyes, hair dyed a flat brown with faded highlights. Her blush stood out like stop signs on her cheeks because all the color had drained from her face.

The front door closed. Finn's footsteps and then his voice, "Hello, Mr. Kincain. I'm Finn, remember? We met a couple weeks ago."

"What are you doing here?" Dad asked him.

Trish stepped around me and walked up to Finn, her hand outstretched. "My name is Trish Lazarev," she said. "I'm an old friend of the family."

Finn shook her hand. "Finnegan Ramos, ma'am, new friend of the family."

"You told me you'd be with Gracie and her brother," Dad said.

"We were. We were just calling it a night," Finn said. "I walked Hayley home because she was cold."

"You're cold 'cause you're not wearing any goddamn pants," Dad said to me.

"It's a Halloween costume, Andy," Trish said mildly. "It's very cute."

"You should see the mask," Finn said, holding out the bird face.

"Stop it!" I shouted, not willing to let them turn this into a game of plastic people talking about nothing while hungry lions paced in the middle of the room.

"Hayley, please," Trish said.

I pointed at my father. "This isn't about Halloween or pants." I pointed at Trish. "It's about you. Did you drug him? Is he having a brain bleed? I mean, God—"

"That's enough, young lady," Dad growled.

"No, Andy, don't!" Trish shouted.

And this, always this. The part where Dad loses it, except he was supposed to grab her, not me, that's what it said in the script; she'd bitch at him and nag, or he'd yell at her and no matter how it started, it ended with shoves and screams and broken things, and sometimes the broken thing was her, and sometimes it was him. Never me because I was small enough to hide in the closet or under my bed.

But that wouldn't work anymore. I was too big.

Dad's breath smelled like whiskey and apple pie. This

close, his eyes were dead flat, with no expression, not even anger. He looked at me like he didn't know me. Maybe if my hair was still in pigtails, maybe if I was two feet shorter and missing my front teeth, then he'd see me.

Finn shouted something and suddenly he was next to me. Dad shoved him away. Finn came back and Dad grabbed his coat and there was Trish right in the middle of everything, her face inches from mine, from Dad's. This was where she'd slap me or maybe Dad or maybe even Finn. This was where the screaming would pitch up and then something would fly through the air, an ashtray, a beer bottle, a table, and they would roar at each other and somebody would bleed and—

"Andy." Trish's voice was barely above a whisper. "Look at me."

Dad squeezed the front of Finn's coat tighter.

"Please, Andy," she said. "Please look at me." She put her hands on my father's fists. "What have we been talking about all night?" she whispered.

Daddy closed his eyes and opened his hands.

Finn and I both stepped out of range. I mouthed "Go," but he shook his head. Dad sat heavily on the couch, expressionless. Spock hopped up next to him and laid his shaggy head on Dad's lap.

"How about we let Hayley get her sweatpants and go to her girlfriend's for the night, like she planned?" Trish asked.

The only sound was the *whump, whump* of Spock's tail on the couch cushions as Dad scratched his ears.

"Or I can leave," Trish said. "Whatever is going to make you comfortable."

Whump, whump, whump, whump, whump.

Dad looked at the dog, but spoke to me. "You should go, Hayley."

"But—"

He shook his head. "I need to talk to Trish. Will this guy walk you to Grace's?"

"Of course, sir," Finn said.

"Would you mind waiting for her outside?" Trish asked. *Action*

—*— **56** —*—

I emptied my backpack on my bed, then stuffed it with a pair of jeans, socks, underwear, a couple of books, and all the money in my secret stash . . . *heart pounding legs running lungs heaving* . . . I pulled on leggings and then sweatpants . . . *get out get out get out* . . . Put on a turtleneck and my heaviest hoodie . . . *run hide watch your back* . . . Took the hunting knife out of my sock drawer and put it in the pouch.

Fought the urge to set my room on fire and scream while the windows and mirrors shattered. Fought the urge to reach inside and punch my own heart until it stopped beating or until I stopped caring, whichever came first.

I walked out of my room. Down the hall.

They were sitting at the table again. She had the coffee cup to her mouth. He stared into the candle flame.

I grabbed my feathered shawl off the floor. Slammed the front door behind me, hoping that it would make the roof cave in. I did not look back to see if it did.

—*— 57 —*—

"Wait!"

I turned right at the bottom of the driveway and kept walking.

"Wait, where are we going?" Finn called after me.

Walking, walking . . .

He fell into step next to me. "Gracie's house is the other way."

What if she kills him? What if she upsets him so much, he shoots her, and then turns the gun on himself?

"I'm not going to Gracie's."

"So where are you going?"

Walk. Just walk.

"Bus station."

"That's ridiculous. You don't run away because you don't like your dad's date."

What if he's been getting worse because she's been messing with his head? What if he has truly lost it, as in he needs to be tied to a bed, he needs them to shock his brain again? What if he's already gone over the edge and can't come back?

"Come on, really?" He jogged ahead, then turned and walked backward a few paces in front of me. "What time does the bus leave? Where is it going? You don't know, do you?"

"Doesn't matter. I'm getting on the first bus out of here."

"What if it's going to Poughkeepsie?" he asked. "Nobody in their right mind would go to Poughkeepsie."

"Stop following me."

"You're following me," he said. "I'm in front."

"I'm not playing, Finn."

"I know. That's what's scaring me."

Just walk.

"You're going in the wrong direction, you know," he said. "Unless you were going to walk twenty-five miles to the Schenectady station."

"If you get your car, you could drive me."

"If I go back to get my car, you'll disappear."

I kept my mouth shut, head down, and feet moving because he was right.

Five minutes. Ten.

We left the last streetlight behind, but the road was lit by the stubborn moon. We passed an abandoned farm and walked through the smell of something dead and rotting in the weeds.

Without any warning, Finn suddenly tripped and went down hard.

I wanted to walk past him, over him if necessary, but the sound he made when he hit the ground, a soft "ow," was so real that I almost felt it.

I stopped. "Break anything?"

He sat up. "Not sure." He reached forward and felt his right ankle, then slowly flexed his foot, wincing a little.

I put out my hand and helped him up. He dusted off the back of his coat and took a few steps.

"Ankle's okay, but I think I sprained my butt bone." He walked a few paces and turned to look at me. "Let's go."

The Halloween wind that had blown us all over town hours earlier cut through me, slicing through my clothes, biting my skin, and breaking the fever that had been boiling in me ever since I opened the door and saw Trish at our table.

"Do you think we've crossed the border yet?" I asked.

"Canada is that way." Finn pointed north. "A very long walk."

"I meant the border to the next town."

"Why?"

The moon chuckled. It did. I heard it.

"I wish they painted black lines on the ground to show you where the borders are, like on a map." I wiped the tears off my face. "You know, like when you're little in an airplane, and you look down and you expect to see fat lines on the ground dividing one state from the other?"

"The company that made the giant paintbrushes to do that went out of business," Finn said quietly, stepping closer to me. "Sabotage, I think."

I shivered. "Why are you doing this?"

He pulled a feather out of my hair and held it between us. "I have this thing for Sexy Big Birds."

I tried to keep my face hard, my fists clenched, but a smile crept up. We kissed, gently at first, then harder. Hotter. We kissed in the moonlight in the middle of nowhere, our arms winding around each other like vines. For a moment, I didn't feel lost.

"Are you hungry?" he finally asked.

"No."

"Good." He lifted my hand and kissed the knuckles. "Let me cook you breakfast. I'll call Topher, tell him to stay away. We'll eat and then I'll take you to the bus station, Scout's honor, whatever bus station you want."

"You were never a Boy Scout."

"Pancakes or waffles?"

— *— 58 —*—

Night vision goggles turn the dark into shades of green, Oz-like, but they can't see everything. Thermal-imaging goggles show the heat signature of the hidden enemy. Kill him and you can watch the heat leave his body like a spirit reaching for the moon.

I am a good soldier, a good officer. I believe in my country and my mission. I still believe in honor, but sand plugs my heart. It sifts through the holes in my brain. Some days I see the world in the green of night vision. Some days I see the heat.

I blink and I forget why I walked into the room. I forget why I am driving on this road. The remembering takes up every breath until there is no room for today. I pour a drink, ten drinks, so I can forget that I have forgotten today. I smoke. Choke down pills. Pray. Eat. Sleep. Shit. Curse.

Nothing chases away the sand or the memories engraved on the back side of my eyelids. They play on a continuous loop, with smells and sound and sorrow.

Finn's house was a narrow condo in the middle of a row of other condos lined up like slices of white bread in a plastic bag.

"You won't believe how much they charge for this place," he explained, unlocking the front door. "Mom's moving as soon as I graduate." He flipped on the lights as we walked in.

"You're positive she won't turn up?" I asked.

"She hates driving at night, don't worry."

In the bathroom, I tried to repair the damage the tears had done to my makeup. The past rushed in through the mirror . . .

> . . . *Trish taking me on a city bus to get my library card, riding bikes under tall dark trees, baking lopsided birthday cupcakes,*
>
> . . . *me wiping the tears off her face with a little-girl hand, her wrapping me in a blanket and carrying me to the car,*
>
> . . . *running from the beast daddy who roared and threw bolts of lightning, her holding me tight* . . .

I turned the light off.

*   *   *

Finn opened the refrigerator. "Milk, chocolate milk, orange juice, or the red diet stuff my mom likes? Or I could make hot chocolate."

"Vodka."

"Milk, chocolate milk, orange juice, red stuff, hot chocolate," he repeated. "Or tea."

"I'll buy vodka off a homeless guy outside the bus station."

He sighed, took the orange juice out of the fridge and a vodka bottle out of the cupboard above it. He set them both in front of me, with a scratched plastic cup. I unscrewed the vodka cap and poured a couple inches.

"Aren't you having any?" I asked.

"Chocolate milk is my drug of choice."

I looked him in the eye, squinted, and looked closer, under the bright light. "Are you wearing eyeliner?"

"Took you long enough to notice," he said. "Like it?"

"Yeah." I chuckled. "Kinda hot. But no mascara, okay? I can't be seen with a dude whose lashes are longer than mine."

He stared at the plastic cup, then kissed the end of my nose. "Are we really talking about this?"

"No." My gut made a decision for me and before I realized it, I had poured the vodka back in the bottle and filled my glass with juice. "Definitely not."

As Finn cooked the bacon and pancakes, he tried to keep me distracted by chattering about his years as an apprentice chef at an emir's palace in the middle of the Sahara Desert. It didn't work. Worries boiled up, wrapped in a twisting gray ribbon of panic.

What was Trish's plan?

She always had one, always stayed four or five steps ahead of everyone around her, especially my father. Was she after his disability check? She probably thought it was huge. Was she going to make him fall in love with her again, let her move in? Get on his life insurance and then help him kill himself?

"Hey!" Finn snapped his finger in front of my face. "You need to eat." He set down a steaming plate of pancakes in front of me, a smiley face of butter melting on top.

"Cute."

"And bacon," he set down a separate plate of crispy bacon strips, "and real maple syrup." He poured dark syrup from a leaf-shaped glass bottle.

"Is that all you have?" I asked.

"My people come from New Hampshire; we only eat the real thing."

"Your last name is Ramos."

"There are Hispanics in New England, you know."

"I'm sorry," I said, "I didn't mean . . ."

He grinned and raised a hand. "No worries. It gives me

permission to say stereotypical things about white girls."

"Great," I said. "What about your mom's family? Do I dare ask?"

"WASPs from Conway."

"Where people like funny-looking maple syrup."

"Which you are now going to try." He speared a forkful of pancake and swished it in syrup. "Open up."

"Forget it. I only like the cheap stuff they make out of corn syrup."

"You'll stand on the edge of a cliff, but you're too chicken to try the best maple syrup in the world?"

He was being a pain to cheer me up and it was starting to work, even without the vodka. "Maybe you're trying to poison me."

"Wuss."

"Now you're picking a fight." I dipped my pinky finger in his syrup and lightly touched it to the tip of my tongue. "People pay money for this?" (After putting up such a fuss I could hardly admit that it tasted amazing.)

"It's boiled-down sap, totally natural," he said. "No chemicals or preservatives."

"It's tree blood. That makes you a tree-sucking vampire. I bet you have splinters in your lips."

"Maybe you should check," he suggested, swooping in for a bite.

The doorbell rang.

"We're ignoring that," he murmured.

"All trick-or-treaters should be in bed," I said.

But it kept ringing, and then came the heavy pounding. Finn cursed and sat back, his shoulders slumping.

"Damn," he said. "I forgot to call them."

—*— 60 —*—

Gracie tripped over the threshold. Topher trailed behind her with a stupid grin on his face. Both of them were red-eyed and buzzed.

"Did you drive?" Finn asked.

"Got a ride," Topher said. "We escaped just in time."

"So many police cars," Gracie said with a giggle.

"Police?" Finn opened the door again to check.

"They busted the party at the quarry." Topher grinned like a ten-year-old. "We ran. They didn't see us."

"We flew," Gracie said, eyes wide. She pointed at Finn. "We have to sleep here tonight. In fact, we're moving in. We'll be hippies and have a commune and raise chickens. And goats."

Topher put his arm around her. "Sorry, dude," he said. "She's a little messed up."

"You two," Gracie's swayed her finger back and forth between Finn and me, "are good. Friends."

"I made pancakes," Finn said.

"Dude!" Topher let go of Gracie and headed for the kitchen.

"Hurry up," Gracie called after him. "I want to talk to dead people."

Finn looked at me. "What did she just say?"

By the time we finished eating, Gracie had somehow convinced Finn to take the big mirror off the wall of his mom's bedroom and set it on the floor of the family room with a fat red candle in the middle of it.

Gracie curled up under an afghan on the couch, her head on Topher's lap, her fogged eyes losing the fight to stay open. Topher tilted his head back and fell asleep, too. I thought about dragging the two of them outside and letting them sleep under the bushes, but that could create massive deposits of bad karma for me, and I needed all the help I could get in that department. By the time Finn came in from the kitchen with the rest of the bacon and a small bowl of maple syrup, the two of them were snoring, Gracie's soft alto alternating with Topher's bass.

"Turn off the lights," I said.

Finn muttered something I didn't catch, but shut the lights off and groped his way back in the dark. He sat across from me, the mirror between us.

"Now what?" he asked.

"Haven't you ever done this?" I wrapped my shawl of feathers around me to shield me from thoughts of Trish and my father. "The veil between the worlds is thinnest on Halloween night. We're supposed to be able to see dead people in the mirror."

Finn crunched a piece of bacon. "My mom would never buy a mirror that had dead people in it."

"You can be an old fart sometimes." I leaned forward and lit the candle, holding my shawl away from the flame.

He pointed at the mirror's surface. "See? You and me, very much alive."

"Take off your glasses," I said. "Let your eyes go out of focus."

"If I take my glasses off, my eyes go out of focus automatically."

I snorted. "Just do it, okay?"

Finn removed his glasses. "All right," he said. "Bring on the dead. They better not like bacon."

I took a deep breath, half closed my eyes, and let them go blurry until I could only see shapes. Oval silver mirror. Square red candle. Circles and then crescents of flame colored blue, yellow, white, and then gray until it faded into the lanky Finn-shaped shadow that melted into the darkness.

Time stretched itself like a cat waking from a long nap, luxurious and patient. I took a deep breath, held it while I counted to seven, and let it go. The candle flame jumped. I tried to lose myself in the light rippling across the face of the mirror. Another deep breath, *hold it.* . . .

An owl hooted a long, eerie call. *Hooo-hooo-hoo-hoo!*

"Whoa," Finn said.

I put my finger to my lips. "Shh."

The owl hooted a second time, much closer, and then a third time, so loud it seemed like the bird was about to shatter the window and fly into the room. A shadow crept into the mirror, a vague shape trying to take form. I was afraid to look at it directly, afraid that if I did, it would vanish. I wasn't cold, but I shivered again, my feathers shaking.

Finn broke the spell. "This is creepy."

My eyes snapped back into focus. "You ruined it. Someone was trying to get into the mirror."

The owl hooted again, much fainter, like she was flying away.

"Sorry," he said after a moment.

I didn't answer.

"Think it was Rebecca?" he asked. "Your mom?"

I stared at him through the waving, watery candlelight. "How do you know her name?"

He pointed at Gracie.

"Did she tell you anything else?"

"No." He unfolded his legs and lay on his side, his head propped up on his hand. "Just that she died when you were little."

I waited, hoping the owl would come back.

"Tell me something about her," he said.

"Like what?"

"I don't know. Something fun. Something you never told anyone else."

I pulled a long feather out of my shawl, slowly thinking over the tiny handful of things I knew about my mother.

"True story about Rebecca," I said. "She jumped out of an airplane when she was pregnant with me. She didn't know she was pregnant, of course. Teaching people how to parachute was her job. She had to give it up when she realized I was on board, too."

I dipped the tip of the feather in a pool of melted wax and dragged a shiny thread of it across the mirror. "I swear I can remember that jump. That's impossible, right? But I do: the falling, the rush of air, the jerk of the parachute, and then the sound of laughing, her laughing. I think she gave me the memory, like it was the first thing she wanted me to know."

Finn put his fingertip in the cooling wax and carefully lifted it, leaving a fingerprint behind. "So who is Trish?"

They were coming, on wings from far away, all the pictures and voices, smells, tastes, all the everything from the past was flying toward me as fast as it could.

I passed my hand through the flame.

"Don't do that," he said. "You'll get burned."

"So?"

Finn blew out the candle.

"I told you a secret," I said in the dark. "It's your turn."

"Only if you tell me about Trish."

"Only if your secret is true."

"True," he echoed, playing with his lighter. He rolled the striker wheel slowly, sparks leaping out like miniature fireworks, the flame never quite catching. "You already know I have a sister, Chelsea. The secret is that she's an addict. She'll smoke or snort anything she can get her hands on."

"Wow, really? I . . . I don't know what to say. Where is she?"

"Boston." He set the lighter on the mirror. "That's why Dad took that job and why Mom drove there this morning. Chelsea is claiming she's had another 'big breakthrough.' Woo-hoo."

"What does that mean?"

"It means she wants to screw my parents over again. They burned through their retirement money to pay for her first two rehabs. She ran away from both. The third time, they took out a second mortgage to pay for a clinic in Hawaii. She didn't run away from that one. She came home with a great tan and stayed clean for eight whole days."

His voice sounded older in the dark.

"Now she says she wants to ask forgiveness so we can all start the, quote, unquote, healing process. Such bullshit. She'll guilt Mom into giving her money and then she'll take off again."

The lighter flared, breaking his face into waves of light and shadow.

"True enough?" he asked.

"Yeah," I said quietly. "I'm sorry."

He lit the candle. "Your turn, Miss Blue. What's so awful about this Trish beast? Why did you freak out?"

She put me on the bus, lunch box packed with a peanut butter and banana sandwich, crusts cut off. She coached my soccer team. She fired the babysitter who spanked me. Took me to work with her for a week until she found a new sitter. She drank wine, not vodka. Sometimes forgot to eat. She only smoked cigarettes when I was asleep. She forgot to answer the phone when I called for a ride home. She forgot to lock the door when she left.

"She used to be my mom," I said. "And then she quit."

—*— 61 —*—

So I told him . . . most of it.

Rebecca, my biological mother, was T-boned by a drunk driver when I was a baby. Dad was fighting insurgents in the mountains, but the army gave him a couple of weeks to come home and sort things out. Battle zones don't have day care, so he took me to his mother's. Gramma raised me until she died, just before I turned seven. That was when Trish took over. She was Daddy's base bunny, his stateside girlfriend who said she loved babysitting.

(I skipped the part where I really loved her and I used to call her Mommy because it sounded so dumb and pathetic.)

"What about your mom's relatives?" he asked.

"I don't remember meeting them. At some point they died. My grandma was all the family I needed."

I glanced in the mirror. No one was waiting there.

"What happened to your dad?"

The kindness in his voice almost sent me over the edge.

I took a moment to clear my throat, then gave the short, clean version: two tours in Iraq, two tours in Afghanistan. How he earned the Purple Heart. Talked about the number of stitches in his leg, visiting him in the hospital, watching him in physical therapy. The drinking, the fighting, and how happy I was when they sent him back overseas again and how bad I felt about being happy. The IED that blew up his truck and his brain and his career. More months in the hospital, then the big welcome home, dog tags turned in, army days over. (That was before we knew about the fraying wires in his skull. Before we knew that he could turn into a werewolf even if the moon wasn't full.)

Trish drinking wine at breakfast. Trish walking out.

"Did he get a new girlfriend after she left?"

I shook my head. "That's when he became a truck driver. He couldn't figure out anything else to do with me, so I rode with him."

"What about school?"

"He homeschooled me. Unschooled me. It was kind of awesome for a while: him driving, me reading out loud, the two of us talking about everything, fractions and evolution, Abraham Lincoln's cabinet and which Hemingway book is the best. Every once in a while, he'd get a bug up his butt that we needed to settle down in a little town somewhere, but a few weeks or months later, he'd get a different bug and, *boom*, we took off again."

Finn crawled around the mirror and sat next me. "How'd you wind up here?"

I took a deep breath. "He got arrested in Arkansas last year. Public drunkenness."

Finn leaned against me, warm and solid.

"He was only in the jail overnight, but he came out completely set on moving back here. Said I needed to go to a regular school to get ready for college."

"Makes sense."

"I thought the move would be good for him, that he'd hook up with old friends and get a decent job. Instead it's like a bomb has started ticking in his head."

"What about Trish?" he asked quietly.

"She'll make it blow up early."

My stomach hurt from going too far, telling too many secrets. I should have kept the past locked away so it couldn't screw up the way I was trying to get by one day at a time. That was Dad's problem, right? His worst yesterdays played on a constant loop in his head and he couldn't (or he wouldn't) stop paying attention to them. At least on the road, there had been times when we'd outrun the memories. Now they had us surrounded and were closing in.

"I don't want to talk about this anymore." I leaned forward and blew out the candle. "Can we go to bed?"

We walked up the stairs, Finn a step in front of me, reaching back to hold my hand. He turned on the desk lamp in his room. The walls were covered with posters of indie bands I never heard of, Russian travel posters, and mostly naked women posed on gleaming motorcycles. A floor-to-ceiling bookcase overflowed with paperbacks, and gaming controllers crowded around the computer monitor and keyboard on his desk. It smelled like body spray and Fritos.

"I wasn't sure," he said. "If, you know, you were going to come up here. But I cleaned, just in case."

"Just in case?"

"Yeah." He closed the door and hit the space bar on his computer. The screen lit up with an image of a fire burning in a fireplace and jazz poured out of the speakers. He shut off the desk lamp, wrapped his arms around me, and kissed me. He tasted of maple syrup and butter and pancakes and bacon.

Now. I will stay in right now, this minute. Build a fortress with Finn and keep yesterday locked out.

And . . . somehow we found ourselves on his bed. And our clothes started falling off because everything felt good, felt right. The world on the other side of his door didn't exist. His mouth, his hands, the muscles of his shoulders, the curve of his back; that was all that mattered. Tomorrow . . .

Shit.

I sat up.

"What?" He sat up, too, breathing hard. "Did I do something wrong?"

"I thought of a bad word."

"A dirty word? I know all of them. Do you have a favorite?"

"Tomorrow."

"Tomorrow isn't a dirty word." He brushed his hair out of his eyes. "Is it?"

"I said it was bad, not dirty." I shivered and pulled the covers up to my chin. "Tomorrow as in reality, as in we can't go as far as we want. Reality sucks."

"Don't think about tomorrow." He ran his fingers down my arm, making me shiver again. "It's not sexy."

"You know what's not sexy?" I pushed his hand away. "Babies. Babies are not sexy."

"But I bought condoms," he said. "I even practiced putting one on!"

The lost-puppy look on his face made me smile. "I'm proud of you, Boner Man, but that's not enough. I have the worst luck in the whole world. If anyone on the planet was going to get pregnant tonight, it would be me. The last thing I need to think about is a baby."

He groaned and rolled on to his back. "Stop saying that word!"

"Baby, baby, baby." I picked my shirt off the floor and put it on. "I can't. I just can't."

"Why are you getting dressed?"

"You have to take me home."

He dug around in the covers for his shirt and pulled it on. "Do you want to go home?"

"No. But if I stay, you'll be too tempting and we'll be stupid and my life will be over."

"I'm not going to ruin your life and we're not going to be stupid." He opened his closet door and reached for something on the top shelf. "You mind a sleeping bag?"

"Why?"

He tossed a tightly rolled sleeping bag at me. "Postmodern bundling," he said. "You stay in yours, I stay in mine."

"Sleeping bags can be unzipped," I said.

"I don't break promises," he pulled down a second bag, "and I'm pretty sure you don't, either."

It took a little while to rearrange the pillows and figure out how to keep the sleeping bags from sliding off the bed, but finally we crawled in and set our phones to wake us up just before dawn. We fell asleep instantly, without even kissing each other good night, like we'd been enchanted.

When our alarms went off, we staggered downstairs and woke up Topher and Gracie. Finn dropped me off at the bottom of my driveway and watched as I keyed Trish's car on my way to the front door. I snuck in the house without waking up the dog, crawled under my covers with my clothes on, and fell back asleep just as I was getting ready to cry.

—*— 62 —*—

When I finally rolled out of bed that afternoon, they were watching football in the living room. Trish was curled up in the recliner, rocking slightly back and forth, a thick book in her lap and hideous reading glasses pinching the end of her nose. Dad sipped a beer on the couch. A half-eaten sub rested on the table in front of him, and the dog was sprawled at his feet. An ugly, wooden cuckoo clock hung on the wall above his head, ticking loudly.

"Look who's up," Dad said.

I pointed to the clock above the couch. "Where did that come from?"

"Trish found it in the basement," he said.

She looked at me over the top of her reading glasses. "You look tired, Lee-Lee. Did you get enough sleep?"

Without any warning or asking for permission, my

eyes teared up again. I should have ignored Finn. Should've walked to the bus station and gotten on the first bus without looking back. Spock rolled over and whined for a belly rub. When Trish looked at him, I wiped my face on my sleeve. Not that I was going to tell her, but she was right. I needed more sleep to deal with all of this, to deal with the bite of the blade, the ripping sound, and the flood . . .

> . . . *she handed me the pen and I signed my first library card and they let me take out eight books that I could read as many times as I wanted* . . .
> . . . *the snip of scissors and the smell of the glue, chaining one loop of paper to the next, red, green, red, green to hang on the tree* . . .
> . . . *rows of M&M's laid on the scratched kitchen table, her trying to teach me that multiplication and division could be fun* . . .

Trish looked up at me. The light from the window was behind her and made it impossible to read the expression on her face. Focusing on the shadows made it easier . . .

> . . . *she threw an ashtray at him and he ducked and it exploded into an ice storm of glass* . . .
> . . . *finding her passed out on the couch with a stranger, both of them missing clothes* . . .

. . . the sound of the door slamming the last time she left . . .

to lock down the memories that kept trying to seep out.

Trish held up her book so that I could see the cover. "The new Elizabeth George. Do you like mysteries?"

Spock whined again and thumped his tail. He could smell the bullshit, too. Trish was already acting like she lived here. If I ran away, she'd make him fall in love with her again and God knows how that would end this time. But if I stayed and she stayed, I'd have to kill her, and murder was still illegal.

Dad and Trish exchanged one of those grown-up looks that meant whatever happened next, I wasn't going to like it.

He turned off the game and cleared his throat. "We need to talk."

"I don't think so," I said, heading for the door. "I'm going to mow the lawn."

"Not yet," Dad said.

"Please," Trish added.

I stopped. Crossed my arms over my chest.

"Don't look at me like that." Dad scratched his head. "Should have told you she was coming, I know. I tried to the other day when we were shooting hoops, but I got distracted."

Trish rocked faster. The recliner started to squeak.

"And I'm sorry I lost my temper last night," he continued.

"Well," I said, "as long as you're sorry, I guess that makes everything better, doesn't it?"

"I screwed up, okay?" Dad cracked his knuckles. "You weren't exactly on your best behavior. Anyway. Trish needs to stay here."

Trish jumped in. "Only for a week or so."

"No sense in her wasting money on a hotel room," Dad said.

"What about the pig barn down the road?" I asked.

The squeaking recliner sounded like a mouse caught in a trap. They exchanged another annoying glance and my last nerve snapped.

"Don't look at her like that!" I yelled.

"Hayley, please," Trish said.

I whirled around. "Shut up!"

"Hayley!" Dad said.

Trish shook her head. "Give her some space, Andy."

"Give me space?" I echoed. "Did you learn that from a fortune cookie?"

"You can't have it both ways," she said.

"What does that mean?"

"You tell me to shut up and then you ask me a question. You can't have it both ways. You have to choose." She pushed the reading glasses into her hair. "I'm a nurse now, Hayley. Got my degree. I'm up here for some interviews.

Andy offered me a place to stay, as an old friend, nothing more."

"Just as a friend," Dad repeated. "She's staying in Gramma's room."

I hoped Gramma's ghost heard that. I hoped she was gathering her dead lady friends together to haunt and terrorize Trish. Maybe she could get Rebecca to help, along with the Stockwell family and everyone else from the graveyard, hundreds of dead people to crowd into the bedroom, Gramma tapping Trish's shoulder and politely suggesting that she get the hell out and leave us alone.

Spock jumped up and shook himself, raising a cloud of fur and dander that hung in the sunlight.

"All right, then." Dad slapped his knees and stood up, as if everything was decided and I wasn't on the verge of running in the garage to get the splitting maul.

"Where are you going?" Trish asked him.

"The choke on the lawn mower sticks," he said. "I'm going to start it for her."

"Don't bother," I said. "I'm going to Gracie's."

"Tell me this is a nightmare." I sat heavily on the swing, making the chains jingle. "Maybe that bacon we ate last night was spoiled. Maybe food poisoning is screwing up my brain."

Grace moaned. "Please don't talk about food."

"It's like Halloween got stuck or something," I said. "I wake up and there's a witch in the living room and my dad is wearing a mask that almost looks like him, but not totally. Everything is weird."

"I don't know why you're so surprised." Gracie carefully sat at the bottom of the slide. Her little brother was playing with his friends over on the new climbing equipment. We'd headed for the old stuff to get away from the noise they were making. "Trish and your dad were together for a long time, right?"

I spun the swing in a circle, twisting the chains around each other. "That's not the point."

Gracie's little brother, still wearing his Iron Man costume, came running over. "Kegan's mom brought oranges. She said I can have one if you say yes."

"Yes," Gracie said. "But eat them over there, okay?"

"Can I have a bologna sandwich, too?" he asked loudly.

"Shh!" Gracie hissed. "My head hurts, remember?"

Garrett leaned close to her face and whispered loudly, "Can I have a bologna sandwich, too? Kegan's mommy makes them with mayonnaise and ketchup."

Gracie blew out a slow breath. "Eat what you want, buddy. Just don't tell me about it."

I waited until he was out of earshot. "You should puke and get it over with."

"I hate puking." She licked her lips. "What's the point about Trish?"

I spun in one more circle. "The point is that she's a terrible person."

"Fix her up with my dad," Gracie said as she leaned back on the slide. "That would solve both of our family's problems." She groaned. "Can a person die of a hangover?"

"If that was true, Trish would be dead by now." I unspun quickly, the ground whirling beneath my feet. "Dad, too, I guess."

"I can't believe I did this to myself," Gracie said.

"The worst part is that she's in our house." I dug my toes into the dirt and spun in the other direction. "Why can't he see what she's trying to do?"

"Stop stressing. You can't change anything." Gracie winced as the little girls chasing each other around the sandbox shrieked. "Parents get to do whatever they want. Will you stop talking and let me die now?"

"I didn't realize what a whiner you are. Be grateful you didn't get arrested."

"I wasn't going to drink anything." She covered her eyes with her hands. "What was I thinking?"

"You weren't thinking, dumbass, you were drinking. They're opposites. Now focus: How do I get rid of her?"

"You don't." Gracie sat up, grimacing. "The world is crazy. You need a license to drive a car and go fishing. You don't need a license to start a family. Two people have sex and *bam!* Perfectly innocent kid is born whose life will be screwed up by her parents forever." She stood up carefully. "And you can't do a damn thing about it."

"You're wrong."

"Then you're the dumbass." She sat on the swing next to me. "Maybe this is a sign."

"Of what?"

"A sign that you need to look ahead. At college and stuff. You gonna apply to Swevenbury?"

"Funny," I said.

"Too close? What about California, lots of schools there. Get as far away as you can."

"What about our commune?" I spun in another circle, bringing the twisted chains so far down that I had to lean forward so my hair wouldn't get caught in it.

"What are you talking about?" she asked.

"Last night you said the four of us—you, me, Topher, and Finn—should raise goats on our commune."

"Liar," she said. "I don't even like goats."

"Sissie!" Garrett ran over to the swing set and shoved half of his bologna and mayonnaise and ketchup sandwich in Gracie's face. "Want some?

"Oh, God," Gracie said, lurching for the trash can.

"Give it to me, buddy," I said. "Sissie doesn't feel so good."

—*— 64 —*—

Finn was less Finn-like in the days after Halloween, distracted and quiet. His junkie sister was playing head games with his parents, but he didn't want to talk about it. His phone was usually turned off (or maybe he was screening my calls), but he showed up faithfully to drive me to school every morning and home in the afternoon. We didn't joke as much in the library or in the halls. Sometimes we barely talked, but his arm was always around my shoulders and my hand liked to slip into the back pocket of his jeans.

(Honestly? I was relieved. The secrets we'd shared at his house belonged in the dark. Seeing him in the light of day or the light of the cafeteria made me feel like my skin had become transparent and the whole school could see inside me.)

Wednesday morning, he picked me up late, yawning and bleary-eyed. He said he hadn't gotten any sleep, but when I asked why, he shrugged and turned on the radio. I leaned against the seat belt strap and tried to doze.

Having Trish around was making Dad worse. He'd woken up screaming around two thirty that morning. It was the third time in four nights that he'd woken up like that, hollering that the truck was on fire or trying to call in air support to take out a hornet's nest of insurgents. After he settled down, he and Trish had spent the rest of the night talking in the living room. I tried to hear what they were saying, but the ticking of that damn clock made it impossible.

I must have fallen asleep because the next thing I knew we were at school.

Topher took one look at the two of us, bleary-eyed and yawning, and bought us both huge cups of coffee to go with our deliciously greasy breakfast burritos. He waggled his eyebrows. "What were you guys doing last night?"

"Nothing fun," I said.

"We had a family Skype meeting." Finn blew on the coffee. "Chelsea and Dad in Boston, me and Mom here."

"Really?" It was the first I'd heard of it. "Sounds nice."

Finn shook his head. "It wasn't. Chelsea wants to go to rehab, but there isn't any money. Mom is thinking about selling her jewelry and her car."

"Dude," Topher said.

Gracie scratched at a piece of gum that had hardened on the table. She was short on sleep, too, from eavesdropping on her parents' custody arguments. Her father was demanding Sundays through Wednesdays. Her mother was demanding that he not be allowed to introduce his girlfriend to Gracie and Garrett.

"What happens then?" I sipped the coffee and burned my mouth. "Will she take your car?"

"She said she'll take the bus to work."

"What about grocery shopping and stuff?"

"My car," Finn admitted.

Grace looked up. "Did you trying saying no to her?"

"What about the insurance bullshit?" Topher asked. "What did she decide about that?"

"Something's wrong with your insurance?" I asked, confused why Topher knew more than I did.

"Last week she said I have to pay for it. Gas, too. Yesterday, Coach hired me to lifeguard during swim practice. I start this afternoon."

"When were you going to tell me?"

"Sorry." He looked into the coffee cup. "I forgot."

"Sounds stupid if you ask me." Gracie stole a sip of my coffee. "Your mom's enabling your sister and screwing you over."

Finn shrugged and bit into his burrito.

"Not to mention the obvious holes in her plan," Gracie continued. "What if she gets fired? What if her boss doesn't want employees who ride the bus, 'cause they're always late?"

"I don't want to talk about it anymore," Finn said.

"You should," Gracie said. "You're enabling your mom the way that she enables your sister."

"Your family calls it enabling, we call it taking care of each other." Finn looked at Topher. "Changing the subject now. Did you hear about the shooting at the middle school in Nebraska?"

"The news is too depressing," Topher said. "You should watch more cartoons."

"Why do we have to change the subject?" Gracie asked. "We all have crazy parents, except for Topher."

"They are pathetically well-adjusted." Topher shook his head. "It's so embarrassing."

"Shut up, goof." Gracie punched his shoulder lightly. "Shouldn't we talk about this stuff and help each other?"

"She has a point, Finn-head," I said.

"No, she doesn't." Finn turned to face me. "She's being nosy and pushy. So are you. I seriously do not want to talk about this anymore."

"Nosy?" I asked.

"So!" Topher said loudly. "Sports! Who wants to talk about sports?"

I should have stopped there, but I couldn't. I was tired, frustrated, possibly a tiny bit in love and horrified by the thought. Plus, I was tired. (Did I mention that already?) My irritation was growing fast, the way a cartoon snowball gets bigger and bigger as it rolls down a mountain.

"The first thing you did when we sat down was to tell us about your family's Skype visit, Chelsea wanting rehab, your mom selling her car and jewelry," I said. "You told us that without anyone sticking their nose in your business."

He didn't say anything.

"And then you casually mention that you got a job that starts today, not that my life could possibly be impacted by that at all."

"I already apologized for that."

The snowball was the size of a dump truck.

"Apologies mean nothing if you don't mean it."

"So what am I supposed to do?" he asked.

"Not yelling at her would be a good start," Gracie said.

Finn pointed at her. "Nosy and pushy, see?"

"Don't yell at her when you're pissed at me," I said.

"I'm not pissed at you, but you're picking a fight."

Conversations at the tables around us were dying down. Zombie heads turned, smelling blood. My irritation had snowballed big enough to crush an entire village.

"I'm not picking a fight!" My fist pounded.

"Stop yelling," Finn said.

"Okay, kids," Topher said. "Time out."

"Stop lying and I will!"

"I didn't lie," Finn said.

"You didn't tell me about the insurance or the job, or the latest Chelsea disaster."

"You don't exactly give me minute-by-minute updates about your dad, but I don't make a big deal about it."

"Don't talk about him," I said. "Not here."

He acted like he didn't hear me. "I figure when you're ready, you'll tell me what's going on. Why can't you do the same thing for me? My family's not half as crazy as yours. It's not like you have to worry about my mom swinging an ax around or getting wasted and doing something stupid, right?"

"Stop it!" I stood up and pushed the table, sending the coffee cups flying and everyone scrambling to rescue their burritos and books.

"That's enough!" called a cafeteria aide, pushing his way through the crowd to our table. "You boys need to move."

"Whatever," Finn muttered as he walked away.

The aide handed me a roll of brown paper towels, the kind that don't absorb anything. "You caused the mess," he said. "You clean it up."

"Whoa," Gracie said after the zombies in the cafeteria stopped staring. "You guys just had a fight."

I ripped a useless handful of towel from the roll. "Shut up, G."

—*— 6**5** —*—

When the announcement came, Ms. Rogak was reading the scene where Athena tells the Dawn to show up late so Odysseus can enjoy a long night with his wife.

"This is a lockdown," said the principal's voice. "Anyone in the hall must find a room now. Staff please follow all lockdown drill procedures."

Ms. Rogak rolled her eyes, closed her book, then locked the door and pulled down the blind to cover the window. By the time she got back to her desk, we all had our phones out, trying to connect with the outside world, just to make sure. I texted Finn first, Gracie second.

There was a 99.99 percent chance this was another drill, but we'd all seen security camera footage of armed lunatics and small bloody bodies on stretchers being raced across playgrounds. Memorials of soggy teddy bears and dead flowers. Sobbing friends. Catatonic parents. Graves. Even with a 99.99 percent chance, it felt like I'd just stuck a fork into an electric socket and someone had turned the power on.

"It's a prank," said Brandon Something. "Someone called in a threat to get out of a test."

Threat

"Wish they'd done it earlier," a guy on the far side of the room said. "They would have canceled school and I'd still be in bed."

"Quiet," Ms. Rogak said.

Gracie texted me back; she knew nothing. Finn didn't answer.

I thought I heard a siren. My heart thumped hard. Was it headed for the school? I couldn't tell.

Assess

The door was the only entrance. In theory, we could escape out the windows, except that we'd need a crowbar to break the thick glass, and we'd have to survive a three-story fall. I texted Finn again:

> *what's going on?*
> *???*

Still no answer. The siren had stopped.

"What if it's real?" a girl asked.

"Don't get worked up, it's just a drill," said Ms. Rogak.

Jonas Delaney, sitting in front of me, gnawed on his thumbnail like he hadn't eaten in days.

BANG!

The sharp noise in the hall made everyone hit the floor. I curled into a ball next to Jonas.

"It's okay," said Ms. Rogak, "it's okay, um, but let's stay on the ground for a minute. Okay? Stay quiet."

My adrenaline screamed, rocketing me into hyper-awareness, senses cranked to the max. Time fattened and slowed down so much that each second lasted for an hour. I could smell Jonas's sweat, the mold growing in the old books on the shelves, the dry-erase markers at the board. I could feel the hum of the building under me, the air moving through the heating ducts, the electric current that tied the rooms together, the Wi-Fi signal pulsing in the air.

Jonas rocked back and forth, his lips pressed together, his eyes squeezed shut. I replayed that noise over and over. The more I thought about it, the less it sounded like a gunshot.

BANG!

The second noise made Jonas shake, but I was convinced.

"Don't worry," I whispered to him. "It's not a gun. That's some idiot kicking a locker, trying to freak us out."

"Shhh," he warned.

Static burst from the loudspeaker. "All clear," the principal's voice announced. "That was much better than last month. Thank you."

Ms. Rogak stormed to the door muttering about suspending the chucklehead in the hall. The room held silent for a second after she left, then exploded into nervous laughter and loud conversation. A girl showed her shaking hands to her friends. Brandon Something joked about who had been afraid and who had been cool. I crawled back into my chair, pulled up my hood, and tried very hard not to puke.

Jonas stayed on the floor.

"Dude!" Brandon shouted at him. "Get up." He walked over and nudged Jonas with his foot.

Jonas rolled and leaned against the front of Ms. Rogak's desk, his knees tucked tightly under his chin and his head down. I smelled it then. Unfortunately, so did Brandon.

"He pissed himself!" Brandon's face lit up with horror and delight. "He literally pissed himself!"

Jonas wrapped his arms over his head as Brandon and his trolls laughed. A couple of girls said, "Eww!" The rest of the class looked away. Jonas was a quiet freak, not a zombie. The horde would not protect him. They'd stand by and watch the culling.

"Get up." Brandon pulled on Jonas's arm.

Before I knew what I was doing, I was out of my seat. "Leave him alone."

"Shut up." He grabbed Jonas by the shirt and hauled him to his feet so everyone could see the soaked crotch of his jeans. "The Urinator, ladies and gentlemen!"

Jonas thrashed, trying to break free.

"Really," I said. "Let him go."

Brandon sneered. As he shoved me backward, I grabbed ahold of his wrist and pulled him off balance. This allowed

Jonas to break free. He sprinted for the open door and disappeared down the hall.

Then Brandon came for me.

Action

Hours later, after letting the nurse check me out and meeting with Ms. Benedetti and the vice principal and talking to
Dad and turning down the chance to go home early, Finn
found me at my locker.

"I just heard what happened," he said, panting. "Are you
okay? Oh my God, did he do this?" His fingertips hovered
above the swollen bruise on my cheek.

I pulled away from him. "It's nothing."

"Nothing? Some douche bag tried to beat you up."

"He pushed me, I pushed him, we both fell down. Rogak
walked in before it got serious."

"I heard you kicked his ass."

"It lasted two seconds."

"I heard he's suspended."

"I guess." I closed my locker. "I feel bad for Jonas."

"Yeah," Finn said. "He's a good guy."

We stood there, my backpack on the ground between
us, staring over each other's shoulders. The loudspeaker
announced that boys soccer practice had been canceled
and requested that the owner of a white Camry move
their car from the fire lane or it would be towed.

"You didn't get in trouble at all?" he asked.

"I didn't start it."

"Doesn't mean they'd pay attention to that."

"True enough, but they did, this time."

He picked up my backpack, but I pulled it out of his hands. "I got it," I said.

"You're mad at me."

I shrugged, too tired to think about anything.

"I had my phone turned off," he said. "I didn't see your text."

"I don't want to miss the bus."

"You could stay," he said. "Hang by the pool or in the library, then I could drive you home when practice is over."

Down the hall a locker slammed. The noise made me flinch.

"You're not okay." Finn took hold of the bottom edge of my hoodie. "Can we forget about that stupid argument this morning?"

"Seems like it happened years ago."

"The warped perception of time is a hallmark of trauma," he said. "I've counseled a lot of superheroes. They all struggle with it."

"Oh, really?" My hand dropped to touch his.

"Superheroes can be a pain in the balls," he said. "Always acting tough, pretending nothing hurts."

"What do you do with them?"

"Most of them go to a llama farm in New Mexico to

meditate and spin wool. I don't dare send you there." He tugged gently, pulling me closer. "You'd scare the llamas."

"You defame me, sir," I said. "I am a kind and gentle friend of llamas."

"You still mad at me?"

"A little." I laid my cheek against his. "Mostly, I'm confused."

—*— 66 —*—

While Trish washed the dishes after dinner, I sat on the couch and killed hordes of attacking zombies with a double-barreled shotgun. Dad sat next to me, passed out. I could barely hear the sweet, wet sound of exploding heads between his snoring, the irritating *tick-tock* of the cuckoo clock, and Trish whistling in the kitchen like a demented mockingbird. She'd gotten a temp job on the pediatric floor, but wasn't showing any signs of looking for an apartment. As far as I could tell, she really was sleeping in Gramma's bedroom. (Thank all the gods.)

I turned up the volume on the television, chambered another round, and pulled the trigger, taking out three zombies with one blast.

Along with tacky clothes and cheap makeup, Trish had smuggled shards of my past in her suitcase: the way hair ribbons felt on my shoulders, the name of the girl next door at Fort Hood, the taste of pimento-cheese sandwiches, the sound of tennis balls being served into the net, and Trish telling me to toss her another one. I'd hear her voice as I was waking up and I'd open my eyes expecting to be in third grade. I'd catch the murmur of them talking when I was in the shower and it was the summer between fourth and fifth grades, only I didn't take showers then, I took baths. And then I'd have to find my science notebook or remember the word for "bathing suit" in Chinese and I'd be seventeen again and confused.

Every time I stepped out of the house, I looked up, expecting to see a bomb or a meteor hurtling toward us. It was just a matter of time.

More zombies clawed their way out of the ground while I was waiting for my health status to turn green. I paused the game and stared at the screen, trying to find an escape. My only choice was to fight my way out, even if I didn't think I would make it.

Trish walked into the living room, zipping up her jacket. "I'm going to the grocery store. Do you need anything?"

I put down the controller. "I'm coming with you."

Trish threw out a few questions in the car, pretending that she cared about my life: did my face still hurt, was Brandon Something a bully to everyone or just me, was I going to play any sports, did I have friends. She asked about Gracie, said we should invite her for dinner one night. She asked if I had signed up for my SATs, and if I wanted her to talk to Dad about anything for me.

Blah and blah and nosy none-of-your-business blah.

I didn't show her the shortcut that would have saved us ten minutes. I texted Finn and when he didn't answer, I pretended that he had.

At the store, I stayed a few steps behind her, waiting until she had a cart, then grabbing one for myself. In the fruit-and-vegetable section, she picked over the heads of lettuce until she found one that met her high standards of lettuceness. Then she went through the same routine choosing bananas, apples, broccoli, and cucumbers. I scanned the prices to figure out what cost the most, then piled boxes of raspberries, gourmet salad dressings, and a couple of bizarre-looking organic things grown in Central America in my cart.

In the meat department, she picked out hamburger and pork chops. I loaded up on steak and packages of buffalo sausages. I skipped the bakery and went to International Foods where I selected canned lemongrass shoots, curry-flavored almonds, and dried baby crabs, among other things.

An announcement about tasty ways to turn tuna into a terrific treat interrupted the Christmas music. Trish passed me without a word on her way to cereal and crackers.

I hit the jackpot in the fish department: lobster, shrimp, and a couple of small jars of caviar. I had about five hundred dollars' worth of food in my cart and there were still three aisles to go.

I turned into coffee/tea/creamers and ran right into Trish's cart.

"I'm not paying for any of that," she said, looking over my bounty.

"I know," I said, wanting to kick myself for having been so obvious.

She pushed past me. I followed so close behind that when she slowed down to take a box of chamomile tea off the shelf, my cart rammed into the back of her legs.

I braced myself for the explosion, but it didn't come. She tossed the tea in her cart, quickly maneuvered around a couple of old ladies and the guy restocking the condensed milk shelves, and took a right at the end of the aisle. The old ladies slowed me down, but I found her in frozen foods, comparing labels on two kinds of burrito.

She put both burritos in her cart and closed the freezer door. "How long do you plan on acting like you're five years old?"

Here we go.

"Until you leave," I said. "He's broke, you know. The house is falling apart and he can't keep a job. He gets high now, too. There is no money for you to steal."

"Roy told me to come," she said. "That's the only reason I'm here. He's worried about you both."

"You suck at lying," I said. "You talked to my guidance counselor long before Roy showed up. He didn't tell you anything."

"Why do you think Roy visited you guys in the first place?" she asked.

A man driving an electric cart squeezed between us.

"What do you mean?" I asked.

"Andy started emailing me six months ago, right after you two moved here," Trish said. "At first, it was friendly, which was more than I deserved. Around August, he started to sound desperate. Wrote some weird stuff. I forwarded the email to Roy and it bothered him, too. He was already planning the hunting trip, so he tacked on a day to stop at your house. When he told me what he saw, I quit my job."

"Sure you did."

She gave an exasperated sigh. "I haven't had a drink in twenty-seven months, Lee-Lee. Twenty-seven months, three weeks, and two days."

"Don't call me that."

"I don't blame you for being mad at me," she went on. "What I did was inexcusable. I am so, so sorry that I left you. It was the worst thing I ever did to another person, worse than what I did to Andy, because you were just a kid.

We can't go back and fix that. I came up here to see if I could help because I still love you. Both of you."

"You're so full of shit."

"I don't think you realize how serious this is," she said.

"You show up for a couple of days and suddenly you know everything?"

"Can you stop being childish for one minute?"

I gripped the handle of my cart.

"He's scaring me," she continued. "Not like he used to. I'm not afraid he's going to hurt me. I'm afraid he's going to hurt himself and I think you are, too."

"He was doing fine until you showed up," I said.

"We both know that's a lie," she said. "When you're ready to start dealing with the truth, you let me know."

The desire to ram my cart into her gut and push her through the glass door into the freezer made my hands sweat. But if I did, she might see it as a "cry for help" and then she'd never leave us alone.

"The truth is, I hate you," I said.

The first snowstorm of the year (eight inches) that hit late on Thursday night should have canceled school, but all we got was an hour delay because the superintendent didn't care if we died fiery deaths in chain-reaction pileups. Finn's tires sucked but since his mom was home sick, he drove us to school in her ten-year-old Nissan. If she sold it, she'd be lucky to get enough to pay for half a day of rehab. The smell of her hair spray made me wonder if I was ever going to meet her. I shoved that question to the back of my mind and buried it under the mountains of junk stored there.

Topher and Gracie pulled in next to us. We fell into the migratory flight path of students converging from all corners of the parking into a reluctant line that led inside the building.

"Why are they wearing shorts?" I asked, pointing to a group of guys walking ahead of us. "It's barely twenty degrees out."

"Baseball," Topher said cryptically.

"The team wears shorts all winter," Gracie explained. "It's like a badge of honor, proves they're tough."

"Look at the leg hair!" I said. "Are they all related to bears?"

A snowball skirmish opened up by the flagpole. We ducked and ran for the door.

"If they were really tough," I continued, "they'd shave their legs every day and *then* wear shorts."

"Exactly!" Gracie said.

"If they did, maybe girls like that," I pointed to the girl in front of us, who was wearing fake Uggs, a pink miniskirt, and a tight black sweater, "could grow out their leg hair to stay warm, and another gender inequity would be balanced, right?"

"Hmmm," Finn answered, mesmerized by the twitching miniskirt.

Fake-Uggs Naked-Legs Girl slowed down and looked back at Finn over her shoulder like she had testosterone radar.

"Did you hear me?" I asked him.

"His other head is doing the thinking right now," Topher said.

"That's gross," Gracie said.

Fake-Uggs Naked-Legs Girl winked at Finn. Before I could growl or rip her face off, she disappeared inside the building.

"She'll get frostbite, you know," I told him as we walked through the doors. "Frostbite so bad they'll have to amputate her legs and big hunks of her butt. Then she'll die of despair, all because she forgot to wear pants on a day when it was fifteen degrees outside."

"Guess that means you're stuck with me," he said, stopping in the middle of the crowd. "Cleveland asked me to stop by his room before first period."

Before I could answer, Ms. Benedetti appeared out of nowhere and wrapped her cold fingers around my arm.

"I need you in my office, right now," she said.

Finn gave me a quick salute and melted away in the crowd.

"What if I say no?" I asked Benedetti.

"I'll follow you," she said with an unnerving smile. "I have all day."

We both pushed against the wall as a group of impossibly pretty girls strode past, bare-legged and acting like it was eighty degrees outside.

Benedetti tapped my shoulder. "My office."

"I'm claustrophobic," I said. "It's too small in there."

The bell rang.

"Follow me," she said.

The auditorium was cool and damp as a cave. Dark, too, with just a few of the wall lights turned on. I followed Benedetti down the aisle and across a row to the dead center of the room.

"Is Finn in trouble because the newspaper isn't done yet?"

"We need to talk about you," she said as she sat. "Will this work? I imagine it's hard to feel claustrophobic here."

"You're real funny." I left an empty seat between us. "Am I suspended after all? Is that what this is about?"

She shook her head. "No, but that little altercation gave me another chance to talk to your dad. Did he tell you? I bugged him again about joining us for the Veterans Day assembly."

I tried to think of something witty, but it was too early in the morning and I was freezing. "Not a word."

"I also told him that you didn't take the SAT."

I shrugged. "What did he say?"

"That he'd discuss it with you."

"His schedule is kind of booked right now."

"Why haven't you asked any of your teachers for recommendation letters?"

"Don't want to watch them laugh at me."

"Some of your classmates applied early decision. They've already been accepted."

"You told me the deadline wasn't until Christmas."

"Doesn't mean you can't apply now. The sooner you apply and get accepted, the better your chances at getting financial aid. Now look." She leaned over the empty seat, crowding my air space. "It's been a huge transition for you, coming here, but it's time to suck it up."

"Do you yell at all the new kids like this?"

"You haven't turned in homework for almost two weeks. Before that, your effort was sporadic at best."

"I do the interesting assignments. It's not my fault that most of them are boring."

"Colleges will scrutinize your grades this year, especially because you're not a traditional student. You have to step up to the plate, get in the game."

"Baseball metaphors don't work with me."

"Damn it, Hayley!" She pounded the armrest. "Quit screwing around. This is your future."

"The present can't be the future, Ms. Benedetti. It can only be the present."

"What are you so afraid of?" she asked.

"Do you get a bonus for every college application we file? Is there a quota you have to meet?"

Benedetti paused, licked her lips, then continued like I hadn't said a word. "I'd like to see a list of the colleges that you're interested in by Monday."

"What if I don't want to go to college? What if I don't know what I want to do? I don't even know how to think about it."

The doors opened and students streamed in, led by an English teacher.

"Hope this is okay," he called to us. "I want to show them how much better Shakespeare is onstage."

"Good idea," Benedetti said.

"So we're done?" I asked, standing.

"One more thing." She glanced at the class making their

slow way to the stage. "The school board had an emergency session last night. They cut a number of extracurriculars."

"So?"

"They canceled Model United Nations, Latin Club, the Brass Ensemble, and the newspaper. Their revenue projections for this year were way off. That's why Bill Cleveland wanted to talk to Finn, to break the news to him."

I shouldered my backpack. "If they really want to save money, they should just shut the whole school down."

—*— 68 —*—

And suddenly, it was the tenth of November.

The day before Veterans Day was traditionally the day when the crazy trapped inside my dad chewed its way out of the cage. This time a year earlier, we'd been in a small town outside Billings, Montana. Driving under bridges had started to become a problem so we stayed there a while. Dad got a job working the grill at a diner near the motel where we lived. I hung out in the library and sometimes fished in the small river that ran behind it.

That Sunday, his day off, I caught three tiny trout. I burst through the motel room door to show him. He was deep into a whiskey bottle, watching the 49ers play Seattle. He mocked me about the size of the fish, slurring his words. I turned to leave, but he told me I couldn't.

I didn't want to upset him. I stayed.

I didn't see the gun until the fourth quarter. (It was a pistol, a new one.)

In the last second of the game, the refs blew the call that would have given Seattle the winning touchdown. Dad exploded, throwing his glass across the room, leaping to his feet, and yelling at the screen. As the official review dragged on, he acted like they were doing it on purpose just to piss him off. He cursed, his face red and sweaty. He stomped his boots on the floor. I wanted to tell him it was only a game and we didn't like either team, anyway, but I didn't open my mouth because I didn't want him screaming at me. The station went to commercial. He paced—back and forth, back and forth—muttering things that didn't make any sense, almost like he didn't know where he was or what he was doing.

The commercials ended. The camera focused in tight on the ref. Dad sat at the end of the bed.

"The ruling on the field stands," announced the ref.

He never got a chance to declare the game over because Dad grabbed the pistol and shot the television in the guts. Then he picked it up and heaved it against the wall and sent a table lamp flying after it. I sat, paralyzed, while he raged, until finally he slid down the wall, crying, his right hand a bleeding mess.

I wrapped a towel around his hand and packed our stuff in the truck. By the time I was done he'd pulled himself together enough to drive, which was good because we needed to get out of there fast. After a while, he made me drive, telling me when to push on the clutch and shifting the gears with his left hand.

We found a town with an urgent care center that took his insurance. The doctor who stitched Dad up was a Seattle fan whose brother was shot in the Korengal Valley. He understood everything. He prescribed a new pill (the seventh new pill? the eighth?) that he promised would mummify Dad's memories and keep the crazy in its cage, even when Veterans Day approached or the moon was full.

Dad never filled the prescription.

That morning, I was tired and angry and late. The only cereal left in the cupboard had been purchased by Trish and was "healthy," which was another word for "tasteless." My clothes all looked like they'd been bought at Goodwill and my hair lay flat on my head like a dead jellyfish drying in the sun. Dad knocked on my door, said something about how he wasn't going to work. My head was in the closet, trying to find something to wear that didn't make me look like a refugee.

I wasn't thinking about the date.

A few minutes later, Dad knocked again and asked if he could come in and I grunted and he opened the door.

He said, "Breakfast," set a plate with toast on it on my desk, and left.

The crusts had been cut off the toast. He'd spread a little butter and a lot of honey.

"Thanks," I said. "What are you going to do today?"

But he was already gone.

Trish paused at my door like it was an ordinary morning, like she might remind me about a dentist appointment or tell me I had clean clothes in the dryer. The sight of her filling up my doorway, as if she belonged there, as if everything was fine, we were all just fine in the morning—it chased me out the door without a jacket, without my books, without a bite of toast.

Finn's car had no windshield wiper fluid and we were surrounded by trucks without mud flaps spraying road gunk on the windshield, plus his wipers were worthless. We had a stupid argument and I made him pull into the gas station and buy a gallon. When I realized he didn't know where to pour it, I yelled at him and did it myself. And then he yelled at me and said I should chill, but I knew he was upset about the stupid newspaper so I didn't let it bother me too much.

We were so late we missed first-period lunch. I went to the library, grabbed a book from the new fiction table, and read it during class for the rest of the day. If anyone said anything to me, I didn't hear it.

After the last bell rang, the final injustice was that I had to ride the bus home again because Finn had to lifeguard. It seemed to me that anyone who needed a lifeguard to make sure they didn't drown shouldn't be allowed on a swim team, but when I said that to Finn, he gave me the "whatever" look and stalked away.

The driveway was empty and the house was still when I got home. I couldn't remember the last time I'd slept more than a couple of hours at a time, and the sun had warmed the living room and the next thing I knew I'd been asleep for hours and the house was dark and I was hungry. I stumbled to the kitchen, opened a can of chicken noodle soup, and put it on the stove. Someone had taken the fossilized toast out of my room and put it on the kitchen table, right below the calendar that hung on the wall, still showing the month of September. I threw out the toast, untacked the calendar, and flipped it to November.

That's when it finally dawned on me that the shitty day I'd endured was the day before Veterans Day. I looked around and realized that I did not know where my father was. I turned off the stove.

I won't get upset, I thought. *That would be silly. Maybe he went to the grocery store for milk.* There was no reason to worry. Maybe the truck needed a new oil filter. Maybe he decided to drive into the Hudson River. Or he offered to take Trish to work and drove them both into the Hudson River. Maybe he went for a walk and flashbacked and he was lost somewhere walking point on a patrol through a valley of insurgents.

I shook the thought out of my head.

No, no, no. He went for milk.

Still, I checked. The guns were locked in the safe. Ammo locked in its own storage box.

I sat on the couch with Spock. One deep breath. Another. Shadows were trying to turn into monsters. One more breath. *We're fine. He's fine.* The furnace kicked on, blowing the smell of stale cigarette smoke out of the curtains and across the room. I'd give it an hour; one minute past and I'd call the police, though I wasn't sure what I'd say to them.

Fifty-five minutes later, the front door opened. Trish walked in first, her face pale and eyes red. Dad followed a few seconds later. He glanced at me, then turned his face away, but not fast enough. He walked down the hall to his bedroom without a word.

"What happened to your eye?" I called after him.

He slammed his door.

"What did you do to him?" I asked.

"He did it to himself." She sat in the recliner and hugged her knees to her chest. "It was supposed to be a date."

I fought the urge to throw her out the door. "Did you punch him in the face?"

"No, the bartender did."

"You took him to a bar, tonight of all nights?"

"Can I tell you what happened before you start with the accusations?"

I nodded once.

"We were supposed to meet at Chiarelli's at five," she said. "I was only half an hour late. He'd gotten there three hours early. By the time I walked in, he'd bonded with a couple of losers over the Giants' defense and bourbon. He didn't want to eat in the restaurant anymore. I ordered pizza, but he said he wasn't hungry."

My stomach started to hurt.

Trish sighed. "The bar got crowded. Andy's new friends left and he went quiet, not wanting to talk, but determined to stay there. It was the first time I'd been in a bar since I joined AA. I must have drunk a gallon of ginger ale." She tilted her head back and closed her eyes. "Anyway. I left to use the restroom. Everything was fine when I walked out."

"And when you got back?" I asked, dreading the answer.

"The bartender had him in a headlock on the floor. Andy thought some guy was staring at him, insulting him. They got into it and the bartender tried to break it up. Andy turned on the bartender, who was half his age and twice his size. By the time the police got there—"

"They called the cops?" I interrupted.

"This wasn't a biker bar at two in the morning, Hayley. This was a nice restaurant, filled with families who wanted dinner, not a show. Yes, they called the cops."

"Did they arrest him?"

She shook her head. "I smoothed it over, gave them the background. God, how many times have I done that before?"

I was thinking the same thing.

"I paid for his tab and our meals. They won't press charges as long as he stays away."

We sat without talking for a long time, the clock ticking against the wall.

"Has he ever hurt you?" Trish finally asked. "I know he'd never do it on purpose, but . . ."

"Of course not," I lied as the scene in front of the bonfire and the confrontation on Halloween night played out in my mind. "He wasn't this bad before you got here. I think you should leave, go back to Texas."

She stood up. "You could be right."

After a long shower, I got into bed and texted:

not going to school tomorw

Finn didn't answer.

69

A sharp knock woke me up.

"What's-his-name is going to be here soon," Dad said through the closed door.

"I'm not going," I said with a groan. "And his name is Finn. Why are you up so early?"

"Are you sick?" he asked.

This was the day he'd normally stay in bed past noon, resting up so he could drink himself blind by midnight. "Have you been up all night?" I asked.

"Are you sick?" he repeated. "Honest now."

"No, but the bus has already left," I said. "I told Finn not to pick me up."

"Trish can take you."

"I'd rather crawl over broken glass."

Silence.

"Can I borrow your truck?" I asked.

He sighed loudly.

"I'll come straight home after school, I promise."

"No," he said firmly. "I'll drive you. Be ready in ten."

Five minutes later, I was ready. Dad was still in the shower so I headed to the kitchen. Trish was pouring water into the coffeepot, wearing a robe and slippers.

"Coffee will only take a minute," she said.

I took an apple out of the fridge. "Thought you were leaving."

"Never did like mornings much, did you?"

I took the keys off the nail by the back door and went out through the garage. The truck started on the first try, and the cab was toasty warm by the time I'd finished my apple. Ten minutes had come and gone. I turned on the radio and watched the front door, fearing the steadily increasing chance that Trish was going to come through it and say that Dad had changed his mind. I put my foot on the brake and shifted into reverse. The second she showed her face, I'd take off.

The front door opened.

A soldier stepped into the cold sunshine, an army captain in full-dress uniform: polished black boots, regulation-creased pants, blindingly white shirt, and black tie under a blue wool jacket decorated with captain's bars, Ranger tab on his left shoulder, Purple Heart, Bronze Star, oak leaf clusters, and the fruit salad of ribbons and hardware that meant he had led troops into battle and tried his best to bring them all home.

I turned off the radio.

He walked slowly toward the truck, his eyes on me the whole way, black beret tilted at exactly the right angle on his head. The swelling around his eye had gone down. The plum-colored bruise looked painful.

I put the truck in park, opened the door, and got out.

"Well?" he asked.

One side of my heart *tha-thump*ed like I was a little kid and he'd just come home and I could run across the hangar floor when the order releasing the troops was shouted, and Daddy would pick me up so I could hug him around the neck and, nose to nose, look into his sky-colored eyes and tell him that I missed him so much. The other side of my heart froze in panic because now I was old enough to understand where he got that limp and why he screamed in his sleep and that something inside him was broken. I didn't know how to fix it or if it could be fixed.

He tugged at the bottom of his jacket. "There's some stupid assembly at your school. I never promised your counselor that I'd go. I might change my mind in five minutes, just warning you."

I nodded, speechless.

"You okay?" he asked.

"Is this a good idea?" I asked.

"Figured it was worth a shot."

I nodded again.

He wiped away the tears rolling down my face. "What's all this about?"

I cleared my throat. "Sun's in my eyes, Daddy."

"Bullshit, princess."

"Allergies."

He kissed my forehead. "You drive."

70

After signing in at the office, I took Dad to Ms. Benedetti's office. She melted a little, the way a lot of women do when my dad is more-or-less sober, cleaned up, and in uniform. They chatted about her brother and a few wild things Dad had never mentioned he did in high school. Benedetti did not ask about the shiner. She explained how the assembly was going to be run: boring speeches, a short video, more boring speeches, and then each veteran onstage would be presented with a bouquet of flowers and a Belmont High Machinists stadium blanket.

A muscle twitched below Dad's ear. He clenched his jaw.

"The vets will be onstage for the whole thing?" I asked.

"Absolutely! We want our veterans to know how much we appreciate their sacrifice."

"How many in the audience?" Dad asked.

"Eight hundred or so."

He blinked like she'd just slapped him.

"How many vets?" I asked.

"Thirty-two," Benedetti said proudly.

"That's a lot of guys to crowd on the stage," Dad said.

"Four of them are women," Benedetti said.

She did not point out that thirty-two people were not

going to crowd the stage. They wouldn't even fill a corner of it. Just when I thought she was being deliberately dense, she added, "You're probably sick of these things, aren't you? I imagine they get a little repetitive after a while."

"That's one way to put it," Dad said. "Plus, I'm not real fond of crowds."

"Oh," she said.

"You could hang out with me in the cafeteria," I suggested. "If you want."

"Great idea!" Benedetti's enthusiasm returned. "Wait until you see the changes in there." She scribbled me a pass. "Hayley could take you on a tour of the building during second period, after the halls have cleared." She shook Dad's hand again. "Thanks, Andy. It's really nice to have you here again."

Dad paused at the door to the cafeteria and scanned the nearly empty room. Most of the students who belonged there were at the assembly. Two dozen kids were scattered in small groups, the floor was abnormally clean and the aides were eating sticky buns and joking with the server ladies. I knew he was assessing the space: no visible threat, clear line of sight, and quick access to all exits. He should have been cool with it, but he didn't move.

"You okay?" I asked quietly.

"Fine," he said.

"I usually sit over there," I said, pointing to the corner where Finn sat, staring at us in wide-eyed surprise.

He wasn't listening.

"Dad?"

He'd made eye contact with one of the cafeteria aides, the old guy whose belly bulged over his belt buckle. The older man checked out Dad's rank and the Ranger tab, then stood straighter and nodded, a brief dip of the head, to my father. One vet greeting another.

Daddy nodded back and said, "Let's go bother what's-his-name."

What's-his-name said, "Hello, sir," and gave Dad a carton of chocolate milk, without commenting on his black eye. A guy I'd never seen before, a baseball player, judging by the hairy legs sticking out of his shorts, came over and asked to shake my father's hand. "Thanks for your service, sir," he said.

I held my breath, hoping that if this triggered Dad, he'd just leave without doing or saying anything I'd regret later.

"It was my honor," Dad said, extended his hand. "Care to join us?"

The guy grinned and asked, "Can my buddies come over, too?" He pointed his thumb at three hairy-legged dudes watching from a couple of tables away.

Dad opened the milk and took a long swig. "If they bring me more of this."

He held court for the rest of the period, listening to their questions and not quite answering them. They asked about the guns and the helicopters and the enemy, and he made jokes about MREs and camel spiders and having to burn the poop bags.

The old cafeteria aide came over and introduced himself. "I'm Bud."

Dad asked him to join us and he settled in, wiping the sticky bun glaze off his fingers with a napkin.

One of the baseball players finally asked the questions that I knew had been the reason they came over in the first place. "Did you kill anybody, sir? Was it hard?"

Dad studied his hands and didn't answer. Just as everyone started to squirm in the awkward silence, Bud jumped in with a story about being lost on a mountain in Vietnam. The guys listened but kept glancing at Dad, waiting for the answers.

When the old soldier's story was finished, Dad asked, "You know how Veterans Day started?"

"The armistice, the end of World War One," Finn answered. "At eleven o'clock in the morning of November 11, 1918, all the troops on both sides stopped fighting. That's the day we honor vets."

"Here's what you don't know," Dad said. "By five o'clock that morning, the officers had all gotten the message that the war would end that day. But lots of them ordered their men to keep fighting."

Bud snorted and shook his head.

Dad continued, "The end of the war meant that career officers would have fewer chances to move up in rank. The goddamn war was officially ending in hours and they sent their boys in to be sacrificed. Almost eleven thousand soldiers died on November 11, 1918. That's more men than died on the beaches of Normandy on D-day in World War Two, twenty-six years later." He cracked his knuckles. "Politics beats out freedom, honor, and service every time. Don't ever forget that."

The monitors around the room flickered to life, scrolling the day's announcements and breaking the spell that Dad held over his audience.

Bud glanced at the clock. "Bell rings in a few. When it does, all hell breaks loose around here."

"Good to know." Dad stood up. "You guys are pissed, aren't you? You're thinking I didn't have the balls to answer your question."

The dudes didn't say anything.

"Killing people is easier than it should be." Dad put on his beret. "Staying alive is harder."

We made it to the flagpole just as the bell rang.

"I can find the truck on my own." Dad wiped away

the sweat on his forehead. "You should go to class."

"I have second period free, remember? She wrote me a pass."

"Very funny."

I walked him to the end of the sidewalk. "See you tonight?"

"Yep." He stepped off the curb without looking back.

"Thank you, Daddy," I called.

He raised his arm so that I'd know he'd heard me, then jogged to the far edge of the student parking lot, where his truck stood isolated from all other vehicles. He opened the passenger door, took off his blue wool jacket, and laid it on the seat. He removed his beret and his tie, unbuttoned the top two buttons of his shirt and rolled up his sleeves. He closed the door, went around, and got into the driver's seat, where he sat like a marble statue, his hands gripping the steering wheel, eyes focused on things that weren't there.

The good soldier swears to kill. Fire the cannon, mount the barricade, lock and load. Smell your brother's blood on your shirt. Wipe your sister's brains off your face. Die, if you have to, so they'll live. Kill to keep your people alive, live to kill some more.

Odysseus had twenty years to shed his battle skin. My grandfather left the battlefield in France and rode home in a ship that crawled across the ocean slowly so he could catch his breath. I get on a plane in hell and get off, hours later, at home. I try to ignore Death, but she's got her arm around my waist, waiting to poison everything I touch.

I wash and wash trying to get rid of the sand. Every grain is a memory. I scrub my skin until it bleeds, but it's not enough. The named winds of the desert blow under my skin. I close my eyes and I hear them.

Those winds blow sand across the ocean, turning into hurricanes, tornados, blizzards. The storms crash into me when I'm asleep. I wake, screaming, again. And again. And again.

The worst of it is seeing the sand sweep across the deep sea-blue of my daughter's eyes.

Showing remarkable maturity, I went to Mr. Cleveland after school to find out what I had missed by chilling in the library with my free pass after Dad left. He helped me figure out how to solve a problem about a kid on a spinning Ferris wheel with a bizarre formula that required the calculation of revolutions per minute to degrees per second, and cosines. I suggested that the carnie in charge of the ride could just hit the KILL switch and take all the measurements with a tape measure. Cleveland was not amused.

I sat in the lobby and opened my math book, waiting for Finn to finish guarding the lives of the swim team. I couldn't make sense of anything on the page. My dad in uniform, that's what I kept seeing, his eyes wavering between confidence and panic. He'd tried something hard and he did it. It was a start.

"Your dad got in a bar fight?" Finn checked his mirror, then turned around before backing up.

"It was a restaurant," I said, "at six o'clock at night. I wouldn't call it a bar fight."

"You don't just get a black eye in a restaurant at six in

the evening." He shifted gears. "What really happened?"

"Trish gave me her version of the story."

"What was your dad's version?" Finn asked.

"We haven't had a chance to talk about it yet."

Finn grunted.

"What's that supposed to mean?" I asked.

He shrugged.

"No, really," I said. "You have the judging face on. Why?"

"I'm not judging. I'm observing uncritically. There's a big difference."

I took my hand off his knee. "So what are you observing?"

"It's just that you're blaming Trish again."

"Only because she deserves it. He was fine till she showed up."

He didn't say anything until the next stop sign. "Not judging, Miss Blue," he took my hand, "but you're wrong."

I didn't touch him after that.

I forgot to kiss him good-bye when he dropped me off.

I opened the front door and walked onto a battlefield.

Trish stormed across the living room, stood in front of the television, and pointed at Dad. "Are you kidding me?" she yelled.

"Nope." Dad, dressed in old jeans and a flannel shirt,

angled the remote so its signal would get past Trish and changed the channel.

"Talk to him, Hayley," she said.

"Don't listen to her," Dad said, his face blank.

"Why am I here if you don't want her to listen to me?" Trish asked. "You haven't done a single thing you promised. Hell, you won't even talk!"

"You're not talking, you're hollering." Dad motioned with the remote. "Out of the way."

Bam! A punch in the gut, that's what it felt like. It was my own damn fault for letting my guard down and believing that anything was different just because he decided to play dress-up for a couple of hours. Make no mistake, the signs were all there: a half-empty bottle of Jack on the coffee table, a second one at his feet, sweat soaking through the collar of his T-shirt though the house was cool, the fact that the dog was hiding. The hard, flat look in his eyes.

Trish took a deep breath and spoke in a calmer, quieter voice. "Your father and I have been discussing his need for help."

"What kind of help?" I asked cautiously.

"Anything," she answered. "Therapy, medication, time with guys who understand, whatever it takes so that he can stop running away."

"I'm not running from anything," Dad muttered.

Time slowed to a cold honey pour, bitter spit flooded my mouth. I could smell his whiskey, the meat cooking in the kitchen, the tea she'd spilled on her uniform. The way she glared at him crashed into the anger that came off him in waves. Lightning could strike at any second. I still had my jacket on, backpack over my shoulder. I reached for the doorknob.

Dad said, "It would only be for a couple of days at a time. Maybe a week now and then."

Time caught up to itself with a brilliant blue flash of light.

I turned around. "What are you talking about?"

"You didn't tell her?" Trish asked.

"Tell me what?" I asked.

Dad poured more whiskey in his glass, sipped, then crunched on a handful of pretzels. He tilted his head to look beyond Trish and see what was on the screen.

"You promised you'd talk to her about this at least," Trish said. "You swore!"

"Tell me what?" I repeated, louder.

Trish suddenly crouched and yanked the television's power cord. The plug flew out, trailing a spark.

Dad swirled the whiskey in his glass. "I'm following your advice, princess. I'm going back on the road. Short-haul mostly." He sipped, watching me over the rim of the glass. "You're not coming," he said. "You have to stay in school."

"No way." I put down my backpack. "You can barely get through a day here, where things are quiet. Besides, what are you going to do? Let me live alone?"

He glanced at Trish and took another sip.

"You lying son of a bitch," Trish murmured.

Shaking her head, she stormed down the hall to Gramma's bedroom. Dad pressed the button on the remote twice before he remembered that the TV was unplugged. And I figured something out.

"Did you bring her up here to babysit me?" I asked. "So you could leave?"

He didn't answer.

Trish stomped back carrying her purse and unzipped duffel bag, clothes hanging out of it. She set the bag by the door and rooted through her purse.

"Don't go," Dad said. "We'll talk tomorrow, okay? I swear it, on my honor. Just not tonight."

She pulled out her keys. "Take your phone out, Hayley."

I hesitated, then pulled it out of my pocket.

"Here's my number," she said, rattling off the digits.

I typed them in and saved the contact as "Bitch."

"What are you going to do," Dad asked, "drive all the way back to Texas? After all the crap you fed me about facing demons instead of running away?"

"I'm going to find an AA meeting, Andy." She opened the front door. "After that meeting, I'm going to find another one, and another one after that until I'm sure I can make it through the night without drinking." She picked up the duffel bag and looked at me. "Call me if you need anything."

She left without saying good-bye. The victory was so

sudden and unexpected I didn't know what to make of it. Cold air poured into the living room as she backed down the driveway and drove off, tires squealing. She hadn't closed the door.

"Shut that, will you?" Dad asked. "And plug the set back in."

— * — **73** — * —

I hummed "Ding-Dong! The Witch Is Dead" and lined up plans in my head like shooting-range targets. Dad needed time to recover from Tsunami Trish. I wouldn't bug him for two, maybe three days. After that I had to get him out of the house, maybe convince him to walk the dog with me, or tell him I was thinking of going out for track in the spring and wanted him to help me get in shape. The next step would be to call his friend Tom and ask him to help find Dad more painting jobs that he could work alone. The work plan was a little vague, but I'd figure it out soon. For right now, he needed to relax and recover.

Two days after she left, I came home to find an envelope taped to the front door. Inside was a short note from Trish giving the address of the motel where she was staying and six twenty-dollar bills. I used the money to buy potatoes, onions, creamed corn (on sale, ten cans for eight dollars), bacon, bread, peanut butter, cheese, chicken noodle soup, and milk. I cooked a vat of mashed potatoes with bacon, but Dad said he was feeling crappy. Thought he might be coming down with stomach flu, he said.

That night I burned Trish's note, then lit a candle that I'd set on a mirror on the kitchen table. Didn't think I'd see any spirits, but figured it was worth a try. The mirror showed an eruption of stress zits that made me seriously contemplate walking around with a knit cap pulled down to my chin.

Dad wouldn't cooperate. He didn't want to walk the dog with or without me, even after I had given him a few days to chill. He thought getting in shape for track was a good idea, but he made excuses instead of taking me for a run. That Tom guy didn't return any of my messages and I began to wonder how much of that story Dad told about the kitchen he painted was an exaggeration.

We argued about everything: my attitude, the weather, how to boil eggs, the size of the phone bill, the smell of the garbage. He shot down my plans and then came up with some of his own, all of them stupid. One night he said that we were going to move to Costa Rica. When I brought it up the next morning, he called me a liar and said I was trying to make him paranoid. He said I should get my GED as soon as possible so he could send me to college in January. Twenty-fours hours later, he forbade me from taking the GED, but told me to start thinking about being a nanny overseas. There were the days when he'd disappear in his head without saying a word. He couldn't sleep more than an hour or two at a time without waking up shouting or screaming. He always apologized for that, once he calmed down.

The second semester started in the middle of all this, looking pretty much like the first semester, except with heavier jackets. They made us memorize and puke up more facts, write more useless essays according to a fascist essay formula and, above all, take tests to prepare for taking even more tests. My conscientious objection to most homework had put my grades in the toilet, but the only class I had outright flunked was precalc. Benedetti finally took pity on me and busted me down to trig.

Then came the night of the phone call.

I was in the middle of a nightmare in which I'd sat down to a history final and couldn't remember anything except my name. At first, I thought the ringing noise was the bell at the end of the period. As I crawled to the surface of waking up, I thought it might be Finn, but he hated talking on the phone and never called.

I pushed the button to answer.

"Is this Emily?" asked a woman's voice. I could barely hear her over the loud music and shouting in the background.

"What did he say her name is? Sally?"

A wrong number. I hung up and fluffed my pillow. I had just closed my eyes when the phone rang again.

"Hayley," the woman said. "Your dad says to ask for Hayley. Is that you?"

"My dad?" I sat up. "Who is this? What's going on?"

"Here, you talk to her." The phone was fumbled and dropped. When it was picked up again, it was my father's voice, but I couldn't understand a single word he said.

"Daddy, what did you say?" I went into the hall. The lights were all on. "What's wrong? Where are you?"

The phone was fumbled again, then the background noise faded. The woman spoke. "Your dad is so drunk he can't remember where he put his truck, which is good because he's too wasted to drive. He got in a fight and the boss is kicking him out. I checked his pockets; he doesn't have any money left."

"Is he hurt?"

"You need to come get him, sweetie. This is a shitty neighborhood after dark. Got a pen?"

"Hang on." I ran to the kitchen and found what I needed in the junk drawer. "Okay, I'm ready."

She gave me the address and directions. "How soon till you get here?"

"I don't know. I have to find a car. Can you keep an eye on him until I get there?"

She shouted, "In a minute!" to someone else, then said, "Hurry."

There was no time to be embarrassed or angry or ashamed. I called Gracie while I was walking to her house.

"Wha . . ." she mumbled.

"I need your mom's car." I explained the situation, then repeated it until she woke up enough to understand what I was saying.

"I can't," she said.

"You don't have to come with me," I said. "Just put her keys on the front seat. I know the code to open the garage."

"Don't open the garage door!" she said. "Mom always hears it, no matter what. If you try to sneak her car out, she'll call the cops, I guarantee it."

"What am I supposed to do?"

"Call Finn."

I stopped in the middle of the empty street. "I don't want him to see Dad like this."

"Do you have a choice?" she asked.

Finn didn't say anything when he picked me up. We didn't talk at all as we drove. The fight on the phone—him saying

I should let Dad wake up tomorrow morning in his own puke in an alley, me calling him a heartless bastard—had drained us both.

(He'd only gotten in his car when he realized I was headed to the bar on foot.)

He didn't say anything until he parked in front of The Sideways Inn. "I can't let you go in there alone."

"You have to," I said.

"It's dangerous." He pointed at a group of guys hanging out in a doorway down the block. "Look at them. They're just waiting to pounce."

"Hardly," I said. "They're hoping that we're stupid enough to leave your car empty so they can break in and steal the radio. This heap is old enough that they could hotwire it. Then we'll really be stuck here."

"But," he said.

I opened the door. "Keep the engine running."

"Get out of here!" the bartender yelled as I walked in. "You're not old enough."

The music was so loud that I could feel it in my fillings. The dark room was filled with shadows leaning against the wall, bending over the pool table, and slumped into chairs around battered tables, all of them staring at me. I wanted to turn around and run, but I put my shoulders back and walked straight to the bar. "I'm looking for my dad."

The bartender scowled. "You got ID?"

"My dad," I said louder. "A woman called me to come get him."

An old guy two stools down looked at me with sad eyes. "She's here for Captain Andy."

The bartender's expression changed. "Did you come alone?"

"My boyfriend's outside in the car."

He nodded at the old guy. "Go get him, Vince. He's in the john."

I kept my eyes on the beer taps. MILLER. BUD. LABATT'S. The music hammered at me, chipping off pieces that fell to the sticky floor. Most of the light in the room came from the television sets, all set to different channels. The couple sitting at the end of the bar stared at the hockey game, their mouths hanging open like they didn't understand what they were seeing.

"Here he is." The bartender's growl made me jump.

Dad had a taken a couple punches to the mouth—his lips were swollen and bloodied. Blood stained his shirt, too, along with vomit and beer. His eyes were open, but nobody was home. He had no idea where he was.

"Thanks," I said. "I got it."

They stared at me, at us. All of them stared. Not because I was young and female, like when I walked in, but because my father was so wasted his little girl had to fetch him home. Total strangers—drunks, addicts, whores, ex-cons—pitied us. I could smell it coming off of them.

Dad's bad leg was useless and his good leg wasn't much better. I put his arm around my shoulder and put my arm around his waist and dragged him through the door, outside to the car. Finn jumped out and helped me get him in the backseat. Dad crawled in and collapsed, his head hanging down in the foot well.

"What about a seat belt?" Finn asked.

"Don't worry about it." I slammed the back door. "Just drive."

We got in and rolled down the windows so we wouldn't be choked by my father's stench.

Finn drove faster than I'd ever seen. "How much longer can you keep doing this?"

"This has never happened before," I said.

"It's not just tonight," he said. "It's everything. You take care of him more than he takes care of you. How much longer?"

I didn't have an answer.

Michael drove Dad around the next day until he found the pickup truck. The window had been smashed and the radio stolen, but other than that it was fine. We both stayed home for a few days after that, feeling like we were coming down with the flu.

75

I pedaled until I broke a sweat. Gracie and I had been able to snag exercise bicycles in gym because so many zombies had blown off school the day before Thanksgiving. (I wondered if they were rampaging in downtown Albany, or maybe took a train to join the larger horde, probably in Poughkeepsie.) The substitute gym aide was working on a laptop in the corner. A half-dozen girls were lying on the gym mats, talking about nothing, and laughing too hard. A couple more sat in the bleachers painting their toenails.

I pushed harder until the sweat dripped off my face and splashed on the floor.

"It doesn't matter how fast you pedal," Gracie said, handing me a water bottle. "That bike's not going anywhere."

I took a long drink. "Now you tell me."

"You look like crap," she said.

"I just need some sleep."

"You need more than that."

I shook my head.

She cycled slowly, like a little kid turning lazy circles on a tricycle. "What's wrong with Finn?"

"What do you mean?"

"He didn't say a single word first period."

I shrugged. "Physics is kicking his butt."

"He didn't touch you, either. You grabbed his belt loop with your finger once and after a minute, he pushed your hand away."

"What kind of pervert are you, counting how many times we touch each other?"

"If you want me to shut up, just say it," she said.

I took another drink. "Don't shut up."

"I wasn't planning on it, but thanks," she said. "I'm worried. You're both so weird and incompatible with anyone else that you're perfect for each other. When he stops touching you and when you stop teasing him, it screws up the universe, know what I mean?"

I held the water bottle against my forehead. "He's got a lot on his mind."

"His sister?"

I set the bottle on the floor. "He's driving to Boston with his mom tomorrow to have Thanksgiving with Chelsea and his dad."

"Sounds like hell."

"I know, right? He was so bummed when he told me and I felt so bad for him that I said I'd go to the mall with him after school. His mom is making him buy a new shirt for the occasion."

"You hate the mall."

"He said he was desperate."

Gracie got a text message. I changed gears and stood up to pedal. Since the night Finn helped me bring Dad home, something had changed. Gracie was right; he wasn't touching me. I wasn't touching him, either, because a token belt-loop grab didn't count. We'd stopped teasing each other. He hadn't broken up with me, but I could smell it coming. He wanted a normal girl with a matched set of unscarred parents. Someone with a "bright future."

"I need to steal a referee's whistle." Gracie stuck her phone in her bra. "The therapist says we have to eat Thanksgiving dinner together, all four of us."

"What's wrong with that?"

"Thanksgiving?" Gracie's eyes bugged out. "Think about it. Carving knives! Boiling gravy! It'll be a disaster." She pedaled faster. "Dad's got to be sleeping with her."

"Your mom?"

"The therapist, dummy. Why else would she recommend such a stupid thing?"

"I don't know, G. Maybe she thinks your parents should stop being idiots and find a way to still be a family even if they are going to split up."

"No way." She stopped. "What are you and your dad going to do? Turkey at home or a restaurant?"

Two years before, we'd been on the road to Cheyenne, getting paid extra for driving on the holiday. We drove until midnight and ate turkey sandwiches to celebrate. Last year, we'd been stuck in a motel outside Seattle. It had a mini-fridge and a microwave, so I'd cooked up a box of stuffing and served canned peaches for dessert.

"How is he doing?" she asked.

"Better," I lied. "Every day without Trish he gets a little stronger."

"Come to our house," she said.

"What?"

"Bring your dad to my house for Thanksgiving."

"Shouldn't you ask your parents first?"

"They'll be overjoyed with the distraction, trust me."

"I don't think it's a good idea," I said.

"You have to do this." Gracie reached over and pushed the button on my console to make it harder for me to pedal. "You owe me."

"For what?"

"I helped you the night you had to bring your dad home."

"No, you didn't."

"I talked to you, didn't I? And I totally would have gotten the car for you if I could have. Besides, it worked out okay in the end, right? Please come to dinner."

"I don't know, G."

"Bring a pie if you want. Pie makes everybody happy. Bring pie and your dad. Maybe it will make them all be on their best behavior. It's worth a shot, right?"

76

"Why didn't your mom call the police?" I asked, trying to keep up with Finn.

"There's no way to prove it was Chelsea," he said, grim-faced.

"Actually, there is." I broke into an awkward half jog. "They have this new thing called 'fingerprints.' Since she was arrested before, they'll be on file someplace."

"Please don't be a bitch," he said. "Not right now."

He opened the glass door of the red entrance of the mall and walked in without waiting to see if I was still with him. While we were at school, someone had broken into his mom's condo and stolen her emergency credit card (chiseled out of its hiding place in a block of frozen ice at the back of the freezer) and a pound of sliced ham. Obviously, it was Chelsea, and it should have been the end of the trip to Boston and his parents' misguided plans for Thanksgiving, but his mother was still acting like everything was fine.

Finn plowed ahead into the crowd of pre-pre-Black Friday shoppers. (His mom said he had to buy a new dress shirt because he had outgrown his old ones. His family always dressed up for Thanksgiving dinner. Utter insanity.)

He didn't realize I wasn't with him until he was ten stores in. He turned in a full circle, looking for me.

I took a deep breath and opened the door. Approximately two billion people were inside, all hollering so they could be heard over the irritating holiday (buy-our-stuff) music. I fought my way through the swarm until I reached him, standing next to one of those fake mini-booths that sell bad cell phone plans.

"It's too crowded," I said. "Let's come back tomorrow."

"We're leaving at six in the morning," he pointed out. "It won't take long."

I followed him into a small, crowded store that was so dark no one could read the price tags. He picked out a half-dozen shirts and we squeezed our way back to the dressing rooms. He went in and closed the door behind him. I called Dad, just to check on him, to tell him I was running late, and I'd be home soon. Also, I needed to hear how he sounded.

He didn't answer the phone.

I counted to sixty and called again. Still no answer.

"Does it fit?" I asked.

"Not the first one."

Five minutes of silence later, I knocked again. "Any luck?"

"Not really."

"Why is this taking so long?"

"What's your problem?"

Where should I start?

"Just hurry up."

Someone turned up the store's music so loud it made the floor shake. A new crowd of people pushed their way into the dressing room area, even though there was nowhere for them to stand. It suddenly felt like I was standing in front of the stage at a huge concert and sixty thousand people had decided to make the place into a mosh pit. I swallowed hard and looked up, above their heads, looking for air and trying not to panic. I called Dad again. The phone rang.

I pounded on the dressing-room door. "Seriously, Finn, it's just a shirt. I need to get home."

He flung a heap of white shirts over the dressing room door. "Can you put those back?"

I tensed as a couple of college-aged guys squeezed past me, waiting to feel their hands on parts of me they weren't allowed to touch. They kept their hands to themselves, which was good because I could feel it, the gray closing in on me like a toxic fog, filling my lungs with poison.

"Miss Blue?" Finn asked. "You still there?"

"None of them fit?"

"They itched."

"They're cotton." The phone at my house kept ringing. "Stop being such a baby."

"What's wrong with you?" he asked.

No answer. No answer. No answer.

The music got even louder. I was sweating. Out of breath, too, because there was not enough air and too many people.

No answer.

I pushed my way toward the front of the store, ignoring the complaints and curses people threw my way, until I finally broke free into the mall.

Finn found me a few minutes later, clenching the railing.

"Where's your bag?" I asked.

"There's another store by the food court."

I licked my lips. Hordes marched past us, shrieking like crows into their phones, carrying small fortunes in big shopping bags, their faces distorted in the reflection of the hanging silver-and-gold decorations.

"Take me home," I said.

"I have to get a shirt," he said slowly and loudly, as if I was deaf.

"Come back and get it after you drop me off."

"Trying to get rid of me?" He leaned in to kiss me.

"Don't." I stepped away from him. "I'm not playing. I hate it here, I want to go home."

"Is something wrong? Is it your dad?"

"He's not answering the phone."

"He never answers the phone. Just give me fifteen minutes."

No answer. No answer.

"No, we have to leave right now."

"Since when did you become a drama queen?"

My legs moved.

I bumped, shoved, slipped into tiny cracks in the crowd, needing to get *Out! Out! Out!* as soon as possible. I couldn't stop the pictures in my head, explosions like a flash-bang grenade was going off behind my eyes: carnage in the street, bodies on the floor of a pizza shop, a movie theater, the county fair. I walked as fast as the crowd would let me, eyes scanning for exits, hair tingling on the back of my neck as if someone, somewhere was pushing the button that would detonate an explosion. Lining me up in his sights and pulling the trigger.

Say the alphabet. Count in Spanish. Picture a mountain, the top of a mountain, the top of a mountain in the summer. Keep breathing.

None of my father's old tricks worked anymore.

Finn caught up with me just before I slipped out the door. He grabbed my arm, spun me around. "What's going on?"

The me of me curled into a dark corner in the back of my skull and some Hayley-bitch version I'd never seen before came out roaring. "Leave me alone!"

"Why? Tell me, please."

"Forget it," the bitch said, using my mouth, balling my hands into granite fists. "Forget everything. I don't know you, you don't know me, and this is all a waste of time."

"But—" Finn started.

The bitch wanted to fight, wanted to scream. She wanted someone else to get in the middle and give her an excuse to kick, to punch, and hurt. She looked at the zombie shoppers who had stopped to watch the sideshow, stared at them, daring them to say anything.

"I'll take you home," Finn said. "We'll talk tomorrow. Or Monday, whenever you want."

The look in his eyes went right through the me of me, piercing my heart, but the bitch was in control.

"We're done," she said in my voice, sounding stronger than I felt, bluffing her way through the end of this game. "I don't want to be with you. I'll take the bus home."

"Are you breaking up with me?"

"Clever boy," the Hayley-bitch said. "Just leave me alone."

—*— **77** —*—

The bitch in me was mostly quiet by the time I woke up Thanksgiving morning. I could still feel her lurking in the back of my skull, reminding me how thin the ice was. I turned on the parade and turned up the volume. The first three giant balloons were cartoon characters I'd never seen before.

I hadn't called or texted Finn. Of course, he hadn't called or texted me, either. I didn't know if he was home or in

Boston or on the turnpike or maybe he was still asleep.

Bitch Voice: better off without him, he doesn't understand, you can't trust him.

I knocked on Dad's door. "It's Thanksgiving. We're going to Gracie's for dinner, remember?"

"Four o'clock," he said.

"Don't drink," I reminded him. "You promised."

I found Gramma's recipe box, pulled the card marked *Mason Apple Pie*, and watched a bunch of videos to learn how to make a pie crust. I took the butter out of the fridge so it could soften. Set out the flour, salt and ice water, bowl and forks. Peeled the apples. Sat on the couch and watched the Hatboro-Horsham Marching Hatters perform in front of the grandstand. Wondered what possessed a school to call itself the Hatters. Looked up why my apple slices were turning brown. Ate half of the apple slices.

The parade ended. Football began.

I ate the rest of the apple slices and pulled some more cards from Gramma's recipe box. *Anna Chatfield's Key Lime. Esther's Pumpkin w/Walnut Crust. Peg Holcomb's Perfect Pumpkin. Edith Janack's Apple Crisp. Ethel Mason's Mincemeat.* And a small surprise: *Rebecca's Lemon Cake.*

My fingers hovered above the keys of my phone, wanting to talk to Finn. Did his shirt itch? Was his whole family sitting around the table, everyone dressed to kill? Was there any way to explain to him why I'd been so mean?

No. I barely understood it myself. I just knew that I

wanted to push him away from me more than I wanted to hold him close.

Dad stayed in his room all day, not even coming out to watch football. My pie came out burnt on the edges and a little watery in the middle, but I thought that for a first try, it wasn't too bad.

Gracie texted just before four o'clock:

plans changed can u com at 6?

I wrote back:

sure

An hour and a half later, she texted:

thxgving canceled
ttyt

I carried the pie to her house. Cardboard turkeys and black Pilgrim hats were taped to the first-floor windows of Gracie's house. (Did they really wear hats like that? If you were on the brink of starvation, would you really care about your hat?) Tall, narrow windows flanked the front door, covered by bunched-up lace curtains that made it impossible to see inside.

I rang the doorbell, but nobody answered.

* * *

Gracie called at ten and gave me the blow-by-blow description of the battle between her parents that had caused the cancellation of the dinner. Instead of being hysterical, she spent the night finishing her applications to four universities in California.

Just before midnight, I texted Finn to say happy Thanksgiving. He didn't answer.

—*— **78** —*—

I became a little unstuck in time after that, drifting like a dead leaf caught in the current of a half-frozen river, bumping into rocks, spinning in slow eddies, not worrying about the waterfalls ahead.

It snowed again on the first day of December. The cold switched my brain to hibernation mode, shutting down the ability to think in favor of keeping my internal organs functioning. The downside was that it also created minor memory glitches. I was halfway across the parking lot that afternoon before I remembered that Finn and I hadn't talked in a week and I couldn't ride home with him. I wouldn't get in his car even if he asked me to. At least, I was pretty sure I wouldn't.

On the bus, I jammed in my earbuds, dialed up Danish

death metal, and played it loud enough to make my ears bleed. By the time I walked up the driveway, my head hurt and I was almost deaf. It felt good in a sick way.

I flicked off the music, turned the doorknob, yanked open the front door, and almost pulled my shoulder out of the socket. The door was locked. Dad hadn't locked it in weeks, but I didn't give it much thought, because something trickled in my ears and I worried that maybe the music had punctured my eardrums and fluid from my brain was leaking.

Get a grip and stop catastrophizing.

I unzipped the front pocket of my backpack and reached for my keys, but they weren't there. I emptied my backpack onto the front porch before I remembered the last place I'd seen them: next to my computer. I'd left in such a rush that I'd forgotten to grab them.

Crap.

I rang the bell and knocked on the door. Nothing. If he was sleeping in his room, I'd have to go to Gracie's or hang out at the park until he got hungry enough to wake up.

Crap. Crap. Crap.

I jogged back down the walk. The rig was still in the driveway, hood down and doors locked. I peered through the dirty window into the garage. The pickup was parked inside. No tools that needed to be put away. No sign of Dad. The back door off the kitchen was closed and locked, too.

I checked all the windows that I could reach. I couldn't tell which were painted shut and which were locked, but none of them would budge.

That's when I smelled something burning. Saw smoke rising from the fire pit, which we hadn't used in over a month. I walked over to it, thinking maybe he'd started a fire to cook hot dogs or something.

He'd been burning his uniform. Scraps of his jacket and pants lay at the edge of the fire. The half-melted boots smoldered in the middle.

I ran back to the living room window, cupped my hands around my eyes to cut down on the glare, and tried to see inside between the curtains. The living room had been trashed. The upside-down couch was blocking the way to the dining room. Stuffing from the couch cushions had been flung everywhere and looked like dirty cotton candy. The recliner had been chopped to bits. The ax handle stuck out from the gaping hole that had been chopped in the drywall. The cuckoo clock lay in a pile of splinters.

My father was curled into a ball on the floor. Blood on his face. Blood staining the carpet under his head, Spock lying next to him.

A girl screamed.

!!!NONONODADDYDADDYNODADDYNONONONO-NONOOOO!!!

Spock howled.

The screaming girl slapped the window with her palms, pounded the window with her fists, bent down to grab her backpack. Spock ran to the window and put his front paws on the sill, barking. The girl threw the backpack at the glass and it bounced off. She was thinking, *Why can't I break it, how do I break it, grab a log, break the window, shatter the glass, a rock, a big rock, break it into a million pieces and get to him, crawl over the broken glass and get—*

The body moved. Uncurled. It sat up, wiped its face on the front of its T-shirt, and turned to look at the wailing girl pounding on the other side.

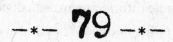

$$-*-\ 79\ -*-$$

"He's dead," Dad said.

I led him to a dining room chair and made him sit down. The blood was coming from his nose and a long cut on his chin.

"Who's dead?" I asked. "Who did this to you?"

He didn't answer.

A burglary? I looked over my shoulder. The TV was still in the living room. Wasn't that what burglars always took? *Michael.* I bet he owed money to a dealer or a shady friend and he didn't pay so the guy came to our house to look for him. Dad had been in the wrong place at the wrong time.

But he burned his uniform and he said "dead." Had he killed the guy? Was there a body somewhere?

"Daddy, look at me. What is going on?"

He closed his eyes, moaned. I ran my hands over the scars on his head. "Should I call the police?"

"No, no," he said wearily. "It was over there." He put his head in his hands and rocked back and forth, breathing hard, like he was in the middle of a race.

The war. Another dead friend.

"You have to tell me," I said gently. "Who was it?"

Dad gulped back a sob. "Roy."

Is there anything worse than watching your father cry? He's supposed to be the grown-up, the all-powerful grown-up, especially if he's a soldier. When I was a kid, I watched him work out, scaling walls, lifting guys bigger than he was, running miles in the heat wearing full gear and carrying extra ammo. My dad was a superhero who made the world safe. He went overseas with his troops and chased the bad guys out of the mountains so that little kids over there could go to school and to the library and use the playground the way I did at home. The first time I saw him cry wasn't so bad because he still had metal rods sticking into his leg. He was in pain. I understood that. After they pulled out the rods, after Trish left, I'd wake up at night hearing him sob, sniff like a child, like me, tears coming fast and mixing with snot. He'd try to keep quiet, but sometimes the sadness came over him as loud as a thunderstorm. Scared the shit out of me, like riding a roller coaster and feeling your seat belt snap just as the track turns you upside down.

I patted his back, waiting for the storm to pass.

It took more than an hour and a lot of whiskey before he'd say anything more. Roy's platoon had been caught in an ambush. Rocket-fired grenades, Dad said. Everyone who wasn't killed was injured.

"They'll never be able to complain," he said. "How can you complain if you're alive? Lose your arms, lose your eyes, a leg, or a foot; it doesn't matter when you think about your brothers buried in the ground."

He was drinking out of a plastic cup.

"Rotting in the ground," he muttered.

His tears made tiny streams down the dried blood on his cheeks. The stubble on his face was speckled with gray and white. The skin along his jaw sagged a little, making him look like he had aged ten years since breakfast. His hands were bruised, the knuckles oozing blood, probably from punching the holes in the drywall.

The dining room curtains had been torn down and sunlight flooded the room, bouncing off the glittering glass shards in the carpet. He had broken all of our glasses, all of our plates and bowls, too, thrown against the walls. The silverware drawer was in pieces and one of the pantry doors had been ripped off the hinges.

A monster had rampaged through the house.

I picked up the dog and staggered to the door. It was a miracle he hadn't cut his paws. The second he touched the ground, he started racing back and forth the length of our yard, from the house all the way to the cornfield and back, ignoring my calls to come, just running until he wore himself out and flopped by the fire pit, where I was able to hook him to the chain.

Dad refilled his whiskey. I went for the broom to start cleaning. I swept up the big pieces of glass and china and drywall, hid the ax in my closet, set the couch back on its feet, and stuffed the guts of the couch cushions into garbage bags. I threw what was left of the recliner in the back of the truck. That would have to go to the dump. I cleaned for more than an hour and still he sat in that chair.

"A shower might feel good," I finally suggested.

I crossed my fingers, hoping he wouldn't start talking about how Roy would never shower again, Roy would never drink whiskey or love a woman or eat Thanksgiving at his mother's house again.

"Nothing feels good." His red-rimmed eyes didn't blink.

I hesitated, not wanting to set him off. "How about something to eat. Eggs?"

He shook his head.

"Pancakes?" I asked. "Hamburgers?"

"I'm not hungry."

"You have to eat something. How about toast? I can make some coffee, if you want."

"I just want some quiet, okay?" He stood up and patted my cheek. "But thanks."

He grabbed the bottle and walked to the living room. The television was the one thing he hadn't destroyed in there. He picked up the remote, turned it on, and clicked through the channels until he found a reporter talking about a late hurricane forming in the Gulf of Mexico. He sat on the cushionless couch, poured himself another shot, and tossed it back.

—*— 80 —*—

I spent the next morning picking out glass and broken dishes from the carpet. Thousands of slivers as thin as pins, sharp on both ends, pricked my fingers. Gloves made the job harder so I finally used a comb, inch by inch through the living room and the dining room. I saved the kitchen floor for last because it was small and easy; just needed to wipe it down with damp paper towels, my knees protected by a scrap of cardboard.

By lunchtime, the floors were safe and I could let the dog out of the basement.

Dad slept.

In school, they were studying Homer, tangents, tonal systems, Dred Scott, and finger whorls. Finn was probably flirting and studying and finishing his applications and saving the world all at the same time. I kept hearing him say, "You take care of him more than he takes care of you" over and over again.

When Benedetti's office called, I said my father and I had flu again.

When the sun went down, Dad woke up, chain-smoked, and ate two bologna sandwiches. After eating, he went outside to talk on his cell. I wanted him to start drinking again so he would pass out. I didn't have to worry about him hurting himself when he was unconscious.

He opened another bottle when he came in, sat me on the couch, and made me listen to stuff I'd heard a million times before: ambushed foot patrols, IEDs ripping open vehicles and bodies, suicide bombers living in ghost villages. The private who was shot in the neck. The guy who removed his helmet to wipe the sweat off his head, and the sniper who blew that head into a red mist that hung in the air for a moment before it dropped to the dirt and soaked the ground.

The thing under his skin took over his eyes and made them look dead. The thing raged and paced, snapped at the dog, yelled at me.

I tried to go to bed around two, but that set him off again. I stayed awake. I listened. Donkeys loaded with weapons. Bloated bodies. The smell of the dead. Flies.

Around quarter after four, he puked all over the carpet and finally passed out. I laid him on his side, put a bucket by his head, and threw a towel over the mess so the dog wouldn't eat it. I took a long shower to wash off the tears and the stench of whiskey puke.

—*— 81 —*—

The sound of submachine guns on automatic fire ripped me out of sleep, gasping. I tried to focus and fought my way over the line that divides asleep from awake. The guns sounded again, a heavy burst of artillery, and then a couple of men laughed. It was a game. Just another shooting game.

I started to pull the blankets over my head and stopped.

Men. Laughing. Men, as in "more than one," as in my father had company and "laughing," as in there was no way Dad could be laughing, so who was in my living room?

I threw off the blankets and scrambled into clothes.

The sunshine stealing through the narrow crack between the curtains sliced the living room into thick patches of darkness and slivers of light. Two men, Michael and some dude I'd never seen before, sat on kitchen chairs in front of the TV, controllers in their hands. Dad sat upright on the couch smoking a bong. His squinted eyes were swollen. The smoke that slipped out of his mouth was the color of his skin, like he was a miserable old dragon slowly disintegrating into ash.

"Why are they here?" I asked.

"He invited us." Michael turned around. "Asked us to come over and cheer him up."

"I wasn't talking to you."

"He's right," Dad spoke slowly. "I called him. Why aren't you at school?"

"Make them leave," I demanded.

He set the bong on a stack of books. "They just got here."

"So?"

Dad gave a half-baked smile. "Kept you up last night, didn't I? Sorry about that, princess. Why don't you make us some coffee, cook up a big breakfast?"

The weed had driven the crazy back under his skin, but it was a temporary situation at best. "I don't want them here."

"Listen to your elders," Michael said.

"Eggs would be nice," Dad said. "An omelet, with lots of cheese."

"Scrambled," Michael said. "How about you, Goose?" he asked the guy next to him.

Goose paused the game and turned around. He had the scabby face of a tweeker, gaunt and haunted. "Not hungry."

I couldn't move. Didn't know what to say. The room looked like the backdrop of a PBS documentary: holes in the wall, messed-up furniture, smoke drifting from shadow to light, the green-lit battle on-screen holding the attention of everyone but me. Or maybe a cheap-ass cable supernatural horror show—the goons in front of the screen ready to morph into demons, the smoke easing in and out of my father really a spirit sent to claim him for the dark side.

"Why, Daddy?" I asked.

He reached for the bong. "I like having them here."

Michael chuckled, his fingers piloting the soldier on-screen through a massacre. "Hear that, Goose? He likes us."

That's when I realized that I wanted to kill Michael. I knew I couldn't, knew I wouldn't. If I jumped him, he'd swat me away like a fly. Dad would come out of his stupor to defend me and then things would get bad and bloody. I could get out one of Dad's pistols, no, a shotgun, and threaten them with it. Not that I'd shoot them—I sure as hell wasn't going to jail over those two morons—but they wouldn't know that. I'd scare them off by shooting over their heads. We were going to have to put up new drywall, anyway.

As fast as that scene—me, shotgun, ceiling, *boom*—unfolded in my head, everything that could go wrong with that plan chased in on its heels. Dad would grab the gun or Michael would grab the gun or Goose would pull out a gun of his own and it would get scary bad and very bloody.

"Do we have any bacon?" Dad asked.

I crossed the room and unplugged the TV. "I'm calling the cops."

"No, you're not," Michael said.

I pulled out my phone. "Wanna watch?"

Goose stood up. "Dude."

"Andy," Michael said. "Tell your kid to put the phone away."

"Come on, Hayley," Dad said.

I opened the phone.

"They'll arrest your dad," Michael said. "Is that what you want?"

I opened the front door and stepped into freezing, blinding sunlight. I turned on my camera and walked far enough down the driveway that I could get the plates of both bikes in a photo.

"What are you doing?" Michael shouted from the doorway.

I climbed into the cab of the big rig, locked myself in, dialed 911, and explained that my father was sick and two men were in my house and they wouldn't leave. As the emergency lady took down my information, Michael and Goose jumped on their bikes and roared away.

Yes! Score!

I set the phone on the dash and high-fived myself. I sighed and picked up the phone. "They're gone," I said. "Those guys I just told you about. We don't need the police anymore."

"An officer has to respond to the call, sweetie," she explained. "Just to make sure you're safe."

"No, really, you don't have to send them," I said, my voice tightening. "Me calling you, that scared them off. I'm totally safe. So is Dad."

"Is he going to need an ambulance?"

"What? No. It's . . . the flu. He needs chicken soup, not cops."

"We have a couple of officers who are sick with it, too. We're a little shorthanded, but I guarantee you, a policeman will be at your house within the hour. Do you want to stay on the line?"

I hung up.

They'd find his weed. What else? Were all his guns legal? What if they brought in a drug-sniffing dog? Would it find hidden stashes that I didn't know existed? What if Dad saw the uniforms and went ape shit? What if they arrested him for assault and possession, or worse because they thought he was a dealer? What if they took him away? Where would they put me?

A wave of nausea hit me hard. I coughed, swallowed bile, and did the one thing I swore that I'd never do.

I called Trish.

By the time she arrived, I had opened every window in the house, sprayed air freshener, and stuck Dad in the shower. I'd thrown the bong as far into the cornfield as I could and flushed his pills down the toilet. I'd cleaned up the now-solid puke from the carpet, poured baby powder on the mess it left behind and tried to vacuum it all away.

Dad stepped out of the shower and was yelling at me to close the goddamn windows when Trish walked in. I explained what had happened in a few quick sentences while she checked Dad's pulse. He'd put on a baggy pair of sweatpants and an ancient sweater and looked more like a homeless man than a war hero or my father. She told me to shut the windows while she got him into bed. I finished a heartbeat before a squad car pulled in the driveway, lights flashing, no siren.

"Can they arrest him if they don't find anything?" I asked.

"Depends," she said. "Keep your story simple. You woke up, Dad was passed out, and you didn't know the guys in your living room. You never saw them before."

"But Michael—"

"No names. They wouldn't leave. You were scared. Okay?"

A cop knocked at the front door.

"Feel free to cry," she added.

Trish took charge, explaining who she was and why she was there, and then taking one of the cops, the skinny one, back to see Dad. The other one was built like a defensive tackle, massive shoulders, neck thicker than his head, and hands the size of baseball mitts. He was on guard, assessing danger with every step like Dad did, but by the time he'd checked out the whole house and sat down with me in the living room, he had relaxed a bit.

I answered his questions. Dad had the flu. I stayed home to take care of him. No, he hadn't been to a doctor. No, I didn't know the guys. No, I couldn't describe them, I was too scared.

He wrote down my answers in a spiral notebook and then he asked me the exact same questions again. I gave the same exact answers. He wrote them down again and then he looked at me and smiled, the lines around his eyes crinkling. He had brown eyes, light brown like an acorn. He glanced above my head.

"Who punched the wall?" he asked.

"It was like that when we moved in," I said. "Squatters."

He did not write that down. "Stay put," he said.

He walked down the hall, his keys and handcuffs and various chains jingling, sounding absurdly close to what I'd always imagined Santa's sleigh would sound like. At the end of the hall, he and his buddy held a murmured meeting. The heat had kicked on and the air was beginning to smell like Michael's satanic cologne. What if this kept happening, what if Dad wasn't on a roller coaster, what if he was on a spiraling slide, turning down and down into the darkness? What would Michael do the next time?

"Excuse me, sir?" I called. "I took a picture of their license plates. Would that help?"

—*— 83 —*—

In the end, they reviewed all the paperwork for Dad's guns and, to my amazement, they were all legal. Dude even complimented him for securing them properly. In the end, they looked through all the photos on my phone and sent themselves the one with the motorcycle license plates. Brown Eyes put the plate numbers in his computer and found something that he talked to his partner about.

In the end, they called an ambulance because Dad was so dehydrated. They put an IV in his arm, strapped him on a gurney, and loaded the gurney in the ambulance. Daddy asked Trish to follow the ambulance in her car. He made her promise not to bring me.

In the end, I was alone in a house that had holes in

the walls and bloodstained carpet. I choked on the words stacked up floor to ceiling, all of them charred black, held over the fire too long, so many words that I could barely breathe.

I made a cup of tea, but when I poured the milk, it came out in sour clumps. We were out of bread and bananas. I ate a spoonful of peanut butter, then I mixed the rest of the jam into the peanut butter jar and ate it until my stomach hurt. I walked the house from one end to the other, back and forth, Spock following close behind me. It felt like the building grew smaller with every step, or maybe I was growing bigger, Hayley in Wonderland, maybe I'd shoot up twenty feet and my head would bust through the roof and my arms would stick out the windows.

Spock got tired of following me and lay down on the carpet in the same spot where Dad collapsed the day he found out that Roy was dead. I stretched out next to Spock and let him lick my face before he fell asleep. The carpet was itchy so I crawled into bed but couldn't get comfortable.

He was alive. I'd been afraid of a day like this forever, but he was alive. At a hospital, getting help. This was a good thing, right? It was all that mattered.

Except.

What now?

I closed my eyes, pretended I was twenty thousand feet in the air, high enough to be able to see where we came from and where we were headed. Borders didn't come painted with lines, but it felt like we'd crossed one. This was a new place with no signs or landmarks. In a land with a million questions, I only had one answer.

In the end, I stole Daddy's pickup truck.

—*— 84 —*—

By the time I got to school, found the only set of doors that were still unlocked, and made it to the swimming pool, the boys' practice was ending. The swimmers each put their hands on the deck at the edge of the pool and vaulted out of the water like seals. Finn was in a bathing suit, too, but he was dry, walking around the pool collecting kickboards as the team filed into the locker room teasing one another loudly, shoving until the coach blew a sharp note on his whistle.

"Can I help you?" the coach asked me.

"Um," I started. "I'm waiting for him. The guard."

"Ramos!" shouted the coach, before he, too, went into the locker room.

Finn lifted his head and finally saw me. I wanted to bolt for the door but was afraid I'd slip on the wet concrete and land on my face. He set the stack of kickboards by the door to the office, took off his glasses, put them on top of the stack, and walked over to me.

"Do you always break the rules?" he asked, squinting a little.

"What?"

He pointed to the sign that read NO SHOES IN POOL AREA.

"Oh, sorry." I kicked off my left sneaker, peeled off my sock, and stuffed it in the toe. I stood on my left foot to take off my right sneaker, but slipped and would have crashed in an undignified heap if he hadn't reached out and grabbed my arm.

"Thanks." I kept my gaze down as I finished removing the sneaker and sock.

I'd driven to the school with the windows rolled down even though it had dipped below freezing outside. The cold wind numbed me from all the nightmares that popped up every time I replayed the image of Dad in the back of the ambulance. But here, instantly, I was sweating.

I unzipped my jacket. "They always keep this place so hot?"

"When the principal isn't paying attention," he replied.

The team was still hooting and hollering in the locker room. Showers were running, too. The loudspeaker crackled with static as an announcement was made, but I could not understand what the voice said.

"You need a ride or something?" Finn asked. "Wait, were you even in school today? I didn't see you."

"I have Dad's pickup."

"Hayley, you don't have your license yet."

"Oops."

He looked ready to make a smart-ass comment, but instead he twisted sideways and dove into the water. He swam all the way to the far end, turned around—still underwater—and surfaced, his arms moving like paddle wheels as he swam butterfly back to me, creating a wave that sloshed over the pool's edge and soaked the bottom of my jeans.

"What are you doing?" I asked.

He bobbed under the water briefly, arching his head back so that when he came up, his hair was slicked back. "What are you doing?" he echoed.

The speech I'd memorized in the pickup melted into the chlorine-scented fog. "Um, how's it going?" I asked. "I mean, how's your sister and mom? And everything."

"You didn't answer my question," he pointed out.

"You noticed that, huh?"

The voices in locker room faded. Metal lockers slammed.

"Chelsea didn't show up for Thanksgiving," he said. "Mom cried all day. Dad went for a drive that lasted seven hours. How about you?"

"We didn't have Thanksgiving." *Could he hear my heart pounding?*

The locker room had grown so quiet that the only

sounds were the buzzing of the overhead lights, and water lapping against the sides of the pool. Finn cupped a handful of water and splashed it over my toes.

"It's warm," I said.

"There's a water aerobics class here in an hour; they get wicked upset if the water is below eighty. Ever had a bunch of scary old ladies wearing swimming caps with plastic flowers on them yell at you? Terrifying." He splashed more water over my feet. "So. Why are you here, Miss Blue?"

I took a deep breath. "Remember that day at the quarry? When you went to the edge? I never paid off that bet. And"—I pointed my toes and drew a circle in the puddle I was standing in—"I don't know how much longer we're going to stay here. Everything's changing and, well, I thought I'd tell you that I always pay up when I lose. And your damn phone is turned off or you blocked me or something, and so I decided to come over and tell you in person."

"That you're going to pay off the bet?" He seemed almost surprised.

"Yeah."

The water lapped at the edge of the pool.

"What's your bra size?"

"Excuse me?"

He stared at my boobs. "Thirty-six B? Or maybe C. They don't make a B-plus, do they? I wonder why."

Instead of waiting for an answer he pushed himself up

and out of the pool (warm water running down his chest, his abs, dear God, those abs) and walked into the office. I reviewed the conversation, trying to figure out how it had gone off course so badly, but before I could, he emerged holding a girl's bathing suit in each hand.

"No time like the present," he said.

—*— 85 —*—

I am so not a thirty-six C. Not a thirty-six B, either, but I decided it was better to have the suit too tight than to have it falling off me, so I put on the B, tugging at the bottom of it until my butt was more or less covered. As long as I didn't stand up straight I'd be fine.

Finn stood next to the ladder in the shallow end. "Looks good on you."

"Close your eyes," I said.

"So you can run away?"

"Just close them." I stepped down the ladder quickly. The water wasn't as warm as I thought it would be. I bounced, arms crossed over my chest. "Okay, I'm in. Can I get out now?"

He chuckled. "No, you goof. You're going to learn to swim. We'll start with floating on your back."

"I don't float. I sink."

"All right." He moved behind me. "I'm going to put my hands on your shoulder blades. Lean into them. I promise I won't drop you."

He put his hands on my back. I hesitated (*What am I doing here?*), then let my weight fall toward him. He took a step backward and pulled me along quickly, much faster than I was ready for. My feet flew up and it felt like my head was going under the water. I jackknifed, trying to stand up and get my feet under me again. I grabbed the edge of the pool and held on for dear life while coughing so hard, I expected both of my lungs to come flying out of my mouth.

"Told you." I coughed some more and adjusted the mother of all wedgies. "I'm hopeless."

"You're scared, not hopeless. There's a big difference. Don't move."

He hopped out of the pool, took a kickboard off the pile by the office door, and turned on the radio. Soft saxophone music filled the air. He hit a couple of light switches and most of the lights went out. A piano played under the sax, with a gentle drum in the background, but as nice as it was, it didn't change the fact that I was in a swimming pool and I did not like it.

"Half an hour," he said. "That's all I need."

"You'll get five minutes if you're lucky," I muttered.

He dove in without a splash and popped up right in front of me. "I heard that."

* * *

He maneuvered the kickboard under my back and, taking my shoulders, began to pull me across the water, slower this time.

"How deep is the deep end?" I asked, trying desperately not to think about the fact that my feet touched nothing.

"Three meters," he said.

"I don't want to go there."

"Kick your feet a little," he said. "Flutter them and they won't drag you down."

He was right, though I didn't admit it. Couldn't because all my energy went into keeping my face above water and breathing. Finn babbled on and on and on, walking me back and forth, back and forth across the shallow end, my feet fluttering, until my arms softened and I let them float out a little from my body instead of holding them stiffly at my sides.

Finn put his hand under the back of my head and gently lifted it a little so that I could hear him. "You're doing great," he said. "Now close your eyes."

"Why?" I asked, immediately suspicious.

"Close them and picture something, maybe the stars we saw the night of the football game. Or the marching band. I don't know, whatever makes you happy."

I closed my eyes and pictured him swimming right behind me. "The stars will work."

He kicked his legs and we were underway again. "You're comfortable now, right?"

"I'm less petrified of dying in the next minute, if that's what you mean by 'comfortable.'"

"Who do you think trains the Navy SEALs how to get through the water? Me," he said modestly. "I also spent a month teaching Antarctic penguins to swim." He took another stroke and we flew across the water. "You're doing great, but you'd be even better if you relaxed a little."

"I'm not screaming," I said. "Give me some credit."

"You need a distraction." Two powerful strokes. "Tell me why you haven't been in school."

It tumbled out before I could stop myself, everything that had happened from my mall meltdown to Roy's death to the sight of the ambulance leaving. Talking made being dragged around the pool slightly less terrifying. I even told him about the holes in the living room wall, and combing the glass out of the carpet. He listened without saying a word.

We paused once so Finn could move the kickboard up, away from my butt. After that, I had to kick my legs harder and push up my hips to stay on the surface. I wasn't going to tell him but he was right, keeping my eyes closed made it easier to focus on the feeling of floating instead of the feeling of drowning.

He stopped again. "I'm taking the kickboard away now, but I'll keep holding up your head." The board started slipping away. "Move your arms."

"How?"

"Pretend you're a bird. Flap your wings."

I smacked the water with my arms, making massive waves.

"Argh!" He pushed me so I stood up, and wiped water off his face.

"Wrong kind of flapping?" I asked innocently.

"Brilliant deduction. Ready to try again?"

I was, to my surprise. I kicked my legs and flapped my arms under the water and I kept my own head above the surface.

He put his lips close to my ears. "Close your eyes again."

I did and we moved across the pool like I was a sailboat and he was the wind. "Trust the water," he said. "It will hold you up as long as you try. Can I take my hand away?"

I bit my lip and nodded.

"Kick and flap, kick and flap," he said. "Eyes closed, kick and flap."

Without his support, my head dropped a little, enough so that his words melted back into the sound of the water, and the saxophone sounded like a faraway whale. I could hear my heartbeat and maybe his, too. I relaxed and found the balanced place between the water holding me up and me staying on top of it. Finn took the fingers of my left hand and pulled just a little until they touched the side of the pool.

"Open your eyes."

I held on to the edge and stopped kicking so that my

feet could drift to the bottom of the pool. Only there was no bottom. My eyes snapped open and I looked down. "You brought me to the deep end!"

"You brought yourself," he said, swimming closer. "You did great."

"I did great?"

He grinned and nodded, his head bouncing up and down like a bobblehead doll on a dashboard.

"What?"

He gritted his teeth and drew in a sharp breath. "I really want to kiss you. But you broke up with me."

"Maybe we were just a little broken up," I said.

"A little broken is still broken," he said.

"But fixable," I said. "Right?"

He smoothed the hair off my forehead. "How do we fix it?"

"I'm sorry," I said. "Will that help?"

He nodded. "I'm sorry, too."

"We're not going to be drama junkies like Gracie and Topher, right? I can't do that."

"Me neither." His toes touched mine under the water. "If I promise to always answer my phone, will you promise to call me?"

"Yes." I let myself sink a little in the water, then kicked hard. "If I promise to listen, will you promise to tell me when things are bad, without joking around or clamming up?"

"No joking?"

"Okay, just a little joking."

"Deal."

"I don't want to shake on it," I said.

Fifteen minutes later, three old ladies in rubber bathing caps decorated with plastic flowers shuffled out of the locker room and were scandalized by the sight of us fixing what was a little broken with an epic kiss in the deep, warm water.

I'd like to think that my grandmother would have understood.

—*— 86 —*—

Trish brought Dad home around eleven that night. He went straight to bed without a word. She asked if she could come in for a while, long enough for a cup of tea. I made two cups and sat with her at the table. (I had no choice. It was the only way to find out what happened.)

The ambulance had taken him to the VA hospital in Albany. It took two units of saline solution to fix his dehydration. His blood work showed high cholesterol, sucky liver enzymes, and a lot of white blood cells, which meant he had an infection somewhere, plus his blood pressure was through the roof.

Trish filled out forms for him and waited and filled out more forms and waited longer until finally the nurse came with signed release papers and a note that he had an appointment in three months to see a doctor. The nurse was excited because the hospital had cut its backlog in half. Now it only took three months instead of six. But, she explained, "If you have a crisis, call your doctor's office immediately and they'll find a way to squeeze you in."

"But he doesn't have a doctor," Trish said. "He doesn't have anyone to call in an emergency. That's why we're here."

The nurse repeated her line about the three-month wait. Trish told me that she'd pulled the nurse to a quiet corner for a conversation that no one else could hear, and after that, the nurse found a spot for Dad on some kind of priority list. His appointment was the second Monday in January.

"Andy wants me to move in," Trish told me. "I told him no. A girl from work is letting me rent her spare bedroom. This way I'll be around, but not close enough to irritate him. I think that would be better, don't you?"

I cupped my hands over the steam rising from my mug. "I guess."

"Are you mad that he wanted you to stay at home? Should I have taken you with me?"

"No. It was probably better for him having you help with doctors and stuff." I blew on my tea, sending ripples across the surface. "Anyway, I didn't stay here."

I explained the bet with Finn, reminded her about my near-drowning, and gave a few boring details about my first swimming lesson. I'd expected a lecture about taking the pickup without permission or a license, but she surprised me.

"You didn't fall in the pool at that party," she said.

"Yeah, I did."

"It was Fourth of July, at the Bigelows'. The docs had discharged Andy too early, but we didn't know it then. He should never have been in a swimming pool by himself." She shook her head. "We were all watching Jimmy and his girlfriend dance; they were good enough to be pros. The music was really loud and everybody was feeling good."

"Was he drunk? Did I fall in because he wasn't paying attention?"

She put her mug down. "He wasn't drinking at all. He was showing off for you, I think. Must have had a tiny stroke or a seizure in the deep end. You were the only one who saw what happened. You didn't fall in, Lee-Lee. You jumped in to help your father, but you couldn't swim. You were, what? Seven? The Bigelows' dog went nuts and someone went to see why he was barking and oh my God." She teared up and looked out the dark window. "Ten guys must have hit the water at once. One plucked you out, laid you on the deck, and started CPR. Your lips were this awful blue, but you came around fast. It took longer with Andy. Damn good thing there were medics at the party."

"Did Dad go back to the hospital?"

"You both did. They kept you one night for observation. He was there a couple of weeks." She cocked her head to one side. "You sure you don't remember this?"

"I remember falling in and I remember opening my eyes underwater and seeing Dad. He had on red swim trunks with baggy pockets. Did he have a shirt on, too?"

She nodded.

"I always thought I was looking up through the water and seeing him on the deck."

"No, you saw him on the bottom of the pool," she said softly. "Do you know what he remembers?"

"He never talks about things like that."

"I know." She looked out the window again. "The last thing he remembers before he passed out was seeing you fly through the air like a little bird. Must have been the moment you jumped in."

"So he knew I was in the deep end and I couldn't swim?"

"He couldn't move. Whatever it was, seizure, stroke. I don't know if they ever figured it out for sure. But he said it was peaceful. He said drowning is not a bad way to go."

I drained my tea. "I'm never getting in a pool again."

"I think you will, as long as the right lifeguard is on

duty." She finished her tea, stood up, and put her jacket on. "Helluva day, huh? The docs gave him something to sleep. I'll call to check on him tomorrow, before and after work."

Spock followed her to the door, tail wagging. He whined a little when she closed the door behind her and nosed aside the curtain to watch her walk to her car.

"Wait!" I ran to the door and opened it. "Wait!" The light from the house barely reached the driveway. I could see where she was standing, but I couldn't see her face.

"What is it?" she asked.

"Thanks," I said. "Thank you for helping us."

—*— 87 —*—

The day after his hospital visit, Dad woke up at the same time I did. As the coffee was brewing, he lined up his new prescription bottles on the windowsill above the kitchen sink. He took his medicine with the first sip, then he went back to bed. He did the same thing the next morning and the day after that.

"Are you doing this to prove to me that you're taking your medicine?" I asked.

"Something like that," he admitted. "What's-his-name is waiting in the driveway. Get going."

I reached for my backpack. "What are you going to do today?"

"Thought I'd write some letters."

"Letters? Like, on paper?"

"Old-school, that's me."

"You're okay?"

"Get going. Stay out of detention for a change."

Trish came to our house for Sunday dinner three weeks in a row. We ate, watched the late game, and then she'd go to work. When she got switched to the night shift, Dad switched, too, going to bed after I left in the morning and waking up in time for dinner. In those weeks, our house never smelled of greasy biker creep or weed. Daddy was down to one bottle of Jack every three days. He didn't explode or cry. He spent his nights writing letters at the dining room table.

It was tempting to let my guard down, but I couldn't, not until he started seeing that doctor.

The swimming lesson changed things with Finn and me, took us to a new level that was hidden from the rest of the world, one that made us laugh more and required a lot more kissing. *Besotted*: that was the word of the month. I went to class, did enough homework to keep me off the naughty list, counted the minutes until I saw him again (praying that he was doing the same thing). I learned to love the smell of chlorine because every day after school, I'd change into a T-shirt and shorts, sit in the visitor's gallery that overlooked the pool, and read while Finnegan Braveheart Ramos valiantly guarded the lives of the Belmont Boys Swim Team.

When I was with Finn, the world spun properly on its axis, and gravity worked. At home, the planet tilted so far on its side it was hard to tell which way was up. Dad felt it, too. He shuffled like an old man, as if the carpet under his feet was really a slick sheet of black ice.

—*— 88 —*—

A tree turned up in our living room the morning of Christmas Eve, the base of its trunk jammed into a bucket of rocks. The bucket sat in the middle of an old tire. The tree leaned toward the window, shedding needles whenever Spock's tail thwacked against it.

Finn and his mom were heading back to Boston that night, so we exchanged gifts in the afternoon. He gave me a coupon book. All the coupons were for swimming lessons.

"Okay, now I really feel like an idiot," I said, handing over his gift. "In my defense, I haven't had an art class in years."

"Ah," he said, ever the diplomat, when he'd removed the paper. "It's an original. I love original things."

I cringed. "You need me to tell you what it is, don't you?"

"Sort of."

"It's a candleholder, see? No, turn it the other way. That thing at the bottom is supposed to be an owl, but it's not supposed to have a giant tumor growing on its back."

Finn tried to keep a straight face and failed. "My first thought was that it was Dromedary Man, the camel super-hero. But you're almost right, it's definitely an owl. But that is not a tumor, that's a backpack, loaded down with overdue library books. I love it." He grinned. "It's very you."

I tried to decorate the tree after he left. I found a small box of old Christmas lights in the basement, but the thought of a flaming tree-sized torch in the living room made me put them back. I baked round sugar cookies and put a small hole in each one so that after they cooled, I could thread yarn through the holes and hang them on the tree. The trick was to hang them close to the trunk and high enough so the dog wouldn't eat them. Too much weight on the end of a branch would snap it off, then Spock would eat the cookie, the yarn, and start in on the branch.

An arctic cold front rolled down from the North Pole Christmas morning. Our furnace ran constantly, but frigid air seeped in through the cracks around the windowsills and overwhelmed the crumbling insulation. I spent the day in suspended animation wrapped in a sleeping bag on the couch, sipping hot chocolate, watching Christmas movies, and waiting for Dad to wake up.

Long after sunset, he came down the hall coughing hard, his nose running. "No hugging," he said. "You don't want this cold."

After a bowl of chicken noodle soup and a lot of Kleenex, I gave him my present.

"You didn't have to get me anything," he protested.

"It's Christmas, duh."

He blew his nose again, carefully removed the wrapping paper and folded it, then flipped the gift over so he could see the front.

"A map of the United States," he said.

"Our map, see?" I pointed at the red lines that squiggled all over the country. "I traced as many of our trips as I could remember. There's a hook on the back so you can hang it on the wall."

"Thank you, princess. I suppose you want a present, too," he teased.

"That would be nice."

He went out to the kitchen, opened a cupboard, and returned with a long thin box, covered in reindeer paper.

He hesitated, then handed it to me and walked away. "Hope you like it."

"Where are you going?" I asked. "Don't you want to watch me open it?"

"No, it's okay," he said, already halfway down the hall.

"Really? You're really going to do that? What is it, a pair of chopsticks from an old take-out order? Did you wash a pair of my socks for me?"

I regretted the words as soon as they were spoken. He turned around, coughing, and shuffled back to the living room. Sat on the couch without a word.

"I didn't mean that to sound nasty," I said. "I'm sorry."

"Just open it."

Under the paper was the kind of box that fancy pens come in. "A pen? That would be way cooler than clean socks."

He pressed his lips together and raised an eyebrow. I lifted the lid, unfolded the white tissue paper, and picked up a pearl necklace.

"Daddy?" I whispered. "Where—"

"That's from your grandmother. Found it in the basement. I doubt the pearls are real, so don't think you're going to get much if you sell it. She wore it all the time."

I rubbed the pearls on my cheek, smelling lemon and face powder and ginger cookies and hearing bees humming in her garden. "I remember."

"Well, good." He stood and patted my head. "She'd like that."

* * *

For three days and three nights after that, it snowed. Our town had giant snowplows so the roads were more or less clear, but poor Spock grew so grumpy about having to stick his private parts in the snow to do his business, I finally shoveled out a potty patch for him and added it to the growing list of things I never thought I would do but did, anyway.

Dad was a dimly seen shadow, only leaving his room to use the bathroom or to make a sandwich or to dump more dirty dishes in the sink. I'd say "Hey" or "How you doing?" or "Want a cookie?" He'd grunt or say "Fine" or "No." His cold was no better, no worse, and he snored so loud that paint was flaking off the walls.

Trish stopped by in the middle of the night on the twenty-eighth and left a card for me that contained a gift certificate for the mall. She scribbled a note on the envelope telling me she was flying to Austin in the morning to visit her sister and that she'd be back right after New Year's.

I had baked her an apple pie for a present, but nobody told me when she going to stop in, and nobody told me she'd be spending the rest of the week in Texas, so I split it with Spock and the ghost of my father.

Why did I voluntarily wake up at seven o'clock in the morning on the fourth day after Christmas? Love messes you up and makes you do strange things, that's why. Finn was guarding at a massive all-day swim meet and had bewitched me into saying I'd spend the day at the pool so we could hang out on his breaks.

It was still dark out, snowing even more heavily than it had been the day before. Frost was etched on the inside of my window, another sign that we needed to re-insulate the house. Finn had promised that the viewing section above the pool would be in the nineties. The thought of being that warm was the motivation I needed to get me out of bed.

I almost collided with Dad, freshly showered, in the hall.

"Sorry," I mumbled, waving at the steam that poured out of the bathroom.

"It's all right. Why are you up?"

"Swim meet, remember?"

"When do you leave?'

"Ten minutes. Don't worry. He's going to have his mom's car. She just got new tires."

"You'll be back for dinner?"

"I think so."

He leaned against the wall, crossing his arms over his chest. "You're getting used to all this, aren't you?"

Something in his tone of voice made me suspicious. "Define 'this.'"

He rubbed his hand over the scraggly beard that was beginning to look like gray-speckled moss on his pale, worn face. "This school. This house. This what's-his-name."

The shower dripped loudly. He was laying the ground-work, getting ready to tell me that when Trish got back, he'd definitely be going on the road again and leaving me with her.

"You seem happier," he continued.

"Maybe," I said. "A little."

The combination of the beard and the fatigue in his eyes made me uneasy, but we were miles past the place where I could ask how he was feeling or even what was wrong.

He startled me with a quick, fierce hug. "Get in the shower. I'll make a classic peanut butter and banana you can eat in the car."

The swim meet was delayed one hour, and then two as the buses from other districts crawled through the storm toward Belmont. It was finally canceled when state troopers shut down the Thruway. The blowing snow turned the fifteen-minute drive back to my house into almost an hour and shook Finn up so much I thought I'd have to pry his fingers off the steering wheel with a crowbar. His mother called while I was making hot chocolate to tell him that the snow would stop soon, but he should stay at my house until the plows got caught up.

We settled in on the couch with our hot chocolate, a bag of marshmallows, the game controllers, and the unzipped sleeping bag spread across our laps.

"Who are those presents for?" Finn asked as we waited for the game to load.

"What presents?"

"Under the tree." He pointed. "Look."

Two small boxes, wrapped in the reused Christmas paper that we'd thrown out days before, had been hidden deep under the tree in the drift of pine needles. One had my name on it, the other was addressed to Finn.

"Those weren't here this morning," I said.

"From your dad?"

"Must be." I shivered. Even with the furnace running, it felt like the house was getting colder. "Let's open them."

"Shouldn't we wait for him?" Finn asked.

"There's a good chance that he's given us something weird. We'll take a peek and rewrap them." I carefully slid my finger under the tape to loosen it. "That way we'll know how to act when we open them in front of him."

The paper on my gift fell away easily.

"Your father gave you a box of Kraft Macaroni & Cheese?"

"Of course." I shivered again. "Doesn't your dad do that? Your turn."

Finn's small box clunked when he shook it. The wrapping paper practically fell off to reveal a box that used to hold four sticks of butter. The tape holding the ends together popped opened. A metal star made of bronze tumbled into his lap.

He picked it up. "What's this?"

My shivering turned into shaking. I ripped open the top of my box and pulled out a faded blue bandanna that held two gold rings, one man-sized, the other a little smaller, and one Purple Heart.

—*— **90** —*—

Me, pounding on his bedroom door. "Daddy, open up! Open up now!"

Me, kicking the door, screaming.

Me, swinging the splitting maul, wood cracking, doorknob breaking off, door falling backward.

(Finn's voice in the distance. Too far away to hear.)

*   *   *

The room was perfectly tidy, ready for inspection. The bed was made; one thin pillow in a clean pillowcase lay at the head, an extra blanket, folded, lay across the foot. His clothes were neatly lined up in the closet. His ancient computer had been cleaned of months of grease smears and cigarette ash. The nightstand, empty except for a reading lamp, the desk, the bureau, all dusted. I checked the closet again; the clothes were still there, still hanging, still quiet. Gun locker closed and locked. I opened it; all guns were accounted for.

I shut the closet door and stood with my back to it. From this angle, the room looked like it could belong to anyone. *No, not anyone.* It looked like it belonged to no one at all.

Garage: pickup truck, engine cold, not running, not pumping out carbon dioxide, no hose leading from tailpipe to driver's window.

Bathroom: empty. No knives. No knives, no blades, no blood.

Basement: empty. No rope. No rope hanging from the I-beam that held up the house, no body twisting, no feet dangling inches above the ground.

He wasn't in the kitchen or the living room or the dining room. He wasn't in my bedroom (he would never have done that, how could I even think it, he would not leave his body on the floor of my room, never that) so where . . .

Gramma's room, which was Trish's room for a little while. In there? In there?

Gramma's room: empty. No fathers. No fathers overdosed on the bed or under the bed or in the closet. On the bed was a box. It was a big, red box that used to hold printer paper. On the box was an envelope addressed to Trish. The envelope fell to the floor. The top of the box fell to the floor. Inside was a photo album I'd never seen, pictures of Rebecca, pictures of Rebecca and me and him. Underneath the album were dozens of crisp, sealed, sharp-edged envelopes. Every envelope had my name on it. In the top-right corner was a date. Half of the envelopes were dated my birthday. The other half were dated December 25, and the years that followed those dates stretched for decades into the future.

This girl was crying again, and the dog was howling again because we could not find my father. A monster had my daddy in its teeth, only this time there was no blood on the floor and no footprints to follow.

Finn's voice had been growing louder and louder until my ears were ringing and he was standing in front of me, his mouth moving faster than I could hear. He held a phone in front of my face and the words finally caught up to my ears, he was saying, "—Trish, stranded in Chicago, the storm, he hid a card in her bag, opened it, she has to talk to you—"

Into one ear, Trish tried to talk, but her teeth clacked together like pearls from a broken necklace bouncing off the floor.

Into the other ear, Finn yelled, "What should I do? What do you want me to do? Who should we call? 911? What about my mom? She'll help. I'll call her. And I'll call 911. What is Trish saying?"

91

My sweet Patricia,

I can't do it anymore. It's not fair to make her carry my bones on her back. She has to live her own life instead of worrying about me.

You said you wanted to help. Here it is: Hayley needs you.

If she ever stops hating me, tell her how proud I am of her and how much I love her.

Faithfully yours, believe it or not,
Andy

P.S.—Tell her she looks just like her mother. Tell her she's strong enough to take on the world.

92

I lost an hour.

I closed my eyes to blink and when I opened them, there were two cops standing in our house talking into radios and phones and looking in every room, as if Dad was playing hide-and-seek. It took a few minutes to register how much time had passed and that a blanket was wrapped around my shoulders and Finn was helping me hold a cup of hot something.

I had been talking, that was clear. The cop had written down Dad's name, his favorite bars, and Trish's phone number. That was her voice shouting from the phone the officer held. Another cop, a woman, was copying down the information from Dad's prescription bottles. She set them back on the table.

"Try not to worry," she said. "Your father has only been gone a few hours. Technically, we can't consider him missing until tomorrow morning. He probably got picked up by a buddy and is drinking in the guy's basement right now."

"But that letter," Finn said.

"If I take that letter to my chief, he'll say that it means nothing until Mr. Kincain has been gone for twenty-four hours. Then he'll chew me out for not being on the road helping with the accidents that this snow caused."

"What are we supposed to do?" Finn asked.

"Sit tight. We see a lot of this around the holidays, especially with vets. He just needs some time and space. Your stepmom says she's on her way back, so I won't call Child Protective Services, but you need to stay here."

The first wave of shock was wearing off. The edges of my mind were slowly waking up, tingling painfully.

"So you guys won't search for him?" I asked.

"We can't," she admitted. "Not until this time tomorrow."

"What if he's dead by then?"

Her eyes were sympathetic. "He won't be, honey. My guess is we're going to get a call midafternoon about him being drunk and disorderly in a bar downtown. Not pretty, but he'll be alive. Here's my number."

Finn took the card from her and said something, but I stopped listening. The engine in my brain turned over. The police wouldn't help until it didn't matter. Trish was on her way back, but she'd be too late.

Finn stood in front of the window, watching the police car drive away. "Want some more hot chocolate? A sandwich?"

"Sure."

I blinked again, eyes so dry. Sunshine flooded the floor. Handfuls of fluffy snow blew off the edge of the roof and floated to the ground like feathers. The wind whirled snow devils in the yard, but the clouds had thinned and the snow had stopped.

Daddy wasn't at a bar.

He wasn't drinking.

He was on a mission. He was sober, clear-thinking, and following a plan. He'd organized everything. He tied up the loose ends. He could not live anymore, so he'd gone off to die alone, like a wounded animal. But where?

I tried to see him, tried to picture what he had been doing here after I left this morning, what he'd been doing when I was asleep. I saw him writing those damn cards, checking to make sure they were in the right order. Had he looked through the photo album before he put it in the box? Had he cried?

The house was quiet except for Finn rattling in the silverware drawer and the distant roar of a snowplow.

I'd always been afraid that he would kill himself at home, but now I realized why he wouldn't do that: he didn't want me to find him. I flashed on the way he had hugged me before I left: sudden and fierce, a true Dad hug.

A good-bye hug.

How was he going to do it? Where?

When we were on the road, there'd been a couple of nights he'd gone on incredible rants when shit-faced drunk. He talked about the all the deaths, all the blood that had soaked him.

(He didn't take any guns.)

He talked about the faces of dead soldiers. Eyes wide in terror. Mouths open in pain. He didn't want their families to see those faces.

(His meds were all here. Did he have an illegal stash?)

What did he want me to see?

Finn set a plate with bologna sandwiches and two steaming mugs on the table, and sat next to me. "I bet she's right." He took my hand in his. "I bet he'll be back before dinner."

The furnace kicked on, making the curtains move like someone was hiding behind them and pushing smells around the room. Hot chocolate. The tang of mustard, lots of mustard. The smell of the swimming pool, overchlorinated, leeching out of our clothes . . .

ripping . . . sun glaring off the pool grown-ups crowded I can't find him music so loud nobody hears when I slip into the deep end water closes over my face I open my mouth to yell for Daddy and water sneaks in my mouth my eyes watching the water get thick and then thicker and grown-ups dancing . . .

"Hayley?" Finn frowned.

The whole room snapped into focus so sharp it made my eyes water. Finn had a smudge on the bottom of the left lens of his glasses. Dog hair on his jeans where Spock had rubbed against him. I could see everything: ghost squares on the walls where Gramma used to hang our pictures, a sliver of glass in the carpet that I had missed, the memory of Daddy under the water.

"I know where he is," I said. "I know how he's going to do it."

—*— 93 —*—

"We should call the cops," Finn said.

"You heard her, they won't do anything."

"But you have a concrete idea now, a reasonable one. You could ask them to drive by, check it out."

I crossed the room and picked up his jacket. "What if they do? What if they find him and he hasn't done it yet? I guarantee if he sees a cop car, he'll end it right then and there. *Boom*."

"What if he does it when he sees you?"

I pulled out the car keys. "You should stay here."

"You're not going without me."

"I'm driving."

He smiled. "I knew you were going to say that."

I didn't know I was right until I turned off Route 15 onto Quarry Road and saw the bootprints that cut through the snow all the way up the hill. I turned the wheel and floored it. Finn grabbed the dashboard with one hand and pulled out his phone with the other.

Ice lay under the fresh snow, making the car fishtail. I steered into the spin, overcorrected, turned the other way, kept my foot hard on the accelerator. The tires spun, then caught and shot us forward, then spun again. Finn shouted as we brushed up against the fence. I fought the wheel and got us pointed uphill again. The car moved forward a few more feet, snow flying in the air, and then it stopped moving, defeated by the physics of ice and incline.

I put it in park, got out, and ran, slipping, falling, scrambling all the way to the top. He'd paced along the fence, north, south, north, south, long enough to beat the snow into a path and smoke a couple cigarettes. I shaded my eyes against the glare and looking along the other side of the fence until . . .

There!

. . . I found the boot prints on the other side and saw something in the snow near the quarry rim.

Climbing up the fence was not hard, one blink, one breath I was on the top and from the top I saw him, my father, a dark lump sitting in a hollow of snow a foot away from where the earth ended. He was in a T-shirt and shorts. The snow had turned his hair white, his skin gray, like dirty ice.

Had he frozen to death? Could it happen that fast?

I wanted to scream his name but was afraid it might

shatter whatever spell he was under. Another bank of low clouds rolled in. The flat light drained all of the color out of the world. The walls of the quarry looked like pitted iron, the water black as coal. Dad hadn't moved. He had to hear Finn shouting, the jangle of the fence as I climbed it, but he sat as still as the rock beneath him, like he was morphing, his bones becoming stone, his solid heart buried forever.

I launched myself off the top of the fence and landed so hard that it knocked the wind out of me and rattled my brains. When I stood up, left knee screaming, the world seemed tilted. Finn's muffled voice sounded far away and the cold didn't bother me anymore.

I struggled forward, angling to the side, afraid of startling him. I didn't know what to do next.

"Daddy," I called quietly. "Daddy, please. Look at me."

I thought I saw his head dip forward a tiny bit. But maybe not. Maybe my eyes were playing tricks. I gimped forward another step.

His gray lips moved. "Stop."

I froze, waited, but he turned back into stone.

"You have to come home," I said.

Nothing.

"You have to stand up and walk with me to the car. Right now. Do you hear me?"

Still nothing.

My left knee quit on me and I pitched forward into the snow. Dad's head snapped around.

"You hurt?" he asked.

"A little." I pushed myself back up to my feet, putting all my weight on my right leg. "I messed up my knee, I think."

Dad turned away, staring straight out at the quarry again. Maybe it was the knife that felt like it was jammed in my knee, maybe the cold froze the part of me that had been afraid as long as I could remember.

"Why didn't you ever show me those pictures of Mom?"

He inhaled slowly. "Thought I'd screwed you up enough already. Didn't think pictures like that would help."

"And letting yourself freeze to death is going to make me feel better?"

"I didn't come out here to freeze."

"So why haven't you jumped?"

He didn't answer. I limped another step.

"Don't!" His hoarse voice pulled me up short. "It's not safe."

"Of course it's not safe, you dumbass!" I scooped up a handful snow and threw it at him. It drifted, sparkling, over the edge of the cliff.

"No, Hayley!" Dad turned around, tried to stand up. "Stop!"

"Shut! Up!" I screamed so loud it felt like my skin split, starting at the top of my head, ripping down the front of me and down the back, unraveling the thin threads that had held me together for so long.

(Out of the corner of my eye, swirling police gumdrop lights colored the snow. Out of the corner of my ear, Finn shouted and shouted, his voice breaking at the same pitch as the crunch of shifting snow.)

I choked up and groaned because everything hurt so much, everything hurt so fucking much. "Daddy! I know you have nightmares and you saw horrible things, but . . ." I choked up again. "But I don't care. I want my dad back. I want you to be brave again, the way you used to be."

"You don't understand." He wiped his eyes with the heels of his hands.

"You can't do this, you can't quit!" I yelled. "It's not fair!"

My voice echoed down the walls of the quarry and rippled across the water at the bottom. The clouds scuttled away from the sun and blinding light reflected off the fresh snow. We were standing in a sea of glass shards, millions of tiny frozen mirrors.

"Nothing is fair, but this is better," Dad said. "Trish will take care of you."

"She won't have to. I'm leaving."

I waited for him to take the bait.

"Where to?" he asked.

"Following you. As soon as you jump, I'm jumping."

"No, you won't."

"Wanna bet? I spent my whole life watching you leave. And then Gramma. And then Trish. Apparently, everybody leaves me. So I'm going to leave, too."

Car doors slammed.

I struggled to step closer to him. I had to drag my left leg, then hop.

"Go back." Dad stood up straight, put his hands out to me. "Hayley Rose, baby, please. You're too close to the edge."

"You first."

"You don't understand." His tight voice shook.

The snow was blue, then red, then blue, then red.

I tried to stand on one leg. The snow under me shifted and I felt it again, the tug of the quarry. The wind pushing.

"You're the one who doesn't understand. I've been standing on the edge with you for years."

Daddy said something, but his words froze in the air before I heard them. He pointed and pointed, his eyes going back and forth: me, the cliff, me, the fence, me, the quarry, trying to calculate something.

The snow shifted again. I thought he was ready to jump and I suddenly realized that he was right. I wasn't going to dive in after him. The past was about to end for us both and it made me sadder than I had ever been in my whole life. So sad that the spinning of the Earth slowed.

My tears hit the snow, sizzling.

"Hayley Rose, listen." His voice caught. "You are standing on an overhang. Just snow. No rock."

"Sir!" shouted a voice behind me.

I looked over my shoulder. Finn stood on the other side of the fence with a cop.

"Don't move," the cop said. "Either of you. We're getting some rope. Don't move. Don't speak."

"Listen to him, Hayley." Dad's deep voice rumbled across the snow.

"You don't want me to fall? Or jump?"

He had moved toward me. "No, sweetie. Shh."

More voices came from beyond the fence: police, Finn, radios squawking, the metal jingling. The snow creaked under me.

"That feeling you have, Daddy, that you want me to be safe, you want me to stay alive? I feel that way about you all the time." I sniffed. "If you kill yourself, then every minute of your life has been wasted."

"I don't know how," he said. "How to live anymore."

"When I got stuck or confused, you used to say, 'We'll figure it out.' I love you, Daddy. My mom did, too, and Gramma. I hate to admit it, but Trish does, your buddies do. With so many people loving you, I know we'll figure it out."

Sirens wailed. "Just a few more seconds," the cop said. "Stay still, both of you."

The wind picked up again. He looked too tired to stand. I could almost feel the quarry pulling him in.

"You're still alive!" I screamed. "You have to try harder because we love you!"

Daddy fought a sob, reached for me. It looked like he had just limped off the plane, the band playing, thousands of hands clapping, mouths cheering, waves of tears raining down to wash away the years of heartache. I stepped toward him, ready to fly up into his arms so I could hug his neck and tell him that I missed him so much.

The snow underneath me cracked, crumbled, and then everything disappeared.

Until my father saved me.

If this were a fairy tale, I'd stick in the "Happily Ever After" crap right here. But this was my life, so it was a little more complicated than that.

Once the video of Trish begging the woman at the ticket counter to give her the last seat on the flight to Albany even though she was not a member of the frequent flyer program went viral, the airline decided not to press charges after all. The nurses said that when I opened my eyes and saw Trish standing over me, her nose packed with gauze (only her nose was broken in the scuffle, not her cheekbone, don't trust everything you read on the Internet), I giggled and sang a song that didn't make any sense. I think they are exaggerating. I don't remember any of that.

Finn had wrecked his vocal cords at the quarry, screaming the whole time that I was too close to the edge. I honestly didn't hear any of it. He was in my hospital room when they brought me back from the MRI.

"Tore my ACL," I said.

"You on morphine?" He sounded like a bullfrog with a three-pack-a-day habit.

"Yeah, but it's not enough. A kiss might help."

"Might?"

"It would have to be a very good kiss."

"Hmm," he said. "I'll try my best."

The winds that had been blowing over the quarry for days had formed a fairly solid rim of snow that extended just beyond the cliff itself. That's what I'd been standing on. That's what collapsed. Dad broke three ribs and hyperextended his left elbow when he grabbed me. Rattled his brain again, too, but he didn't let go. (My shoulder was dislocated, but I only fractured two ribs.)

When I jumped from the top of the fence, not only did I blow out my knee, but I got a grade two concussion, which was why, the docs said, everything had seemed so weird out there on the edge.

They were wrong.

Out there on the edge, the spinning of the Earth had slowed to give us the time we needed to start finding each other again.

They released me first; Trish was a nurse, after all, and we were sort of getting along so I asked if she would move in for a while and help me get better. Dad was transferred to a VA rehab place after the hospital. By the time he came home, he'd lost twenty pounds and looked ten years older, but the shadows had left his face, and he remembered how to smile.

We both had months of physical therapy (aka pain and torture): me for my knee and back, him for his busted elbow and his battered spirit. The demented soul who was my physical therapist laughed and high-fived me the first time I burst into tears when I was rehabbing my knee.

"Progress!" she shouted as she danced around me.

"You're sick," I said.

"And you're getting better." She knelt in front of me. "Can't escape pain, kiddo. Battle through it and you get stronger. Cry all you want, but you're going to bend that knee five more times. And then we will celebrate with pie."

Dad called his version of Happily Ever After "Good Enough for Today." Some days were better than others. He got fired from a pizza place and the bowling alley before the post office rehired him, but he got along great with his therapist and was starting to talk about grad school again. He walked Spock every morning and every afternoon, coming home in the gloaming, just before dark.

Swevenbury let Finnegan Trouble Ramos in (of course) and threw a scholarship at him so big that it made him burst into tears and, after that, hug me so hard I thought I'd broken my ribs again.

The original plan was for me to take the spring and

summer off and finish up the classes I missed next fall, but as my knee got stronger, I got restless and badgered Benedetti until she helped me cobble together classes and an independent study to get enough credits to graduate on time. I even took the godforsaken SATs and did a halfway decent job on them.

The summer days slipped through my fingers. The nights were never long enough. I showed Finn how to change his oil and his tires. He drove me to a half-dozen state schools and helped me find the one that combined flexible admission dates, scholarship money, and a relatively low percentage of zombies in the student population.

And then it was August, and time flew by even faster until it was our last night. We picked up a pizza at ten and drove to the hill that looked over the football stadium. We spread out a big blanket on the wet grass and ate pizza and drank cheap champagne out of paper cups before we lay on our backs to watch the stars parade overhead. Crickets sang. Bats chirped. Mosquitoes feasted. We talked for hours, dancing around the fact that we were leaving in the morning. He was going to travel north by northeast, one hundred eighty miles. I was headed southwest, seventy-four miles. When we didn't talk, we kissed. We held each other and listened to the owl hooting from far away, and the ragged ends of songs that came from the cars driving on the road in front of school. We were determined not to sleep, but it crept up on us when we weren't watching.

We woke at the same time, in the morning gloaming, when the birds started to sing. The sky was light enough that we could look into each other's eyes. I never wanted to look away.

"Why is everything happening so fast?" I whispered.

"It's a conspiracy," Finn said. "Communists. Or maybe Martians."

"Martian Communists?"

"That's got to be it." He stretched with a groan. "You haven't changed your mind, have you?"

"I change it every other minute." I sighed. "What if Dad loses it again? What if he starts drinking or stops seeing the therapist or gets fired or—"

Finn rolled on his side and gently put his finger on my lips. "Shhh."

I batted his hand away. "And what about me? What if my roommate snores and I snap one night and kill her in her sleep or my professors are stupid or you stop calling me or I get bubonic plague or something?"

"Your dad is going to be fine and I'll call you so much it'll drive you crazy and there are no bubonic plague outbreaks anywhere. You're just scared."

"Am not."

"Are too."

"Am not and I'll punch you in the kidneys if you don't shut up."

"You sure know how to turn a guy on, Miss Blue." He kissed my cheek.

"I might be a little scared."

"That's awesome."

"No, it's not," I said.

"Yes, it is, because you can only be brave if you're scared. Being brave in the face of your freshman year of college will add to your already impressive superhero résumé."

"What if I do it again, the not-remembering? What if I get so scared I crawl into a hole?"

"You mean, what if you turn into a zombie again?"

I sat up. "What did you just call me?"

"Oh, come on." He leaned forward and kissed a mosquito bite on my knee. "You were totally a zombie for a while; you wouldn't let yourself remember the past, you had no future, and you were just getting by, minute to minute. You talked a good game about being a freak, about 'owning your soul' and 'following your path,' but the truth . . ."

The truth was that it hurt too much to think about how nice it had been when Gramma braided my hair, or when Trish taught me how to ride a bike, or when Dad read me a book. I had shut the door on my memories because they hurt. Without my memories, I'd turned into one of the living dead.

"What if it happens again?" I asked.

He gently pulled me back down next to him. "That's not merely improbable, you goof, that's impossible."

"You can't say that, you can't know what's going to happen."

"As soon as you get a higher security clearance, I'll show you the crystal ball that I keep hidden in the bottom of my closet, but until then . . ." He kissed me. "Until then we're going to keep making memories like this, moments when we're the only two people in the whole world. And when we get scared or lonely or confused, we'll pull out these memories and wrap them around us and they'll make us feel safe." He kissed me again. "And strong."

The stars folded themselves away as the sun peeked above the horizon and cracked open the sky and I kissed him and we laughed and it was good.

Discussion Questions
— * —

1. While the focus of this book is on Hayley's family problems, no one in the novel seems to be without significant challenges. What kinds of issues are the supporting characters facing? And why do you think the author chose to handle these characters in this way?

2. Roy says of Hayley's father: "His soul is still bleeding. That's a lot harder to fix than a busted-up leg or traumatic brain injury" (101). What does he mean? Support your answer by reviewing the sections of the book that reveal the memories that haunt Hayley's father. What do these memories explain about his behavior?

3. Hayley's father teaches her a number of strategies to employ when feeling stressed. Discuss how or why they might be successful. What strategies have you tried when you are stressed?

4. Hayley says there are only two types of people in the world: zombies and freaks. What does she mean? If you had to divide the world into types of people, what categories would you choose?

5. Describe Hayley's feelings about Trish. Why do you think she feels this way? Do you think her feelings are justified?

6. The scene in which Finn helps Hayley learn to swim is a pivotal one in the story. What does it signify in terms of Hayley's relationship with him? In terms of her relationship with her father?

7. Hayley says, "I needed to hear the world but didn't want the world to know I was listening" (5). What could she mean by this? What experiences do you think cause her to feel this way?

8. The final chapter begins: "If this were a fairy tale, I'd stick the 'Happily Ever After' crap right here" (365). Do you think the final chapter is a fairy-tale ending? Why or why not?

9. Hayley's friends and teachers encourage her to think about her future, but Hayley does not have any plans. Why do you think this is the case? If you were in her shoes, how do you think you would handle thoughts of the future?

Q & A with author
Laurie Halse Anderson
— ✳ —

You've said that this is a very personal story for you. How so?

My father was a WWII veteran with PTSD. When I was growing
up, society did not recognize the emotional trauma that so many
soldiers experience. We didn't even have a name for it. Like many
vets, my father tried to deal with his horrible memories by drinking. His alcoholism almost destroyed him and my family. He lost
his job. He was actively suicidal, which terrified me. One minute
he would be the greatest guy in the world and then he'd transform
into a nasty stranger. It was bewildering and scary.

It took me a very long time to understand how the war affected
him. As I watched our soldiers return from Afghanistan and Iraq
and try to reintegrate into their families and communities, I saw
a new generation of veteran's children who were facing the same
issues with their soul-scarred parents as I had. Any teen who has
parents struggling with depression or addictions carries a massive
burden. That's why I wanted to write about this.

How is your relationship with your father now?

After I left home for college, we had a strained and superficial relationship for twenty years. One of the worst aspects of his alcoholism and "the dark years" we all endured was that my parents didn't
like to talk about the elephant in the room. Actually, they wouldn't
talk about it at all. My father eventually cut back on his drinking
enough to get his old job back, and then they retired to Florida. We
occasionally talked on the phone and saw each other once or twice
a year.

After fifteen years of retirement, my parents' health had deteriorated to the point that they needed much more help than I could give them from a thousand miles away. I moved them back north and took care of them until they died: my mother after four years, my dad after nine.

Being able to spend all that time with them at the end of their lives is one of the greatest blessings I have. We were able to put the pain of the past behind us and concentrate on loving each other. Daddy knew all about this book—it was published a few weeks before he died—and he was very proud of me for writing it.

You are a self-described "preacher's kid." How did that affect you and your writing?

That makes things even more interesting, doesn't it? My alcoholic father didn't work in a factory or an office; he was a minister. We were supposed to be perfect: perfect preacher, perfect preacher's wife, perfect preacher's kids. That meant we didn't talk about what went on at home. When I was younger, I was very frustrated with the Church and confused about the role religion played in my father's life. In time I understood. He became a minister because of what he had seen in the Nazi concentration camps. He wanted to make the world a better place, to operate out of love, not hatred. Daddy was a broken man, but he tried his very best to share the love and glory that he found in the Gospel of Jesus Christ. He was incredibly empathetic and a gifted counselor who helped countless people get back on their feet. His own family . . . well, he gave the best part of himself to his parishioners. It hurt, to be honest. But that is a very common experience for clergy families.

My father was also a poet. His love of poetry and of God is frequently reflected in my life and in my writing.

Where did you get the inspiration for the title? And why did you choose to move away from the one-word title approach?

I spent a lot of time pondering the notion of "memory." We sentimentalize it. Our culture has the expectation that the memories of a happy childhood will somehow ground you and prepare you for adult life. But what about the memories that cut, that wound, that won't heal? The title reflects the hurt that memories can inflict. (Plus, I got a little bored with one-word titles!)

Can you share a bit of your writing process? And what is your favorite time and place to write?

My carpenter husband built me a wonderful writing cottage in the woods near our house. I like to get up before sunrise, start the fire in the woodstove to warm up the place, and write. It's a dream come true.

How do you write such convincing teenage characters? Are there elements of the teenage Laurie Halse Anderson reflected in Hayley Kincain?

People who have known me my whole life would tell you that I haven't matured much since age fifteen. That is my superpower. I was an angry and confused teenager; you frequently see those qualities in my characters.

All of your young-adult novels deal with serious issues. What draws you to this kind of subject matter? And why do you think that it is so important to address these issues with your readers?

Our culture is incredibly disrespectful of teens. We have outrageous expectations of them, but very few adults will actually take the time to listen to them and help them figure out the hard things in their life. (So many of them are struggling with very serious issues!) Growing up in a house where conversation about the ugly truth was not allowed made me keenly aware of the need for transparency. We can't expect teens to mature into healthy adults unless we help them make sense of the more challenging parts of life. Literature is a fantastic way to help with this.

What advice would you give to readers who are struggling with demons—either their own or a loved one's?

First, I'd like to give them a hug. And some Kleenex. And a mug of tea or hot chocolate. I want them to know that they are not alone. Their feelings of fear and anger and sadness and confusion are totally normal and understandable. The best way to deal with the demons (your own, or those bedeviling someone you care about) is to speak up. Tell someone. Tell many people. Tell what is going on, what you are afraid of. Keep telling your story until you establish a network of loving, trustworthy people who can help you deal with what's going on. Speaking up can be scary, but it is the most powerful thing you will ever do.

Resources for readers and their families

— ∗ —

Al-Anon

Provides support and hope for families and friends of those struggling with alcoholism.

www.al-anon.org

Department of Defense Outreach Center for Psychological Health and Traumatic Brain Injury

Provides authoritative information and resources 24/7 to service-members, veterans, their families, and those who support them.

Call 1-866-966-1020 or e-mail resources@dcoeoutreach.org.

Family Caregiver Alliance

Addresses the needs of families caring for loved ones with chronic, disabling health conditions. FCA offers programs at national, state, and local levels to support and sustain caregivers.

www.caregiver.org

National Suicide Prevention Lifeline

Connects suicidal individuals or their friends and loved ones to a skilled, trained counselor at a crisis center in your area, anytime 24/7.

Call 1-800-273-TALK (8255) or visit www.suicidepreventionlifeline.org.

Veterans Affairs Caregiver Support Line

Provides services and support to family members who are taking care of a veteran.

1-855-260-3274

KEEP READING FOR A SAMPLE OF
LAURIE HALSE ANDERSON'S
HAUNTINGLY COMPELLING NOVEL

wintergirls

So she tells me, the words dribbling out with the cranberry muffin crumbs, commas dunked in her coffee.

She tells me in four sentences. No, five.

I can't let me hear this, but it's too late. The facts sneak in and stab me. When she gets to the worst part

... body found in a motel room, alone ...

... my walls go up and my doors lock. I nod like I'm listening, like we're communicating, and she never knows the difference.

It's not nice when girls die.

"We didn't want you hearing it at school or on the news." Jennifer crams the last hunk of muffin into her mouth. "Are you sure you're okay?"

I open the dishwasher and lean into the cloud of steam

that floats out of it. I wish I could crawl in and curl up between a bowl and a plate. ~~My stepmother~~ Jennifer could lock the door, twist the dial to SCALD, and press ON.

The steam freezes when it touches my face. "I'm fine," I lie.

She reaches for the box of oatmeal raisin cookies on the table. "This must feel awful." She rips off the cardboard ribbon. "Worse than awful. Can you get me a clean container?"

I take a clear plastic box and lid out of the cupboard and hand it across the island to her. "Where's Dad?"

"He had a tenure meeting."

"Who told you about Cassie?"

She crumbles the edges of the cookies before she puts them in the box, to make it look like she baked instead of bought. "Your mother called late last night with the news. She wants you to see Dr. Parker right away instead of waiting for your next appointment."

"What do you think?" I ask.

"It's a good idea," she says. "I'll see if she can fit you in this afternoon."

"Don't bother." I pull out the top rack of the dishwasher. The glasses vibrate with little screams when I touch them. If I pick them up, they'll shatter. "There's no point."

She pauses in mid-crumble. "Cassie was your best friend."

"Not anymore. I'll see Dr. Parker next week like I'm supposed to."

"I guess it's your decision. Will you promise me you'll call your mom and talk to her about it?"

"Promise."

Jennifer looks at the clock on the microwave and shouts, "Emma—four minutes!"

~~My stepsister~~ Emma doesn't answer. She's in the family room, hypnotized by the television and a bowl of blue cereal.

Jennifer nibbles a cookie. "I hate to speak ill of the dead, but I'm glad you didn't hang out with her anymore."

I push the top rack back in and pull out the bottom. "Why?"

"Cassie was a mess. She could have taken you down with her."

I reach for the steak knife hiding in the nest of spoons. The black handle is warm. As I pull it free, the blade slices the air, dividing the kitchen into slivers. There is Jennifer, packing store-bought cookies in a plastic tub for her daughter's class. There is Dad's empty chair, pretending he has no choice about these early meetings. There is the shadow of my mother, who prefers the phone because face-to-face takes too much time and usually ends in screaming.

Here stands a girl clutching a knife. There is grease on the stove, blood in the air, and angry words piled in the corners. We are trained not to see it, not to see any of it.

.... body found in a motel room, alone . . .

Someone just ripped off my eyelids.

"Thank God you're stronger than she was." Jennifer drains her coffee mug and wipes the crumbs from the corners of her mouth.

The knife slides into the butcher block with a whisper. "Yeah." I reach for a plate, scrubbed free of blood and gristle. It weighs ten pounds.

She snaps the lid on the box of cookies. "I have a late settlement appointment. Can you take Emma to soccer? Practice starts at five."

"Which field?"

"Richland Park, out past the mall. Here." She hands the heavy mug to me, her lipstick a bloody crescent on the rim. I set it on the counter and unload the plates one at a time, arms shaking.

Emma comes into the kitchen and sets her cereal bowl, half-filled with sky-colored milk, next to the sink.

"Did you remember the cookies?" she asks her mother.

Jennifer shakes the plastic container. "We're late, honey. Get your stuff."

Emma trudges toward her backpack, her sneaker laces flopping. She should still be sleeping, but my father's wife drives her to school early four mornings a week for violin lessons and conversational French. Third grade is not too young for enrichment, you know.

Jennifer stands up. The fabric of her skirt is pulled so tight over her thighs, the pockets gape open. She tries to smooth out the wrinkles. "Don't let Emma con you into buying chips before practice. If she's hungry, she can have a fruit cup."

"Should I stick around and drive her home?"

She shakes her head. "The Grants will do it." She takes her coat off the back of the chair, puts her arms in the sleeves, and starts to button up. "Why don't you have one of the muffins? I bought oranges yesterday, or you could have toast or frozen waffles."

~~Because I can't let myself want them~~ because I don't need a muffin (410), I don't want an orange (75) or toast (87), and waffles (180) make me gag.

I point to the empty bowl on the counter, next to the huddle of pill bottles and the Bluberridazzlepops box. "I'm having cereal."

Her eyes dart to the cabinet where she had taped up my meal plan. It came with the discharge papers when I moved in six months ago. I took it down three months later, on my eighteenth birthday.

"That's too small to be a full serving," she says carefully.

~~I could eat the entire box~~ I probably won't even fill the bowl. "My stomach's upset."

She opens her mouth again. Hesitates. A sour puff

of coffee-stained morning breath blows across the still kitchen and splashes into me. *Don't say it—don'tsayit.*

"Trust, Lia."

She said it.

"That's the issue. Especially now. We don't want . . ."

If I weren't so tired, I'd shove *trust* and *issue* down the garbage disposal and let it run all day.

I pull a bigger bowl out of the dishwasher and put it on the counter. "I. Am. Fine. Okay?"

She blinks twice and finishes buttoning her coat. "Okay. I understand. Tie your sneakers, Emma, and get in the car."

Emma yawns.

"Hang on." I bend down and tie Emma's laces. Double-knotted. I look up. "I can't keep doing this, you know. You're way too old."

She grins and kisses my forehead. "Yes you can, silly."

As I stand up, Jennifer takes two awkward steps toward me. I wait. She is a pale, round moth, dusted with eggshell foundation, armed for the day with her banker's briefcase, purse, and remote starter for the leased SUV. She flutters, nervous.

I wait.

This is where we should hug or kiss or pretend to.

She ties the belt around her middle. "Look . . . just keep moving today. Okay? Try not to think about things too much."

"Right."

"Say good-bye to your sister, Emma," Jennifer prompts.

"Bye, Lia." Emma waves and gives me a small berridazzle smile. "The cereal is really good. You can finish the box if you want."

◀ 003.00 ▶

I pour too much cereal (150) in the bowl, splash on the two-percent milk (125). Breakfast is themostimportant-mealoftheday. Breakfast will make me a cham-pee-on.

. . . *When I was a real girl, with two parents and one house and no blades flashing,* breakfast was granola topped with fresh strawberries, always eaten while reading a book propped up on the fruit bowl. At Cassie's house we'd eat waffles with thin syrup that came from maple trees, not the fake corn syrup stuff, *and we'd read the funny pages.* . . .

No. I can't go there. I won't think. I won't look.

I won't pollute my insides with Bluberridazzlepops or muffins or scritchscratchy shards of toast, either. Yesterday's dirt and mistakes have moved through me. I am shiny and pink inside, clean. Empty is good. Empty is strong.

But I have to drive.

. . . I drove last year, windows down, music cranked, first Saturday in October, flying to the SATs. I drove so Cassie could put the top coat on her nails. We were secret sisters with a plan for world domination, potential bubbling around us like champagne. Cassie laughed. I laughed. We were perfection.

Did I eat breakfast? Of course not. Did I eat dinner the night before, or lunch, or anything?

The car in front of us braked as the traffic light turned yellow, then red. My flip-flop hovered above the pedal. My edges blurred. Black squiggle tingles curled up my spine and wrapped around my eyes like a silk scarf. The car in front of us disappeared. The steering wheel, the dashboard, vanished. There was no Cassie, no traffic light. How was I supposed to stop this thing?

Cassie screamed in slow motion.